Upon the Darkest Mountain

Rachel L. Tilley

Copyright © 2024 Rachel L. Tilley

All rights reserved.
ISBN-13: 979-8323109869
ASIN: B0D131V2QP

The characters and events portrayed in this book are fictitious. Any similarity to real persons, living or dead, is coincidental and not intended by the author.

Without in any way limiting the author's exclusive rights under copyright, any use of this publication to train generative artificial intelligence (AI) technologies to generate text is expressly prohibited. The author reserves all rights to license uses of this work for generative AI training and development of machine learning language models.

Dear reader, thank you for taking the time to pick up this book.

A short intro:

*Thank you to Cat Cover Design, who designed the cover.
Thank you to Charlotte Langtree, who edited this novel.*

This book uses British English spellings, which often includes a letter u, such as: colour, or replaces a z with an s, such as: recognise.

CONTENTS

Copyright
Dedication
Chapter 1 – Duties   1
Chapter 2 – Resolve   7
Chapter 3 – Repetition   13
Chapter 4 – Routine   18
Chapter 5 – Awakening   25
Chapter 6 – Echoes   31
Chapter 7 – Progress   37
Chapter 8 – Changeability   43
Chapter 9 – Mission   53
Chapter 10 – Picnic   61
Chapter 11 – Prisoner   65
Chapter 12 – Flight   71
Chapter 13 – Crypt   80
Chapter 14 – Dharjigs   87
Chapter 15 – Breeze   93
Chapter 16 – Respite   103
Chapter 17 – Complications   106
Chapter 18 – Portholes   115
Chapter 19 – Onwards   124

Chapter 20 – Waterfjord	130
Chapter 21 – Abeyance	140
Chapter 22 – Lost	145
Chapter 23 – Hunted	151
Chapter 24 – Kindness	157
Chapter 25 – Witch hunt	165
Chapter 26 – Unity	173
Chapter 27 – Waiting	177
Chapter 28 – Sentenced	186
Chapter 29 – Simmer	195
Chapter 30 – Flicker	201
Chapter 31 – Culmination	207
Chapter 32 – Scars	213
Chapter 33 – Observation	221
Chapter 34 – Quandary	231
Chapter 35 – Embers	239
Chapter 36 – Nobility	248
Chapter 37 – Teardrops	253
Chapter 38 – Expectations	259
Chapter 39 – Second Thoughts	267
Chapter 40 – Aftermath	272
Chapter 41 – Freedom	278
Chapter 42 – Stasis	285
Chapter 43 – Necessity	293
Chapter 44 – Swimming	302
Chapter 45 – Search	310
Chapter 46 – Sunrise	318

CHAPTER 1 – DUTIES

In times past, the land had supported civilisation, providing crops and shelter. With arable soil and trees growing produce, animals had grazed at leisure, and food had been plentiful.

Supposedly.

It had *not* been that way within living memory. Two, perhaps three, generations had endured through the dust, drought, and famine.

Yet, there was a surprising congruity to the rumours, lending some truth to the suggestion times might once have been better.

An unexpected darkness had taken hold and torn through the world like wildfire, likened more to an intangible dark smoke than the shining crimson flames one might have imagined.

Mysterious and empty, rather than glowing.

No one knew exactly what had happened or what had caused the transformation. Even now, this bleak speck in time was discussed rarely – and only through whispers, in daylight, between trusted relations. Words like 'magic' or 'sorcerer' were not presumed to be uttered.

One fact could not be refuted: there remained very few structures intact which could be aged in excess of fifty years. Stone houses and underground mines alone were preserved from the time *before*. Wooden houses and farms had been built prolifically in the years since, requiring frequent repair as the only affordable timber was weak and rotten.

Hunger was unabating. The ground had been scorched and remained largely infertile. Sheep and cows had been bred – lean, like the rest of the populace – but crops were languishing.

Worse still was the fear. A layer of disquiet hovered, unseen, yet felt by all… as though a spell overshadowed the land. Warning that even now, there was something out there to be afraid of.

Adria waited in the lounge alongside every other member of the Royal staff. The chatter was background noise to her, and rather than focusing on any individual conversation, she daydreamed of the Yule ball the week before. She didn't mind that the Steward was taking his time – preferring to linger on her fond memories of dancing and rich food than engage in the present.

Shortly, the team would find out their responsibilities and shift allocations for the year to come. It was mostly done out of tradition. The butlers were always butlers. Tailors were specialised and usually couldn't be spared elsewhere. Grooms were those good with animals, and so on.

Adria would be assigned to either the kitchens or cleaning. Possibly, a mix of both. She didn't experience any nervousness or anticipation over where she might wind up, which she put down to her easy-going, light-hearted nature. She would apply herself to whichever role they needed her in. Other girls crossed their fingers they'd be able to work with their most trusted confidantes, but Adria seemed to find herself well-liked and at ease amongst whomever she encountered.

In the year just gone, she'd been one of three kitchen

porters. The job had been repetitive, and her peers had rued their lack of inclusion in market day trips – but for Adria, Ember House had always been her home, and she'd never felt any marked curiosity about the world outside. The constant flow of people arriving and leaving brought enough news for her to know she was not missing anything. She had sufficient comfort and diversion right where she was.

The word 'house' didn't really do the place justice – set within acres of grounds, the huge rectangular building stood impressively at the centre. Other than the twelve towering white colonnades that lined the anterior, the building was notable only for its unremarkable plainness and symmetry. It was, as she had heard others refer to it, 'handsome modern architecture at its prime'.

Inside was a veritable maze of rooms, corridors, staircases, and courtyard gardens. It had been a long time since Adria had become lost, but she'd discovered she had a knack for finding others who had wandered down the wrong hallway and setting them to rights. She considered herself too modest to mention her perceived usefulness to others, but inwardly she was at least somewhat proud of her own ingenuity.

When the Steward did, at last, grace the room, she was surprised to see he didn't beeline directly for the desk from which he usually made his address – and instead walked through the crowd. Her interest was piqued even further when it was herself whom he approached.

"Adria, please could you stay where you are following the announcements? I wish to meet with you for a quiet word." Too shocked to say anything, she nodded her assent. Resigning herself to the wait and letting the subsequent task allocations go over her head, she didn't hear her name listed – but she couldn't say whether she actually hadn't been mentioned or she simply hadn't been paying enough attention.

Unconcerned, she reminded herself that the verbal

recitation was just a formality, and she would be able to check the written lists when they were posted later that afternoon.

As the others finally filtered out of the room around her, she remained seated. It would not have surprised her if she'd been forgotten, but as she watched, the man she knew only as 'the Steward' spoke briefly with the scribe, then acknowledged her once again.

"Thank you for waiting."

Adria's mind wandered, considering whether she'd indeed had any choice in the matter.

She *was* slightly prone to reverie… but being aware she needed to pay attention and be respectful, she righted herself the moment she became conscious her thoughts were drifting. "Yes, of course, sir. Please tell me how I may assist you, and I will make my best endeavours."

He paused in thought for a moment, then pulled a chair over to sit beside her. Their eyes were now at the same level. "What I am about to tell you may seem a little shocking, but before I can confide in you, I must gain your assent. This is because I will require you to be ensorcelled to maintain secrecy."

Adria scratched the side of her head while she tried to make sense of his words. Instead of responding, she frowned, bemused.

"Whilst I am asking for your consent before acting, please also understand that I consider this merely a formality."

"I am taken aback by your question and, I guess, the whole situation. It is difficult to pass any reasoned judgment… but yes, I consent. Call it curiosity or whatever you will." Unease over what he might say next was already building inside her. Looking into his eyes, she tried to ascertain the emotion behind them, before concluding his nature was kindly. "It is just secrecy that is required of me. There will be no other enchantment or influence?" she asked, undergoing a momentary panic.

"Yes, secrecy alone. What I am about to tell you, you will be able to repeat to no other." He beckoned over the scribe, who approached them and placed his hand on her head.

Only a few seconds later, he nodded, then resumed his station, where he had been writing up the posting lists.

Adria felt no different than she had before. Internally, she questioned whether his magic had even been effective. Her confusion must have shown on her face as the Steward chuckled.

"Every year," he continued, "we select a member of our team to devote themselves to a specific duty, and to this sole duty alone. Previous aides have agreed to continue to make themselves available for several years in order to reduce the circle of admitted companions. You may offer me some sympathy in being forced to make a new election for the current rotation."

He paused there, as though expecting her to say something – but Adria was still far too perplexed to have any idea as to what. He sighed dramatically.

"In all my thoughts, I kept returning to yourself as being the most suitable candidate. It is in numerous ways I find you thus. I have had the fortunate opportunity to observe your character for the many years you have resided here and feel by – seventeen?"

"Eighteen, sir."

"Yes, by eighteen, your character is well formed. You have proven yourself amiable, courteous, and trustworthy. I also know that you are able to uphold positive sensibilities, and perhaps most importantly of all, do not attach yourself too strongly to any one person or situation."

Adria sucked in a deep breath at this detailed,

hard-hitting assessment of her character. "Perhaps you overestimate me. I… I hope I can live up to your expectations in the task you will be requiring. But please help me to understand what it is you need from me." *As in, please get to the point already.*

Taking her hand, he led her through the room and continued walking until they were outside. Once clear of the grand house's shelter, he turned her towards an extensive shadow. The land around them was hilly, to the effect not much could be seen outside of the Sovereign family's grounds, but standing high, far above all else, was a mountain.

A proud, imposing, lone peak.

Adria grasped for the mountain's name and found nothing in her memories. Until today, she supposed she had never given the mountain much thought at all.

CHAPTER 2 – RESOLVE

Atop the mountain rested a golden palace.

From this distance she could only make out limited details, but she was struck by its overall style – an unequivocal contrast to Ember House. The turrets were uneven and somewhat ostentatious. It was haphazard and majestic, to Ember House's controlled uniformity.

She had always been aware of its existence but had somehow never actually *considered* its presence. Now she wondered how she'd never before looked up in awe. It was beautiful and bold, whilst simultaneously garish and distasteful. Romantic but old-fashioned.

Only when her guide spoke again did she realise she had been lost in thought, mesmerised inexplicably by something she had routinely walked past.

"It is natural for eyes to be turned away from the sight. The inhabitant chooses to live in isolation."

Yet now she was finding the opposite to be true – she simply *couldn't* look away.

"He has given you a gift, Adria. To truly see what is before you."

"This is like magic? My mind has changed?" It was a lot for her to process, and a slight throbbing had begun in her temples. "But… what could you possibly want from me? What is it you're asking?"

"Do not concern yourself with worry. You will not find you feel discomfited once you are used to your duties. Once each day, you must ascend the mountain to bring him food, fresh water, and clean clothing. This is all that is required. You will not be expected to engage with the occupant; he will not speak to you, and I strongly recommend *you* do not speak to *him*.

"There is a sturdy pony trained to take you along the trail, and the way is passable for her until two-thirds of the way up. From there, a staircase embedded in the rock will lead you to the palace, where you must simply dispense him the resources and collect his worn garments to bring back to the Ember House laundry rooms.

"There is nothing difficult about the task itself, only sufferance of the solitude. Attend the stables by sunrise tomorrow, as your first trip will be the slowest. You will quickly find you build some stamina."

He smiled at her, although it didn't reach his eyes. "Take some time for reflection this afternoon, but ensure you save any questions for myself only."

He walked away, and Adria found herself dismissed.

Even several hours later, as she lounged on her bed replaying everything she'd been told, she couldn't decide whether she was pleased or otherwise about her new role – but she did feel apprehensive.

Usually a sound sleeper, that night she woke frequently. In the short periods of sleep, strange dreams infiltrated her subconscious. Come morning, she could remember the wrongness of them, but not specifics. Her mind called up vivid images, but these were merged together with blurry lines such that she saw only indiscriminate patterns.

Although Adria fretted about finding her way and managing the climb, she couldn't deny another lingering concern – that the jinx performed on her could have affected her subconscious. Not knowing the specifics of the magic rendered, she had no way to be certain of its limits. She couldn't be confident all they'd done was lift the glamour and bind her to keep it a secret.

There was something insidious about his lackadaisical use of magic on another person... on *herself*. Until yesterday, she'd only half-believed magic was even truly possible.

Now it felt like secrets she was surrounded by secrets she only half understood.

After dunking her head in a wash basin to freshen her face and hair in one go, she made her way to the stables. The pony awaiting her there – well-cared for and already saddled – was a pleasant surprise. As the stablehand led her out, she saw the basket she was tasked with delivering had already been stocked and securely bound to the tame beast, whose name was Velvet.

She had ridden horses before, albeit only on occasion, so whilst she needed a step-up to help her mount, Adria felt sure she would be able to sit comfortably for the distance. Velvet was as mild-mannered as she had initially seemed and did not complain as her new burden shuffled about, attempting to find the ideal position.

It was difficult to gauge how long it took them to reach the steps, but the sun's arc told her it was mid-morning when she finally dismounted. Only now did she see the full extent of the challenge ahead of her.

Adria's legs were already numb from the ride, and the stairs stretched upwards interminably. Her field of vision had been reduced to steps and more steps – and each one, a foot high.

Her task was arduous.

The basket, seemingly light at the outset, now sat

uncomfortably, looped over her left arm… until the load grew too heavy, and she swapped it back to her right.

Thus, she continued, until a new, unexpected challenge beset her. Although the stairs were wide and deep enough for her to be sure she wouldn't accidentally slip, the height had become dizzying.

"I'm not afraid of heights. I'm not afraid of heights," became her mantra. She wasn't afraid of heights, really – only exhausted and disoriented. However, she was now *so* high there was an obligation to feel at least some semblance of fear at the size of the drop, should she misstep and fall.

Upwards she went, fully disbelieving she'd be able to repeat this journey daily. Utterly convinced that her aching leg muscles would not carry her this way again tomorrow.

Adria was almost senseless by the time she could see an end to the flight. Never before had she experienced this near complete void of thoughts – but at that moment, her mind was empty of anything bar the climb.

The monotony she had suffered during the long journey only served to enhance the strange mirage-like effect of seeing the golden palace up close for the first time. To begin with, she even thought the entire exterior shimmered, but standing on flat ground – and a few blinks – abruptly cured her of *that* ridiculous notion.

The staircase had brought her out on the eastern side of the palace, whilst the façade faced north. Adria had been advised to seek out a side door, and she did not have to search far to find it. The small entrance was a monstrosity in itself. It looked like a huge, heavy, solid gold block. There was no pattern or design ornamenting it and, more disturbingly, there was no obvious knocker or handle.

As the Steward had directed, she moved as quietly and swiftly as she was able. Having seen its size, she began to wonder whether her strength would be sufficient to slide open the lower third of the door.

It was heavy, just as she'd feared, but once she'd dislodged it, the slab silently rolled aside.

Adria pushed the basket through and scooped up the linens she found there. Risking a brief glance inside before she closed it again, she saw there was a second, similar door, only a short distance from the first.

Glad to be starting her return leg, she made her way straight back down the stairs. She'd planned to circle the palace and view the intricacies of its glory, but the idea now seemed laughable. It was an uncomfortable thought, but she knew there would be plenty of opportunity to explore over the coming days. *There'd be a year of this chore, as a minimum.*

As she began to climb, her legs threatened to buckle below her, but she remained steadfast, and soon they eased up enough for her to safely descend.

It was with a mixture of surprise and relief that she found Velvet waiting exactly where she'd left her. A small mercy, the bottommost step provided a serviceable ledge suitable for using to remount. Otherwise, she did not think she could have climbed atop her.

Now she was familiar with the route, the journey back should have seemed to pass more quickly than the way there, but instead, it felt drawn out and left her demotivated. She was consumed by thoughts of her own fatigue.

Resolving to seek out the Steward the first moment she was able, Adria practiced her speech. Explaining why the task was beyond her, she'd declare it to have been an unreasonable request in the first place.

When the end of her journey was at last in sight, she changed her mind. It was too soon to give up. She'd give it one more go on the morrow and see if she still felt the same way.

The same stablehand greeted Adria on her return, and thankfully, he did not seriously entertain her half-hearted offer to brush the pony down. Leaving Velvet in his capable hands, she dragged herself back to her chamber, stopping only to drop off the laundry she'd lugged.

Having been ready to lie straight down to sleep for the night, the sight of the plate of fruit and bread left on her dresser reminded her that she hadn't eaten since the previous day.

Forcing the food down too quickly to enjoy it, it became apparent she had been much hungrier than she'd acknowledged. Not leaving time for her food to settle, she laid down on her bed and immediately fell into a deep slumber.

CHAPTER 3 – REPETITION

Emptiness had been his world – his entire world – for as long as he could remember.

His memories didn't stretch as far back as they should. Or, maybe there was only nothing and more nothing.

Yet… yesterday, something had seeped into his living space. It had been ever so slight, but he was extraordinarily sensitive to even the most negligible changes. It wasn't a feeling or something he had smelt or heard; there had been a subtle shift in his environment, and it had led to the start of a reawakening.

He was once again aware of his own existence.

Adria woke to the sound of ladies bustling along the corridor outside her room. As she began to shrug off her sleep, the awareness of what was actually ahead of her hit suddenly and forcefully.

Not just today but every day.

She was rising much later than she should have been, but even with this knowledge, she couldn't incite herself to action.

Yesterday afternoon, she'd been determined to request a swap to a different duty, but with the clarity of the morning, she realised how unlikely that was to be an option. How could she ask someone else to take her place – if there even *was* anyone else the Steward might consider?

Holding back tears, she lay still, staring at the ceiling. Droplets formed in the corners of her eyes, but she brushed them away before they could fall.

Only when the corridor quietened did she feel willing to brave the day.

With leg muscles stiffened by the day before, she was forced to use her arms to pull her right leg over the side of the bed, followed by her left. The act of standing was arduous in itself, and she had to circle her room a few times just to loosen up enough to dress.

Given it was already past sunrise, Adria figured she might as well treat herself to some breakfast before she set off. As she hobbled awkwardly towards the dining room, she prayed she would run into as few people as possible – whilst simultaneously hating that, by avoiding people, she was only going to worsen her status as a recluse.

Despite her concerns, she took a roundabout route, winding through the narrower corridors. Today, she needed to be alone.

There were no berries left, so she helped herself to a roll and some cheese, then slipped an apple into her pocket for the journey.

It hadn't occurred to her beforehand, but on arriving at the stable, it became clear that both the groom and stable lad had been worried she'd deserted her post. Adria was exceedingly apologetic – to the extent she was worried her remorse had come across as forced – but, outwardly, at least, they seemed appeased.

She determined to try and remember their names – the young man who'd met her yesterday was called Arron, and the older gentleman was Harlan – as the way she was going, they were the only people she was likely to encounter.

Arron had to give her a lot more help climbing onto Velvet than she'd needed the previous day, and as soon as she'd settled in the saddle, she felt desperate to dismount. She did her best to ignore him as he stifled a laugh, although his amusement served to enhance her discomfort.

As she trotted towards the *still-nameless* mountain, she tried to distract herself, once again falling back on pleasant memories of the Yule party. Her glittered, silver mask currently lay abandoned, alongside her sole party dress, at the bottom of her closet. As Ember House had its own mini economy, the dress had been bartered for, and she now owed the seamstress a favour. The mask she had designed herself.

There were a few such events throughout the year, but none felt so liberating as the celebration held at the close of the year. Whilst the masks didn't do much at all to hide anyone's identity from their peers, the revellers still gained a false sense of anonymity, meaning they truly relaxed and enjoyed themselves in a way they usually wouldn't.

The Yule ball was also the only gathering routinely attended by the Sovereign and his heir, which further added to the excitement.

Adria had felt timid at the outset. She'd dreaded to think that during one of the dances where partners were routinely swapped, she might find herself paired with the prince, but after a few glasses of the punch, she had felt extremely at ease. It was out of character for her to be such an obvious flirt, but she had spoken with several young men that night and had greatly enjoyed dancing with a couple of them in particular.

By prolonging her reminiscence, she managed to keep herself entertained until she reached the foot of the stairway.

Dismounting from Velvet was as difficult as getting out of bed had been, and climbing the stairs was slow going. Her efforts were most akin to a crawl, requiring the use of her hands as well as her feet – she was glad no one was around to see how undignified she must look.

The basket bumped into the steps so many times, she was afraid to look inside and determine whether its contents were still intact.

There was one small positive amidst the pain – the stairs did seem a little less high than they had yesterday. She promised herself that was a good sign the route would start to get easier once her legs strengthened.

Hadn't she said she'd be content with whatever job she was allocated? Perhaps she'd brought this upon herself with silly thoughts – or maybe it was true she'd acclimatise, and this was something she could weather. There was no suggestion she was special. Quite the contrary, she'd been selected as someone who was expendable. They would not care to hear of her success, only to chastise her if she failed.

She was nobody, and this trial had come to put her in her place. There was nothing for it but to accept her lot… or leave her home and everything she knew. It was her first true lesson in being forced to come to terms with something she felt was unfair.

By the time she arrived back at Ember House, it was far later than it had been the day before. As well as her delayed start, having slept in, she had unquestionably taken far longer to complete the journey itself. It was not an encouraging sign, but she tried to hold onto the hope that tomorrow would be better.

Finding the stables empty, she brushed down Velvet alone in the waning light – light that had all but completely faded by the time she had finished. She might have quite enjoyed navigating the empty corridors of the manor in the dim candlelight, feeling her way for the most part, had she not felt ready to collapse. As it was, all she could do was focus on each individual step, as she dragged herself closer to the one thing she desperately wanted: her bed.

CHAPTER 4 – ROUTINE

On her third day of this arduous, new duty she again set off in the late morning, and the way itself had still seemed incredibly tough going. By day four – and even more so day five – she started to find she was becoming more accustomed to the journey.

After a full week, a dull resentment that she had no free time and no company but her own settled over her. Whenever Adria overheard chatter about rest days, she could not help but scowl – and that only made the rest of the staff avoid her even more.

No one had bothered to ask what she did all day, and this made her bitter. Having been afraid of what lies she might be required to tell, it was even worse to not have needed them at all.

After a time, she began to suspect this was part of the magic.

It was only once a full three months has passed that she really accepted and settled into her routine.

When things improved, it seemed to be everything at once. Adria began to appreciate the exercise. Spring approached, it warmed up, and she was able to enjoy the fresh air. Best of all, she could now do the journey in roughly half the time it had taken her at the outset.

Every morning, she rose just before sunrise, skipped to the dining hall to grab an apple and a roll for the journey, greeted Arron and Harlan, and then made her way up to the palace. Her legs still tired, but they didn't ache every morning, and her lungs could now cope well enough with the thinner air such that she could still breathe easily by the time she reached the top.

A quick turnaround of incumbencies, and she could be back at the stables by early afternoon.

Most days, the other residents were still at work when she returned, so while she found herself at ease, she had little to divert her.

Come rest days, conversely, by the time she was able to relax and enjoy herself, everyone else was usually already preoccupied in some way – many of them partaking in regular familial or market visits.

Accordingly, Adria found herself going days at a time without speaking to another person.

Even her own mind was playing tricks on her. The worst had been the time she'd imagined herself disappearing into the walls, unseen – having to go so far as running outside into the fresh morning air to convince herself she hadn't.

The girl she had been was now unrecognisable. She'd matured into a young lady focused on her duties, abandoned by her previous life.

Every now and then, she'd remind herself to make an effort to converse with those she'd once fancied were her friends, but it usually ended after an amicable hello. No one had much to tell her, and the sad fact was she had nothing of interest to discuss with anyone else.

The more she faded away, the less she valued her own existence. She'd previously had self-esteem, but now she could barely remember how such a thing had felt.

She dreamt she was relentlessly counting steps, and was haunted by the number seven hundred and ninety-three – by now, she not only knew the total number of steps held by the mountain, but she was also avidly familiar with which were chipped, loose, or uneven.

She wasn't sure if it was self-preservation, resulting from a lack of attention from her peers, or a steady state of depression, but she found herself in a perpetual daze. Her eyes had glazed over in a continual disinterest towards her surroundings. When she wanted to, she could focus, but it always seemed to slip away again, and often, she found it too much effort to bother fighting to retain it.

Adria was consequently even more surprised than she might otherwise have been when she found herself face-to-face with the Sovereign's daughter. Not only that, but the Lady was looking directly at her.

Initially, she resisted the eye contact, using the pretence of bowing her head in respect. After an uncomfortable stretch of silence – in reality, only a handful of seconds – she dared a glance upwards. Lady Jhardi had the largest eyes she could ever remember having seen. Not only were they an unusual malachite, complete with swirls of green and black, but they glowed like a cat's.

Adria was immediately on her guard. It was outside of convention for someone from The Family to engage with anyone in their household – other than the nominated Steward or Matron. For a split second, she wondered if she was daydreaming and instinctively blinked. The eye contact was broken, and so, therefore, was the Lady's hold over Adria.

"Good afternoon," she intoned in a smooth, deep, melodic voice, whilst sweeping her silky black hair behind one shoulder in an exaggerated gesture. Yes, she *very* much reminded Adria of a cat.

"Good afternoon, Lady," she said, tipping into a slight curtsy. "How may I be of assistance to you this day?"

Lady Jhardi smiled. It was a sly smile, not unfriendly as such, but it certainly wasn't warm. She took a step forward, and Adria inadvertently flinched at the narrowing of the distance between them, all too aware of how distinctly the beating of her heart had quickened. She felt like she was being examined. "So, you are the one they have picked to traverse Mount Tenebrae."

Adria nodded her head slightly, unable, due to fear, to do much else. Although, she wasn't sure whether this had even been meant as a question.

"How are you finding your new… duties?"

"Very well, thank you, Lady." A rogue thought popped into her head that this might be some sort of game.

"I'm glad." Lady Jhardi purred. There was that half-smile again. Then, quite as if the conversation had never happened, she turned and walked away. Adria put her hand to her chest and took a deep breath in and out.

Lady Jhardi couldn't have been more than three or four years her senior, but she had a *presence* Adria could only aspire to.

It was clearly a contradiction to say her eyes had been incredibly expressive yet hadn't given away any of the thoughts behind them, but she found that to be her lasting impression of the woman.

As she ate alone – after the first couple of weeks, she had returned early enough for a full meal – and surveyed the dining room, Adria realised something about her encounter that afternoon had shifted her perception. She almost felt like her old self again, as though she had snapped out of the despondency which had been weighing her down.

When she looked at her hand, she spotted a blurred outline around it. It wasn't obvious; she could only just about make it out. Adria turned her wrist slightly. Shimmering, it moved with her hand. The effect was so *subtle*. She could easily have missed it. She probably *had* missed it. Instinctively, she suspected she'd been carrying it with her for some time.

Almost as though she had summoned him purely by virtue of the questions floating around the inside of her head, the Steward took a seat on the bench beside her. They ate their meals in silence, with Adria stealing sideward glances at him as often as she felt was acceptable.

Only when he had finished his last mouthful of soup, having laid down his spoon, did he turn towards her. "I said you should come to me with any questions."

"My hand? Is that…?" *Is that* what… *what was her question?*

"It's part of it, yes. You are on the other side of the glamour to everyone else." He moved his arm from left to right to encompass those in the room.

Adria cocked her head to one side, frowning in thought. Just as she'd believed she'd managed to grasp the concept, understanding seemed to slip away from her instead. She looked at the Steward in confusion.

"As you know, the mountain and palace are spelled to turn eyes away." When he didn't continue, she realised he was waiting for an acknowledgement, which she duly gave, despite feeling slightly irked that he thought she wasn't able to remember something so important. "When you were allowed to see through the enchantment, you passed beyond its reach. For those still inside the web of the spell, you are outside of their vision. They turn away from you in quite the same way they turn away from the mountain."

His closing statement was hard-hitting. There was no coming back from this. She would never regain her old ease around her peers. Or was it more accurate to say *they* would never be at ease in *her* presence?

"Yet they still see *you*? Yes they must, or you would not be able to do your job. Did the scribe not also grant you the same *gift*?"

"He did, but it is a matter of our respective circumstances. I spend more time amongst the living, interacting with those before you, whilst you have been merely subsisting; slowly distancing yourself from the people here as your connection with the mountain increases. It is the same with Harlan, as he knows something of where you go each day too, but the two of us do not wade through the glamour like you must."

Adria was pensive for several moments as she processed his words, and a new comprehension settled over her. Thoughts came pouring in – as though they had been stored up somewhere for three months and had now been allowed to return to her.

"It's unusual." His voice startled her – she hadn't expected him to speak again; she hadn't fully appreciated he was even still sitting there. "Farren never picked up on it, nor the incumbent before her. There have been three of you in my time of responsibility. Farren walked the route for rather a long time… she was very *pliable*."

His thoughts were a bit scattered, and Adria briefly considered whether he was quite meaning to say all of this out loud.

"Usually, the fading of awareness continues. After a year, they barely remembered their own names. So said my predecessor also."

Adria felt slightly nauseous at this particular revelation.

He continued, unashamedly, "I wonder what caused you to wake up again, and if you will maintain it. The shimmer you are seeing around yourself is the spell's lattice failing to touch and enclose you."

"Lady Jhardi spoke to me today." She wasn't quite sure why she offered him this small tidbit. Nay, she had spoken without thinking.

"Yes, perhaps it *was* her acknowledgement that brought you back to yourself. I'm sure the effect was unintentional, but it was not proper for her to have approached you."

Hardening herself, she turned and glowered at him. "Tell me why they are living alone in that palace."

"That really would *not* be my place." With this refusal, he sounded far more assured of himself.

"Regardless." She attempted to stare him down, strangely undaunted by his superiority to her.

"I'm afraid I couldn't. That is to say, I don't actually know."

CHAPTER 5 – AWAKENING

Something felt wrong. The concern trickled through his barriers, permeating the darkness. Had he newly roused? No, he had awoken before and encountered this same nothingness.

He felt like a baby who'd just discovered they were able to open their eyes.

How could he be a child, though, if he had the awareness that he was thinking like a child? The paradox lulled him back and forth. Would it send him back or grant him cognisance?

Change was coming; he knew this with a fundamental certainty.

Adria was herself again, but she was also altered. Only a few weeks had passed since the day of her strange, twinned encounters, but the peace that had previously settled over her had entirely washed away.

She no longer mindlessly traversed her route. Instead, she did so with a bitterness and inherent resentment over her inescapable circumstances.

The basket felt heavy again and it was far too hot. She tripped on a step, then growled at it – as if it were somehow at fault instead of her own carelessness.

Her water flask had run low because she had been

irresponsible and failed to ration it.

She had already started to entertain herself with thoughts of running away. Her task was unbearable now she could see her entire future laid out ahead of her once more, like a tunnel with no light at the end.

One day, she determined, she would conquer her fear and leave.

Having never left the compound of Ember House, Adria had little knowledge of the world outside. Her education was severely lacking, and she wasn't much use to anyone – unless they needed their rooms cleaning or their potatoes peeling.

Ember House was *the* great house, that much she knew, but she had no idea whether there were any other, lesser houses out there. She didn't even know if anyone other than the Sovereign actually employed a staff. She didn't have any money. She didn't know what distance she'd be forced to travel to reach civilisation. Worst of all, she didn't know how far the spell carried. It terrified her that she might leave only to remain ethereal. Forever unseen.

By the top of the stairs, she had managed to get herself so riled up that her anger seethed. She slid the ingress open with more force than was required and shoved the basket in so hard it toppled over.

"Bother!" she exclaimed, without thinking.

A sort of scuffling sound followed.

She hadn't spoken especially loudly. Was it a coincidence this movement had followed immediately after the first time she'd uttered a word aloud? Surely not.

Yet hadn't she known better than to speak? This person was in isolation up here, and whether by choice or otherwise, there had to be a reason for it.

The shift towards terror diffused her anger. She almost

laughed.

Adria struggled to think clearly enough to make a decision. She didn't want to climb into the hatch to right the basket, but she knew she ought to; she should put the spilt pieces back inside. It would be unkind to leave the food splayed across the floor.

She wanted to linger for a while. Once she was assured there had been no more noises, she might be brave enough to rectify things… but the occupant might collect the food while she waited.

Regardless of how curious she might *think* she was, Adria realised she definitely did not want to meet them.

She ducked down and crawled inside.

Having come from bright daylight, she couldn't see anything except her way back out through the open section of the panel. She was forced to feel out her surroundings with her hands. She didn't have to stretch far; the space was just about large enough for someone slightly bigger than herself, but it was by no means a comfortable situation to be in.

Running her palms across the floor, she sought out the escaped items, cringing at the feel of the dry, dusty earth beneath them. It was truly unpleasant. She prayed the items she was finding were actually food. She'd never bothered to look inside her load to see what this person ate.

Thinking about it, all she knew for certain was that she only picked up one load of clothes each day, implying whoever was here lived in isolation.

It now occurred to Adria that she could have – *should* have – asked Harlan for extra water, given the heat. Instead, she had been caught short, with nothing left for the way back down. Perhaps she had even missed a trick by not checking inside the basket.

With hindsight, that was probably why it had felt so

heavy today. Harlan certainly would have thought of it; he'd been considerate enough to provide both her and Velvet with their own flasks each day.

She crawled back out, clutching the day's dirty laundry collection, and scraped her shin right across the frame. She bit her lip to stop herself from crying out – she *really* didn't want to make any more noise than she already had – and drew blood. All of her anger bubbled back to the surface.

Today, she decided, was the day she was going to walk around the palace. It was nonsensical. It was too hot, she had no more water, and it was absolutely the wrong day to choose. Which was why, in her foul mood, she determined she had to.

It was further to walk than she'd anticipated; the palace covered a vast area.

The stones had been evenly laid, meticulously so, and looked to have each been dipped in molten gold. Or else, she wasn't sure of any other way the gold effect could have been achieved. There were no chips or signs of any cheaper building materials below it, even though the gold should have been too soft to support a structure of this scale.

And it really was huge.

It was difficult to say exactly how many floors there were, but she guessed the central building spanned at least four. The towers, which varied in height, looked to hold between six and eight.

She wanted to peer inside, but frustratingly, she couldn't find any accessible windows. All the lower-level openings were so high she would have needed to stand on another person's shoulders to reach them. Long, narrow, rectangular slots, they appeared from this distance to be nothing more than holes in the walls. Stuck at floor height, all she could see beyond them was darkness.

Adria couldn't put her finger on the exact problem, but

she was certain there was one. The palace felt wrong.

She realised her shoulders had tensed up.

Unsure when she'd begun to sense it – probably around the time she had regained her faculties – she was on full alert as she finished her circle, walking as quickly as possible. She could always look again; she had the time and opportunities. Today, her aim was simply to overcome the heavy revulsion she felt towards the site.

It was strange that a structure, which looked almost comically out of place with the rest of its surroundings, could invoke such an aversion. Even the mountain had a sense of haunting beauty about it – one that the palace practically ridiculed by standing so absurdly atop it. Yet, despite this, it seemed proud. She supposed it had been created as an intentional contrast to the surrounding nature, in order to draw people's attention – the irony of which was not lost on her.

Did anyone other than herself and the Steward even see it?

The more she looked, the more Adria noticed the perfect, immaculate appearance of the exterior. There was a suspicious lack of decay.

Ember House required constant maintenance. There were always vines gaining a foothold, squeezing the prone-to-crumbling foundations. Several gardeners were required in order to contain these and to control the aggressive weeds.

This palace had to be vacant. There was clearly no staff to take care of it. The upkeep could only be accomplished… through magic?

A cold chill settled over her, and she noticed the sun was starting to set. *How long have I been standing mesmerised?*

She hastily made her way back to the stairs and carried herself down them, managing to trip and fall down several steps in her haste. Her long-since banished awareness of how high up she was briefly reappeared, but she didn't have time to dwell on either this or upon how much worse her stumble could have been. The light was almost gone.

Her relief at seeing Velvet still waiting at the foot was immense – and her ride proved just how well trained she was, keeping steady footing whilst navigating the usual route.

Once she'd caught her breath and relaxed into Velvet's slow trot, Adria began to feel incredibly guilty about having left her alone in the sun for the entire day. Feeding her the apple in her pocket – the one she'd failed to eat for her own lunch – quite rightly did very little to assuage that.

CHAPTER 6 – ECHOES

He had heard a voice and known *it was real.*

The realisation that he knew what was and wasn't real settled over him.

Going to collect his food, he understood that he was engaged in the act of opening a door. He was about to partake in the act of eating. Had this been taking place before without his perceiving it as such? Did he somehow exist beyond the realms of what was possible and probable?

He was convinced he was capable of intelligent thought, so why did it so frequently elude him?

An exhaustion lay over Adria such as she had not felt since her first three treks up the mountain, although this time, it was her mind rather than her limbs which wearied.

She approached Velvet cautiously, investing some time in petting and flattery before mounting. Her horse was probably intelligent enough to perceive that the attention was thinly veiled guilt, but she'd felt the need to do something to apologise, however small a gesture it turned out to be.

Velvet did not give any hints as to her true feelings and carried her without complaint. It led Adria to wonder whether there might be more magic at work. Spells lying over the top of spells. There seemed to be so many layers of them, she wondered how anyone could keep track. Or maybe no one did anymore. Perhaps they had built up over time, and now not a single soul could break through them.

Privately – not that she had a friend to share her conjectures with anyway – Adria suspected that if anyone could see things as they truly were, then that person must surely be Lady Jhardi. She had seemed alive in a manner quite apart from anyone else. The way Adria had felt whilst in her presence... well, she still shuddered to think of it.

Besides, it made sense. The Sovereign would be the one to issue the Steward's orders, and if *he* knew the secrets of Ember House, then why not his daughter, too?

She didn't know much about them, but then nobody did. The family of the House were reclusive, rarely leaving the separate wing where they and their personal attendants resided. They even had their own private, walled gardens.

The Sovereign himself was thought to be in his late sixties, and his wife perhaps ten to fifteen years younger. Lady Jhardi was their eldest, and Lord Dann Jhardi, who was a couple of years younger than his sister, had recently turned twenty.

Lord Dann was infamous for sneaking away from his family to join the staff celebrations. Adria had seen him from a distance, never having danced with him herself, but knew of several women who claimed to have had the pleasure of his company.

Adria had always been far more curious about Lady Jhardi, frequently finding herself wondering how someone – someone whom she had imagined as not dissimilar to herself – managed to live sequestered away, alone. Adria had never known her parents, but she had always hoped it was less lonely to be hidden from the world in such a manner if you were accompanied by your family.

It was strange to think that the Lady she had dreamt of so often – regularly speculating whether she was in need of rescuing – had lived up to be nothing like her expectations. The painted portrait hanging above the main stairwell, in which she looked innocent, haunted, and even lost, had failed to capture the fiery intelligence and intensity her gaze had owned in the flesh.

Once she dismounted Velvet and began to climb the steps, Adria's concentration turned solely to the task ahead. She visualised herself running to the door, opening the hatch, and quickly switching today's provisions with yesterday's clothing, which she'd take to be washed.

It was a huge relief to finally reach the top. Today, more than ever, she yearned for her lazy afternoon in the gardens. The sun was hot again, and she desired some time to herself to reflect on the strangeness of the previous day.

It was just as she was closing the door that she heard it.

"Hello."

A single whispered word.

She wanted to believe she had imagined it, could almost have persuaded herself as such, had it not been for the hundred preceding days when she hadn't heard a sound.

Adria did the only thing she felt brave enough to do. She ran. She gave little to no thought to her footing as she fled down the stairs, but her memory took over. It would have been tempting to have left the basket behind so she could run more quickly, but then she would have had to return to fetch it, and that certainly wouldn't have been worth it.

Pushing herself, she didn't begin to slow until the ground was within her reach.

Her subsequent one-sided conversation with Velvet lasted the full duration of their trip back.

"Yes, Velvet, but what do *you* think I should do? Of course, I knew there must be somebody there. No one warned me what to do if they attempted to engage me, though. Does that mean I can decide for myself? But is it rude to ignore them?"

Velvet whinnied, which was all the encouragement Adria needed to continue.

"Maybe I shouldn't have bolted. Do you think they will speak to me again? Who do you think they are, Velvet? Why would they live up there all alone? Why would they only speak to me now, today, and never before? Should I tell the Steward? No, you're right; *I* don't trust his judgment much either."

As she whiled away her afternoon, lying on the lawn threading white daisies together, she continued to ponder it.

At some point, it occurred to her there was a chance the library would hold some information of interest – such as the origin of the strange, gilded palace. Nevertheless, today was too hot for her to muster up any effort to go searching through manuscripts.

For now, she was quite satisfied with her own ridiculous musings and speculations.

☆ ☆ ☆
 ☆ ☆

The following morning, Adria spent her entire journey up the mountain readying herself to greet the voice at the top, but she was met only by silence.

Although she was not ready to initiate a conversation, she found herself lingering as long as she could, hoping the individual might react. She even kicked a stone, assuming the noise would attract his attention.

Why had she been so afraid on the previous day? She could only surmise that rather than fearful, she'd been startled. Without having had the chance to deliberate as to whether or not she ought to respond, or consider what was the best thing to say, her instinct had been to flee and avoid the encounter entirely.

Day in and day out, there were no signs of the greeting being repeated. After the passing of three weeks, Adria's disappointment peaked. No longer able to continue demonstrating such patience, she opted to be the one to break the status quo.

"Hello?" she whispered with uncertainty as she opened the door. There was no reply. That is, no one responded straight away. As she turned to leave, she was answered by a reverberation.

"Hello, hello, hello, hello, hello." The voice echoed as though it bounced around a room, reducing in volume with each repetition.

Speaking quickly, so she couldn't second guess herself, she ventured a hopeful "Good morning."

"Hello, hello, hello, hello, hello," she heard back. *That voice*. Its owner sounded… *haunted*. Even without the echo intensifying the dramatic effect.

Adria suddenly wasn't sure she wanted to continue the conversation.

Remembering her situation, it was clear to her now that she was treading on improper territory. This was outside her allowed remit. She would have been equipped with more knowledge at the outset had she been supposed to engage with the occupant.

Returning down the stairs, feeling quite foolish at having overstepped, she resolved to avoid future contact.

Regardless of whether this isolation was optional or enforced, *nothing* about this situation suggested an invitation for company. She had let her *own* loneliness drive her decisions instead of common sense.

Even once she had put some distance between herself and the voice, it continued to repeat itself, mockingly, within her mind. *Hello, hello, hello.*

It seeped through, fixing itself in her thoughts, and she could not halt it.

The floodgates had been opened.

CHAPTER 7 – PROGRESS

He was awake, and this alteration in circumstances was all the girl's doing. He could picture her face, even when he closed his eyes. There was nothing interesting about it. Straight, blonde, lacklustre hair, the only becoming part being the length. A symmetrical face but no striking features.

It was burned into his eyelids now, the only thing he could see when he closed his eyes. It was worse than when he opened his eyes to the darkness.

Was this to be his only memory... or simply his first? Who was she, and why did she matter? This disturber of his peace, with the melodic voice. He hated her.

Hated with the intensity of someone for whom hatred was the only emotion they had discovered how to feel.

Remembered how to feel.

"Foolish girl."

The words stopped her in her tracks, and Adria immediately dipped into a curtsy. With her eyes lowered, her attention was drawn to Lady Jhardi's hand, which held a smooth oval stone. She stroked her finger across the surface repetitively, as though the mundane object meant something to her.

"Heed this warning. Take care what path you tread next. He has awakened, and time cannot be reversed, but perhaps you may still lull this feral beast back to his dreamless sleep. Sooth him, however you can." Her words may have sounded vaguely reassuring, but her tone was direct and commanding. "He is imprisoned for a reason. Do you hear me and understand me?"

"Yes, Lady."

"Your frown; what is behind this?"

"I just don't understand… because… *how* has this happened? Others before me have presumably not misstepped as I have." Adria let out a small, pained sigh. "I'm sorry. I truly am."

"That much is clear to me, but it is not entirely your fault. You became alerted to the enchantment, breaking through it like none have before you. Your predecessors all faded, whereas you have begun to shine. Be careful you do not draw more attention to yourself than you may intend."

Adria bowed her head – in respect and in penitence.

"Alis. My name is Alis." And then she was gone.

Adria paused for a time, reliving the ominous conversation in her head until she was certain she had memorised every moment of the strange encounter. Once again, Lady Jhardi had disappeared so gracefully that Adria almost doubted she'd been there at all. *Like a feline?*

Not Lady Jhardi. *Alis.* Why had she honoured her with her first name? Unlike her brother's, it wasn't commonly known. Had she shared it solely out of camaraderie? It was a strange kindness, and she couldn't suppress her surprise at the gift, whatever the reason for it might have been.

It could have been the meeting with Lady Jhardi which had thrown her off-kilter. Adria wasn't sure. Perhaps she had expected something ominous to happen that day simply because of what had followed their last meeting. What she *did* know was, on reaching the mountain, she immediately became apprehensive. Something was wrong.

Nothing *looked* out of place, at least.

The peak was shrouded in silence, but there were never any sounds up there anyway – the glamour presumably keeping away not just people but also birds and other wildlife too.

It was calm but, again, the air here was always still.

Despite being on edge – despite her expectation that change was imminent – she was caught by surprise when the voice greeted her.

"Good morning." There was no echo this time. It was a clear baritone with an indeterminable age. Whilst strong and confident, this voice was devoid of emotion. It chilled her.

Although unsure what the appropriate honorific was for this faceless adversary, given he lived in a palace it seemed logical to treat him as her superior. "Good morning, sir," she said, then curtsied; purely out of habit, as of course he couldn't see the gesture from behind the hatch.

"Your name?"

Could she refuse? He had spoken as though it were a command. "It's Adria."

"Adria. How apt."

"Apt, sir? Why so?"

"You question me?" There was a long pause, and Adria thought he might not speak again. She worried she may have offended him, and had already become angry with herself when at last he replied, "Do you not know your flora? I refer to the black flowers growing all over this mountainside, which are your namesake."

Confusion struck her. She certainly had not seen any such flowers growing, and something so striking as a black flower... surely she would have noticed.

"Tell me, do you resemble the flowers in any other way? Are you poisonous, too?"

"I apologise – I don't believe I have seen any such flowers."

Just as she thought to wonder quite how long it was since he had left his refuge – since these flowers had still deigned to grace the mountainside – he declared, "You are dismissed." Too stunned to do much else, she gathered her wares for the return journey and promptly departed.

Early in the afternoon, Adria made her way to the library.

Oak bookcases reaching from the ceiling to the floor alternated with display stands holding sculptures of things she didn't recognise. The plaques declared they were people or animals, but they lacked any distinguishing features and Adria found them somewhat uninteresting.

Whilst her intention in visiting the large hall had been to delve into the annals of the mysterious palace, she found herself drawn to the compositions on natural history instead. Having made her choice, she took a seat on a bench in the corner – like the rest of the utilitarian house, the shelves were neat and well-ordered, so Adria dared not lay claim to more than one book at a time.

She had hoped to discover descriptions, but the encyclopaedia of flora also held sketched pictures of the Adria flower. They were hardy, drought tolerant, and known to prefer rocky areas. They each produced only a solitary stem with three large, black petals. She had not travelled, so only knew the local area, but there was something unique about it; a delicate appearance, despite its strength and durability.

As the sun set, there was little she could do but call an end to her attempts for the day. Encompassing this one large room and two private reading rooms, the library was lit only through the windows, as candles and lanterns were not permitted. On entering, there had been several other people around, but Adria realised it had now been a while since she had seen anyone else.

Not knowing whether she was allowed to remove any of the books, she instead returned to her room and made some notes on what she'd read. Her attempts to sketch the Adria flower proved unsuccessful – and she suspected that come a year's time, even she would not recognise the drawing for what it was meant to be.

As she put down her pen, an unexpected longing settled over her. Might her parents have been looking up at this mountain while deciding what to name her? The fake picture her mind conjured faded away only a moment after it had come to her – before she could bring their imagined faces into focus.

Restless, she couldn't drift off to sleep, despite the late hour at which she'd gone to her bed. Her thoughts had returned to more present regrets. Nothing the stranger said had been truly critical, but Adria could not shake the impression of hostility she'd received from his tone.

After struggling to calm her mind for a little over two hours, she was struck by the strange thought that it would be nice to see the palace at night. Once it had entered her mind, the idea wouldn't leave her alone.

Not bothering to change out of her nightdress, she grabbed some boots, as well as a thick shawl to pull over herself, then acted on her strange impulse.

The air was cool and fresh, but not too chill to bear. The breeze blew her hair up in a fierce tempest that obscured her vision. Using one hand to clutch the shawl, she attempted to clear the rogue strands with the other, but they came back more quickly than Adria could right them.

For the first time, she wondered about the world outside. It wasn't that she hadn't considered it before, but now she found herself in dedicated thought – as to what was out there and who she could be. Ember House suddenly felt more like a prison than a home. She had no family here, no other ties to the place, and the only pull was the small measure of comfort she had been afforded.

The stars twinkled at her alone, casting a very faint light over the environs.

It was with a strange kind of satisfaction that she noted the eerie luminescent glow coming from the mountaintop. In this light, the palace no longer looked overly ostentatious or brazen. There was an otherworldly beauty to the shimmering turrets; it barely looked tangible. Perhaps this was the light under which it had always been intended to be viewed, although she had no inkling as to why that may be.

The mountain itself was so dark that if one did not know it was there – if someone had arrived by night and never seen it in daylight – the palace would have appeared to be floating.

She shivered.

For all the nighttime had improved the aesthetic, there was still a sense of wrongness. It shouldn't have been possible for it to be both so mesmerising and so unsettling in the same breath.

CHAPTER 8 – CHANGEABILITY

The girl swam around in his thoughts. Time only seemed to move forward when she was around. He gained a sense of self when she was nearby; she was his anchor to the real world.

The memories were there now, that was something he could be sure of, but they were behind a hazy veil. He couldn't access them yet. It was frustrating.

He was irritable… his bad mood was difficult to shake, but he had to try. This girl was the key to his being; that much had become clear. Perhaps even the key to his freedom.

Alis's warning sat quashed, somewhere in the back of her mind. Despite Adria's tendency towards obedience, the level of curiosity she felt was too high; the temptation too strong. Who else was she supposed to speak to anyway? What other way was there to alleviate her daily boredom? No, Alis had thought only of herself when she'd beseeched Adria to keep her distance from the prisoner.

Besides, what harm could he do her anyway? Simple words did not constitute a means by which he could escape.

Perhaps he was locked away because he knew something he shouldn't. If he held a secret Alis didn't want anyone else to know, it might make the Lady's caution warranted. If that *were* the case, then Adria felt confident she had sufficient morality to determine whether such a matter ought to continue to be kept a secret, should its nature ever be revealed to her.

Over the couple of weeks which followed, Adria's conversation with the man ebbed and flowed. She still did not know his name, but in her thoughts, she'd dubbed him 'the stranger'.

When she attempted to open a dialogue about the flowers she'd researched, he simply replied, "Yes, very well," and then declined to speak any further.

On other days, he initiated the conversation, peppering her with questions about seemingly unrelated topics, but his manner was no more cordial towards her.

Although she couldn't see him, his tone gave away his mood far more than he had perhaps even realised. During the first once or twice he'd spoken, she'd thought he'd been intentionally loud, to ensure the sound travelled through the hatch. Quickly, she'd come to understand he was impatient and short-tempered.

It was difficult to blame him, given his unfortunate circumstances.

Now she'd justified her position – to herself, and Velvet – Adria forgot Lady Jhardi's words entirely, instead focusing her energy on increasing the daily level of discourse and encouraging their rapport.

Adria came to view the man as a puzzle.

Judging he would not appreciate questions about his appearance, she was forced to speculate based upon his personality alone. She decided he had short brown hair and bristled eyebrows, but beyond that she could conjure nothing.

Part of the issue stemmed from her uncertainty as to his age. She wanted to think he was only in his twenties, for there to be at least one way in which the two of them were not so different, but it was difficult to believe it could be possible.

It was inevitable she'd be disappointed, should she find out the truth, so she'd resisted the temptation to ask.

Beyond the reason he was locked away, and how he might look, she wondered what was going on in his mind. His questions were focused, but she could not quite figure out what answers he was trying to attain.

He asked her to describe the décor of Ember House, then quizzed her on specificities such as the colour of the carpets or how many benches there were in the staff dining room. Had he seen it solely from the outside? Why did it intrigue him so? Was it the only thing he looked upon?

She imagined what it would be like to stare at the same thing every day, considering what wonders it might hold, but unable to know for certain.

The windows were tiny… so perhaps he could only see the ground, and *that* was why he didn't know the mountainside was cold and bare of life. For some reason she couldn't quite make sense of his knowledge and the gaps in it.

On another occasion, he asked her intimate questions about her own person, such as how she enjoyed living at Ember House and what had happened to her family.

The questions were always direct, and the conversations themselves always brief. She was lulled into a sense of monotony, thinking her interactions could and would do no harm.

There was no discernible reason for the change, so when she found herself greeted in a warm and friendly manner, Adria was caught entirely by surprise.

"Tell me about the sky. Describe it to me," he opened with. "Please."

Adria had been staring upwards, trying to compose her words, and had obviously paused for longer than she'd appreciated if her silence had elicited a 'please'.

"It… well, the sun is blinding today. It's glowing – not like the palace glows gold, but similarly ethereal. Does that make any sense? Its colour is difficult to determine." A strange uneasiness settled over her. She was babbling, due to distraction from the sudden realisation which had now struck her. She didn't know for certain whether this person had ever actually been outside. He'd claimed the Adria flower grew on the mountainside, so she'd assumed he had at some time… but then, he'd never *described* its appearance.

"Tell me more."

"Today is bright but calm, and the sky is a pale, mostly solid blue. There are a few wispy clouds, and the breeze is so tame they appear motionless. So, there's nothing to obscure the sun."

"Very good. Not poetic, but sufficiently congenial."

Allowing herself a sly smile, she grew brave – and before she could change her mind, asked him, "How about your palace, sir? Would you care to describe it for my benefit?"

"Lord."

"Pardon me, Lord."

"Better. My 'palace', you say. What a word to describe it." He sighed, sounding more like he suffered from pain than frustration. "Nevertheless, I will enlighten you. I can walk seven paces in one direction and four paces in the other. Is this what you wanted to know?"

Her brain struggled with his numbers, as she attempted to imagine the scale in her mind.

"The walls feel smooth to touch, silky almost. The ceiling is of indeterminable height – I cannot reach it. There is one side area with a small drainage pipe for waste. The cuboid's darkness is absolute. I cannot open the door unless the outer hatch is closed; no light ever penetrates through. I cannot see my own hands if I hold them in front of my face."

That served as confirmation he couldn't see outside. So, he wasn't looking down upon Ember House? Adria frowned.

"You greet my situation with silence?"

"I apologise... *Lord*, I just do not understand. What I am seeing is a palace, but you describe only one room."

"Enough!" he bellowed. His turn of character was clear, and Adria knew they were done for the day. It was time for her to head back; to trudge miserably down the stairway, until she reached her waiting friend – her *only* friend – Velvet.

☆ ☆ ☆

As if nothing had happened, the next day he was genial once again.

"A palace, you say. Would you care to describe it to me? Maybe I will have some memory of it, stirred by your words."

"Of course. I will try to do it justice." Adria did her best to describe the magnificence of it, while downplaying the antiquity angle and omitting to mention her own personal distaste for its gaudy appearance.

"Thank you. And I am inside this structure you describe?"

"Yes, my Lord."

"Curious."

"Are you certain... that is... have you *fully* satisfied yourself there are no doors in your room?"

"The impudence! Do I not pass half my time wondering how I can leave? I have run my hands over every inch of these walls. Over the rough, muddy floor, too. I tried to squeeze myself through the food hatch, but on my side, it is too small for my shoulders to breach – it must be smaller than your side, as I know you have climbed inside. I have tried to break apart the frame, but I cannot even make a dent."

Adria was so completely lost for words that the conversation went no further. Deep in thought, she seated herself a small distance from the door in case he wanted to speak again. However, he did not, and after a time, she took her leave.

☆☆☆

Adria described the grass and the trees. Her descriptions were gradually improving, and alongside the visual aspects, she attempted to convey the smells of Ember House and its grounds too.

She told him about the current fashions, the latest hairstyles, and recent grooming trends.

In return, he offered up the only information he claimed to own, explaining that Tenebrae, the name of the mountain, meant 'the dark'. He still did not recall his own name, although his conviction that he had at some time had one could not be shaken.

When he asked her about the outside world, she was unable to tell him anything.

"Make something up then," he instructed her.

Adria composed stories while she sat atop Velvet in the mornings – careful to always disclose what was fact and what was fiction before she performed them for her eager audience. She spent numerous afternoons browsing storybooks, hoping being better read would help prevent her from running out of ideas.

Sometimes, she would find herself sitting outside his door for hours. Depending on his mood, they would either talk incessantly or spend their time in companionable silence.

One day, she woke to discover small, purple-black

flowers peppering Tenebrae. The Adria flower was far more spectacular in reality than it had been on paper. She picked a handful and set them in a jar in her room, hoping, though she passed them every day, that she'd never tire of them.

He seemed to enjoy her stories, even though many of them were repetitive and lacked any meaning. Despite his lack of complaint, Adria found she was not especially pleased with her own skills in wit or imagination. Although her offerings were slowly improving, she had no doubt that many others would have put her to shame, had they been given the same opportunity.

Presently, the weather turned cold again. She described the fall colours, trying her best to do justice to the landscape of reds, oranges, and yellows, which were even more spectacular from her high-up perch.

"I hardly recall what colour is," he admitted. Having grown used to his captivity, the words made her feel sad for him all over again, but put an end to any worries that she wasn't adequately capturing the full range of hues visible.

Their friendship had lost much of its previous uneasiness, and he had transformed into a kind, amiable acquaintance. While he had lost his patience with her regularly before, she now found his outbursts had all but ceased.

Adria had intended to maintain an element of scepticism at his change in demeanour. She was concerned he had simply become better at *not showing* his temper.

Over time, her barriers seemed to have relaxed.

Knowing she was the only person he ever spoke to, she began to share secrets with him as a way of unburdening herself. Things she had never told anyone, things which must have been bothering her for years without her even *realising* as much, came tumbling from her mouth.

"My family," she found herself telling him. "I have no idea who they were, and there is no record of them, so I do not suppose I shall *ever* know. Yet… I cannot help but feel *less* for not knowing. I do try my best not to feel resentful. Resentful towards whomever they were… and resentful that I will never know the answer to the one question I most want to."

"I understand," he told her. "I cannot remember my family or any details of my life. I would say that is tantamount to the same circumstances."

Adria grimaced. "I'm sorry, that was insensitive of me. I have never spoken to anyone about it before, and I knew you would understand… but I should have thought better before speaking all the same."

Only silence followed – but by the next day, his joviality had returned.

☆ ☆ ☆

Already it was time for the year's Yule ball. It seemed to have come around more quickly than it should have. Adria, having regained much of her old self-esteem, looked forward to it with considerable anticipation.

Hidden from the world behind a pretty costume, she'd be allowed to dance and laugh amidst the crowd as if she were still one of them.

Having remained fond of the dress she'd worn the previous year, she decided to wear it again but fashioned herself a new mask. It didn't turn out quite so well as her last one, but the thin material had grown tattered, and she'd been unable to restore it. Inspired by the Palace, she'd opted for gold instead of silver, and imbued it with glitter until it was bright and fun. Two attributes she had always aspired to.

The evening did not fail to meet her expectations.

The dance hall had been lavishly decorated. Tables were dusted with icing – to appear as though they were coated with snow – and embroidered, white cloths had been hung over the chairs. Delicate white and blue paper chains hung down from the ceiling. The dancefloor was made from frosted mirrors.

Perhaps it was the masqueraded nature of the party which confused the glamour magic, but through Adria's perception, all the guests appeared both seen and unseen, in equal measure. It added to the ethereal quality of the night but, imagined or otherwise, she felt as though she glided amongst them with a sense of... *power*.

Like she was strong. Free. Whilst they were oblivious. No other partygoer knew they were wrapped in a spell.

Except, that was, for Lady Jhardi, who appeared to move around completely unnoticed. It was clear she did not wish to have any attention to drawn to her. Adria wondered if she had done the same in other years. More than likely she had, having previously been immune to her own observation, too.

They shared a tentative smile but no conversation.

Adria twirled and spun around the dance floor until she forgot everything but the fun, the party, and the boys. In a corridor, after the dancing, she and Arron kissed. Lost in the moment, she didn't care who it was or what it meant.

When she went to collect Velvet on the following morning, she greeted him with the same shy smile she'd always given, wondering whether he had known it was her behind the sparkly mask.

☆ ☆ ☆
 ☆   ☆

The stranger asked dozens of questions about the ball. In her answers, Adria showed him a part of herself – a vulnerability – that she did not think she had shown anyone before.

He didn't care what she had drunk or eaten, or which songs she had enjoyed the most. He wanted to know how she had *felt* and what she had experienced. Throwing herself into the challenge, she found herself reliving the whole evening, letting him see it vicariously through her eyes.

Had he bristled slightly when she mentioned the kiss? She wasn't sure, but once she had described it – caught up in the reminiscence – she couldn't take the words back.

It continued to sit over her uneasily all that night until she had returned the next day to find him cordial and unaffected. To all intents and purposes, nothing had changed.

Announcement day came and went.

Adria sat alone, spoke to no one, and was, of course, not listed among the tasks handed out. Uncertain whether she'd be wanted, she had attended solely out of protocol, then spent the whole morning wishing for it to be over so her day's visit was not cut too short.

The realisation came to her that, at some point, she had begun to think of it less as a duty and more as a challenging, unrelenting role she was playing – with one man alone whom her performance was required to please.

CHAPTER 9 – MISSION

A year had passed. He knew this only from her tales of the changing seasons.

His confinement had made it interminable.

Constant darkness. Emptiness. Reliance on another like a child...

The girl still dominated his waking thoughts; her silhouette was etched onto his brain. Her inferiority was so marked it infuriated him, but he had come to enjoy her worship. Which was ironic, given she would be *his saviour. He would make sure of it.*

She just needed some encouragement... and perhaps a small dose of flattery.

"You must leave," he exclaimed, much to Adria's surprise. "I need you to find me a way out of here. There *must* be answers in that house somewhere."

"I am not sure how I can be of help... I think you're overestimating me." Silence. "But I could try if it would please you?"

"Yes, you must try. I need to see you. I cannot bear not being able to be close to you any longer." He really had overdone it a bit – presumably in an attempt to get her to do his bidding. Or maybe he really had grown that fond of her; a side-effect of Adria being the only person he ever had contact with... an inevitable by-product of his reliance on her.

Either way, Adria was too daunted by the difficulty of the feat being requested of her to pay his motives much heed. It was perfectly logical he would want to leave, so making such an appeal seemed completely reasonable.

Whilst she understood the reason, she was disappointed at being dismissed.

The library was the most sensible starting point. The Steward, she was certain, knew less about the man's situation than she did. She imagined Alis Jhardi would hold invaluable insight, but Adria was afraid to ask; approaching her wasn't even an option she would consider.

She did not stop to question whether this course of action was right or wrong. She'd long wondered why he was imprisoned, and Adria had yet to determine whether he was telling her the truth that he remembered nothing. The ethical dilemma didn't matter unless she could actually find him a way out – it seemed unlikely she ever would – and until then, any in-depth contemplation on the matter would mean worrying needlessly.

Adria's daily trips to Tenebrae became increasingly brief, and although she'd visited the library most days already, she no longer spent her time in the fiction section.

It didn't go unnoticed.

"It has not escaped my attention what you are doing."

Adria, hunched over a book on the desk, had been entirely unaware of Lady Jhardi's approach. She would have scrambled to a standing position in order to curtsy, but the Lady put a hand firmly on her shoulder as if to hold her in place.

"You must cease."

"Thank you for the instruction, Lady Jhardi. Would you consider letting me know why, so that I might…" she tailed off. Adria suddenly wasn't sure that questioning the ethics of keeping this man incarcerated would sit well with someone who might be the cause of said imprisonment.

Nor would it be a good idea to explain she needed an excuse to give him as to why she was not able to release him.

"I have granted you permission to call me Alis. This was not a trivial decision; please don't forgo my offering." She seemed genuinely put out. "As to the matter at hand, I cannot tell you the why. My lips are sealed by the magic, which, as you have observed, lies heavily over this place. Know, however, that whilst it was not *I* who sealed his fate, I fully believe he should remain where he is." Alis wavered slightly. Adria had never seen her this agitated. "He… I… Just please heed my words. You can either trust him or me. I implore you to choose wisely."

Adria tried to respond but, as often seemed to happen, words failed her.

Alis, on the contrary, regained her composure abruptly. "You will not find what you are looking for here anyway. It cannot be found because it cannot be done."

If that was the case, then there was no harm in continuing to look. She wasn't sure how she could face the stranger each day otherwise. She might not fully trust him, but she did enjoy his company very much. There was no way to prove as such but, instinctively, she believed him when he claimed his memory was lost. Perhaps whatever vice he had previously been disposed to had also vanished, along with whoever he had at one time been.

Whilst Alis had so far been proven correct and Adria had not found any information as to why the stranger was sealed away or how to release him, she had learnt a good deal regarding the place's history. This, she hoped, would go some way towards helping soothe his growing frustration at her lack of progress.

Adria understood his disappointment. She could not

imagine what he had done that someone would be cruel enough to mete out such an exacting punishment.

"The palace, its name is Lucis," she told him proudly.

"That doesn't help me. Did you find a way to free me?"

"Oh… I… perhaps I should go."

"No, don't. Wait. I'm sorry. It does mean something to me. It's familiar. Truth be told, it's as though it has touched something hidden in the back of my mind. I'm just impatient for news. I can't help it; it's all I think about."

"I have tried every book on either the history of Ember House or the palace that I've been able to find. I was even warned off and kept looking regardless." Adria clapped her hand over her mouth. She hadn't quite meant to tell him that.

"Warned off? Warned off by whom?" She could hear his temper rising. It had been unintentional, but she'd upset him.

"A member of the Sovereign family. She told me I would not find anything of use."

"Speculation you will not find an answer is not equivalent to telling you to cease looking."

"That's true. I guess, in all honesty, she also asked me to desist." Adria cringed. She hadn't meant to turn her allies into each other's enemies. She might know this stranger more familiarly, but she trusted Alis's good intentions.

"Understood. So, weeks of progress aggregates to only a name? You know how I feel about names."

"No, my Lord." She threw the 'Lord' in to appease him, knowing he took kindly to the flattery. Despite his internment, she was still intimidated by his person. "The palace here is old. Very old. It was built over two hundred years ago; closer even to three hundred years, they think."

"That does not seem such a long time to me." Adria could tell he was questioning himself as he stated this. His memories only spanned a year... didn't they?

"Oh... apologies. Shall I continue?" She waited for an affirmative response, but none came. Feeling like it was what he would want, she elaborated regardless, "That is why the fashion of it is so bygone. It was built by the Sovereign family back then, and at that time, it was considered rather extravagant. Its construction cost more money than Ember House has in its entire treasury – or, at least, so the documentarians speculate.

"It would have taken *decades* to build, but the use of techniques requiring magic meant it was completed in only eight years. It's difficult to believe it's so completely abandoned. This huge, expensive residence, and no one even lives here.

"About a century ago, they started work on Ember House. After a few years, everyone moved in, and Lucis palace was entirely closed down. I just can't fathom why they would leave this place behind – and even set a spell to turn people away from it. What can be so awful about this place that they would want to ensure it was left permanently untouched?"

The stranger laughed. Was this the first time she had heard him laugh? It was a loud, hearty sound and not at all how she had expected his laugh to be. "I believe that may be due to myself. Surely, I am the evil they are keeping people away from. I must be *truly* terrible. It's almost a shame I cannot remember how awful I am."

Adria was slightly disturbed at his reaction, but she rationalised it to herself by asking how else he was supposed to respond to the facts she'd set out before him in such an insensitive way. "I'm sure that isn't why. You have not seen the inside of the palace. Perhaps the magic keeps the outside pristine, but the inside has rotted."

With his humours good, the conversation flowed, and it turned into one of those days – days that seemed to be happening more and more regularly – where Adria left the mountain only just in time to return before dark. She had been missing dinner so frequently that Harlan had begun to pack extra food in her basket.

They had ended up in a discussion on the concept of magic itself, and she now had even more unanswered questions.

Although his memory seemed to include an impressive depth of knowledge, Adria could not make any sense of how he could recall some strange things so clearly – and even if she was sceptical, *he* clearly believed them to be true – but then knew nothing of himself. Months ago, he'd told her about the Adria flowers, and now he was insisting that use of magic was prolific.

"Not everyone has magic," he'd told her, "but many people do, and its benefits to the field of structural engineering are only one of the many ways in which society has been improved by wielding it."

Adria did not know much of the world, and somehow it felt like she knew even less than this phantom, but she was certain that magic was *not* being used in this way. She'd suggested he must be mistaken, but he had been unconvinced.

It was typical of him to be so sure of himself that he would not budge in his views.

Although magic was not seen as evil per se, at Ember House it was a taboo subject. Only extremely basic magic was possible, such as the moulding of the glamour required in her own case. Everything she had heard of the world outside Ember spoke to the preclusion of magic.

The more she thought about it, the more she decided that there was no, or very little, creation of new magic; rather, use was limited solely to the manipulation of existing magic.

On locating and questioning the scribe, Adria had her suspicions confirmed. He seemed surprised she had figured it out without any instruction on the matter, which left her feeling quite pleased with herself.

In fact, he even went so far as to test her, to see whether she could influence the glamour herself – but she had been found lacking. He seemed a little disappointed at this. Adria, on the other hand, didn't mind at all; she was quite content to consider herself ordinary.

It was only now, armed with this knowledge, that she finally felt certain he had performed no magic on her at that announcement ceremony a little over a year earlier. All the scribe could have done was give her a nudge towards the other side of the glamour – and although he refused to give confirmation when she suggested any claim she'd been spelled not to reveal the truth was nonsense, his face had given much away.

Whilst Adria had no intention of testing what would happen if she tried to tell someone about the stranger, she was certain there would be no barrier preventing the words from leaving her mouth.

She was a little doubtful the scribe had done anything to her at all. Rather than any magic – or manipulation of existing magic – having occurred, wasn't it more likely that the Steward had been the trigger, when he'd first directed her attention towards the mountain?

Armed with the knowledge that magic was all but inaccessible, Adria realised she was happy to encourage the stranger to share his preposterous stories, which she took enjoyment from hearing.

He told her how magic could be used for the plumbing of

running water.

He told her about farms reliant on magical irrigation and harvesting methods.

"How about medicine?" she asked him one brisk afternoon. "Could magic be used to make people recover from sickness and injury?"

"Is there someone you wish to help? It's an experimental field and I wouldn't advise trying it."

"There isn't. I'm merely curious about the subject."

"Small things might be possible to do safely. Closing over a cut, preventing infection, or helping to mend a bone. Anything bigger would be too risky. There has been a lot of research on the subject, but in general, the use of magic in medicine is still fairly primitive."

The possibilities seemed endless. Whenever she thought there could be no more to learn, the stranger would surprise her with a new anecdote, or some simple but powerful science being employed in an everyday way.

Preferring to lounge in the fresh mountain air enjoying her companion's stories, Adria's trips to the library tailed off even further, to the extent she was only making the effort once or twice a week. Her attempts to find the answer to her friend's troubles had become half-hearted at best.

Right now, she was the centre of his world; and a small part of her worried what might happen if she *did* enable his release – surely, he would quickly lose interest in her.

CHAPTER 10 – PICNIC

Lucis, Lucis, Lucis. The name echoed in his mind. He hadn't needed her to speak it; ever since she had read the word, since she'd had the thought in her mind, it had been carried to him in whispers. Whispers that surrounded him. Whispers that never seemed to cease.

The palace of light atop the dark mountain. Why did it taunt him? Was it the absence of all other diversions, or... was it something further?

If only he could simply remember himself, if he could feel whole again, he might know the answer – to this and more.

Spring was almost over, and each day felt noticeably warmer.

"I fancy a picnic," proclaimed the stranger, who was no longer a stranger. "Can you ask..."

"Harlan," she supplied.

"Yes – Harlan. Will he prepare us a solstice feast? That should give him plenty of time to make arrangements. The nights will be far more pleasant by then, too."

She smiled, pleased he'd considered her own comfort. "Harlan won't mind at all; there's always plenty of food at Ember." The idea appealed to her. She barely socialised these days, and the opportunity to do something outside of her very limited routine was quite exciting.

"Perhaps… perhaps you could sleep here under the stars for a night or two and keep me company."

Delighted by the suggestion of camping atop Tenebrae, Adria practically gasped in response. She made no attempt to contain her enthusiasm. "That's a great idea. I can bring a cloak, and I'm sure they will have a spare sleeping bag for me to borrow, too."

"I will look forward to it. Just make sure he knows to ensure the food has been preserved – so we will still have enough for a few days, even if it's out in the heat. Fresh food will be fine to start, but bring salted meats, hard rolls, and apples for the other two days, and then we can make a whole celebration of it?"

☆ ☆ ☆

Harlan had been perfectly amenable to her suggestion, even if he had looked at her a little oddly. The idea she would want to sleep outdoors to keep a recluse company made no sense to him, that much was clear, but he was jovial enough not to pry. And she was too excited to care.

Only after she'd asked him did Adria realise the magic likely prevented him from having any interest in their schemes; he'd merely accepted her request at its most basic level.

Usually reserved and modest, Adria started to connect ideas in her mind. A Lord was asking her for her company. A Lord who had bristled when she had, albeit stupidly, mentioned a boy she had kissed at a party.

For the next few weeks, she strode around Ember House as though she owned the place. Fantasies of moving into residence at the huge palace filled her mind, alongside visions of the imagined face behind the voice.

Adria was sure his looks would match his confidence – and surely once he was free, his spirits would improve. Any fears that he wouldn't choose *her* had all but had disintegrated.

She realised she'd need to find a way to broach the subject with Lady Jhardi in a way that didn't garner her disapproval. A task almost as impossible as finding anything helpful in the library.

The day she'd been long anticipating finally arrived, and her good mood was tested before it had really begun. Having packed far, far more than she needed – or at least, far more than she could comfortably carry – poor Velvet was overburdened, and her trip up the staircase was slow and cumbersome.

Her arms ached, and a sheen of sweat coated her back and face. She had, at least, managed to resist the temptation of bolstering her energy by eating some of the contents.

At the top, she was forced to wait while she caught her breath, not wanting to alert him of her presence until she'd recovered, so she could arrive in a more dignified manner.

He knew she was there before she was ready.

"Come hither," he called. "I have a favour to ask you. It is okay if you don't want to, but it would mean a lot to me."

Adria faltered, feeling nervous as to what he might be about to ask of her.

"Would you mind awfully if you joined me in the darkness for a short time? I'd like to feel you close. Maybe you could sit between the doors for a while. Of course, when we eat, you can go back outside."

She was rather relieved that had been all he wanted. "It's okay, I'm sure I'll adjust to the darkness," she said optimistically. Pushing through the basket, Adria slid herself into the opening, ensuring she was careful not to graze her knee this time.

Her relief was short-lived.

"Close the door? Then can I open mine. Remember, it won't budge unless the other is shut."

She hesitated.

"I haven't made contact with another person in so long."

She cautiously slid the access panel back across and was left to rely on her ears to hear his side opening.

"Take my hand?" he said.

She felt around for it, but he found her first. He grasped her wrist… and pulled.

She was dragged *through* the door and into his prison.

Apparently, it was only *his* shoulders which were too broad to fit through the opening.

CHAPTER 11 – PRISONER

The moment they had clasped wrists, he had been struck. Not by a spark of passion or love. No, by something far more valuable. A memory. He knew his name. He remembered his own face.

His gamble had paid off.

Her heart raced.

The darkness was absolute, just as he'd said it would be.

He was somewhere in here with her.

"I can hear you breathing, child." She started at the sudden sound. "You can try to quieten it, but it won't stop me. I know exactly where you are. Living like this, in darkness, has heightened my ability to detect sounds."

"I can just leave again." Her voice shook, and she couldn't steady it. "You won't be able to keep me here; you will have to sleep at some point." How close by was he? She could hear her own breath too, but nothing beyond that.

"Tut tut tut, accusing me of capture already? I am not stopping you from leaving. Although, the magic might. I don't know. *I* can't leave. I'd say it's as equally likely the magic is attuned to only prevent myself from leaving as it is that it will prevent anybody at all leaving."

Adria knew then and there that she did not like this person. She had been terribly foolish.

She was afraid to feel her way around the room in case she collided with him – she was too afraid to move from the very spot in which she stood.

"Varick. My name. I remembered. In case you wanted to be happy for me."

She pictured him smiling and felt sickened. "How convenient for you! You expect me to believe you just *happened* to remember, right now, in this ludicrous situation. I do not believe a word you say – and I don't think I ever shall again!"

He mostly ignored her ravings. "Of course it was not a coincidence. You did something to me that made me remember."

Adria found herself torn between curiosity, fear, and anger, all three of which now seemed equally intense – and she wasn't sure which one she wanted to prevail.

"Take my hand again? I want to try something."

Before she could respond, Adria felt him touch her fingers and immediately flinched. The reek of sweat pervaded her nostrils, unnaturally sweet but with a hidden tang – like a melody with a discordant note.

"Wait. Hold it."

She closed her eyes – redundantly, but it had been a reflex. As though her body had thought it would somehow make her less afraid.

"Nothing. Hmmm. That is strange."

"Please, can I leave now?" Any pretence of manners on Adria's part had been disposed of.

"Wait. Stay with me a while?"

"This is so ridiculous. If I have a choice, I want to leave.

You're scaring me."

"It's still me. We can do this nicely, or you can obey me."

Adria fumed.

"Put your hands against the wall. Please." She did not move. Evidently too proud to deign to explain himself, he grabbed her hands and pressed them against the wall. "Just hold them there for a few moments."

She narrowed her eyes at him, wishing her glare could sear him. Until... a *tingling* started to spread through her fingers. "What are you doing to me?"

"You, Adria, are my salvation. You are draining the magic out of the walls. The air is already less oppressive." He took a deep breath in victory. "Keep going until I say otherwise."

"Are you sure this won't affect *me* somehow?"

"I honestly have no idea."

She was too afraid to do anything but comply regardless.

Eventually, he told her it was okay to stop. Personally, Adria couldn't sense any difference in the room itself, but her hands felt uncomfortably numb. "What are you doing now?" she asked, feeling more than a little exasperated.

"I'm seeing what has changed. Help me search the walls if you want to be helpful."

She made a token effort to help, unable to suspend her disbelief, and finding the whole charade silly – until he called, "Aha! Over here." Adria bumbled around until she found where 'over here' was.

To her tremendous surprise, she could feel the edges of a doorway. Although, she supposed there was no proof it hadn't been there the whole time. "You must have missed it before. Why would it have suddenly appeared?"

Ignoring her, Varick applied a modest amount of pressure, and it opened outwards. "Grab the basket!" he commanded her.

"Hold on one second. *You* can go through this door and see where it leads. I, on the other hand, am more than happy to go back out the way I came in." Her desire to see whether he would allow her to leave far outweighed any curiosity she felt towards seeing the palace.

"Of course. If you are sure that is what you want? Don't you wish to look inside?"

"I think I will be happier returning, thank you."

He changed tact. "And you think you *can* just return to Ember House? Having freed me? However will you explain yourself?" This did give her pause. Alis Jhardi's face was the first thing to enter her mind, painting an intimidating picture.

Only now did the realisation of what she had just done actually strike her. She had always assumed that, should she find a way to free him, she would have time to consider the correct course of action.

It was much too late for that now.

"I would appreciate your company, besides," he continued, apparently taking her silence as encouragement. "Aren't you intrigued to see inside Lucis palace? See the world? You and I together." She wasn't really sure *what* she wanted. "You can always turn around and come back after we've ventured in and done our exploring."

Egged on by his words, despite her continuing disbelief at the situation, she found herself stepping through the doorway – with Varick left to follow behind her, carrying the basket. She could imagine he was scowling at this, but right then, she was not inclined to care. "How long have you been planning this? You made me bring extra food." She frowned. "How did you even know what would happen?"

"Aha, you have comprehended my scheme. Well done you. I didn't know for certain, but I suspected. It was a gamble in which I had nothing to lose."

She stopped abruptly and turned around to face him, registering on some level that it was the first time she had seen a hint of his appearance – and he was *young*. "How could *you* possibly have known my hands would do that when I had no inkling of my own?"

"As you well know, I hate being asked to explain myself."

"You're completely detestable. Who are you that you think you have the right to Lord it over everyone else?" She stepped away, and folded her arms. A pointless gesture, as it went largely unseen. The corridor they had emerged in was quite dark, even if not the unadulterated darkness they had experienced before.

"You know full well I can't remember." He let out a slow sigh. "Fine. Firstly, you kept leaving an impression of your profile in my mind. I could usually tell when you were nearby, and sometimes even hear you, when your thoughts leant in my own direction. I heard it when you were thinking names such as Lucis and Tenebrae aloud in your mind. Other than that…"

"Yes?"

"Well… had you never wondered how you managed to see what the glamour was doing to you, when none before you had ever come close? You must have drained away just enough magic to alert you that something was amiss."

Adria had a lot of new information to digest, and remained silent as they walked. Whatever this magic she possessed was, it seemed a little pointless. Perhaps she could make people notice the palace, but it wasn't clear there would be any other potential ways to use it, never mind any ways that could actually be helpful.

It wasn't exactly like she had an easy way to practice it

either.

"I was tested, though!" she exclaimed, having only now remembered the scribe's assessment. "They tried to see what I could do, and I couldn't do anything at all."

"That, Adria," he said patronisingly, "is because you are not creating your own magic. Nor are you able to manipulate it. You are merely draining it."

He didn't elaborate, and she was left to contend with the slightly uneasy feeling there was something rather *distasteful* about this alleged newfound ability she had unknowingly come by.

With luck, she could keep it a secret, and wouldn't have to use it ever again.

CHAPTER 12 – FLIGHT

He had lied to the girl.

Every time they touched, it brought a little more life back to him. There had been a magical block on his memories, and now, finally, she was draining it away.

She was a siphon, in control of the rarest type of magic.

The chance that he'd found one seemed incredible. Impossible.

Seeing. Seeing something... anything... after all this time. He was trying not to stare like a child. He would not *show any weakness. He would not let her see how affected he was by his escape.*

Most of all, he would not let her know how invaluable she was.

Let her see only disdain, not his dependence on her. Never that.

They emerged into a narrow hallway, identifiable as the servants' area. The rooms to each side were small and mostly bare.

Thin, high-up slits, which passed for windows, let light filter into the main rooms. This light, in turn, trickled through into the long corridors. It was dim, but sufficient for them to make out their surroundings.

Once they determined the servants didn't have their

own separate way in and out, there wasn't much of interest in that wing, and they sought the main entrance hall instead.

Their path led them to an upward stairwell that spiralled round to take you into a tower – this was not where either of them thought they ought to be heading, given they wanted to find their way outside. The cell had been situated at ground level, that much they were able to be certain of, and therefore this was the floor they wanted to stay on.

Unhappy at having been tricked, Adria made a concerted effort to speak to Varick as little as she possibly could, and simply grunted in agreement when he suggested an alternative route, which avoided heading upwards.

As the quality of the furnishings and adornments increased, she knew he'd steered them correctly, and they were heading away from the more functional areas.

It dawned on her now, why it felt like there was something unusual about this place. There were no sheets to protect the furniture, and none of the belongings had been collected. Its appearance suggested it had been abandoned in a hurry.

At least, there were plenty of things Adria would have chosen to take with her should *she* have lived here.

As soon as they stepped through the kitchens and out into the dining hall, the forgotten wealth confronted them.

Adria had always thought Ember House was prosperous, but this was something else entirely.

Great glass chandeliers hung from the ceiling – or they might have been some sort of crystal, she wasn't certain, and they were too high up for her to touch. They reflected the light in a spectrum of colours, and she couldn't help but think this was the first example of extravagance she'd seen that had actually appealed to her artistically. She wished she could have seen one with all its candles aflame.

Numerous pairs of golden candlesticks lined the centre of a long table below. There was a richly woven tablecloth, displaying no obvious signs of disrepair, and the thirty-six chairs were uniquely carved, each showing its own woodland scene.

Luxurious, thick rugs ran across the floor to either side of the table. Adria slipped off one of her boots and pressed her foot against it, enjoying the feel of it sinking into the soft cushioning.

She was astonished. It wasn't even that different from what she had expected; from how she had pictured it, during those days she'd lain on the grass imagining this place.

That hadn't prepared her for actually *seeing* it.

Yet, from her few stolen glances, Varick seemed suspiciously nonchalant.

Disconcerted, she folded her arms and tried to appear less enamoured. Adria knew she shouldn't care what he thought, but she couldn't help herself. She didn't want him to think her childlike.

The moment she turned her back to him, she ceased any attempts to hide her wonder. This was the first time she'd been inside anywhere other than her home, and the contrast was striking.

Gradually, she became aware of the eyes boring into her back. Self-conscious, and remembering her situation, Adria decided she'd had enough anyway and stopped her gawking. Although she remained where she was standing, she frowned at Varick to indicate it was his move. Forced to lead the way, he strode off. She followed, arms still folded, and rolled her eyes behind his back, if only to make herself feel slightly better.

He led her directly to the palace door, essentially confirming her suspicions that he already knew his way around.

The large, gold door had a locking mechanism – which Varick promptly undid. "There is a path we can use to exit Tenebrae on the opposite side to Ember House. Given they think you're sleeping up here, no one will be any the wiser – probably for several whole days."

Drat his stupid plan and the fact she'd told everyone she needed three days' worth of food.

Although, would anyone care if I went missing anyway? No – I mustn't *think like that. Besides, they would care about their captive escaping... which is my fault. Does that mean that... maybe... I'll* never *be able to go back?*

This is a disaster. An absolute mess.

She composed herself, then turned her attention back to Varick. "Are you going to open the door then?"

"I can't. That is to say, I've unlocked it, but there's some sort of magical seal on it, too. Pretty please, may you siphon it?" His arrogance grated on her in a way it never had before.

"Sarcasm? How childish. Fine." She put her hand to the door and waited for a few minutes. When Varick nodded, she tried to push, but it still wouldn't budge. "It's too heavy for me. Stupid solid gold. You try. *Pretty please*."

Varick lent on it again. "The seal hasn't been removed. Hold on. Put your hand on it again." He placed his own hand over hers. "Nothing is happening." He thought for a second. "Okay."

She waited. She didn't want to have to speak, but apparently, they were at an impasse. "This is one of those times where 'okay' isn't really sufficient."

"Whatever. This will probably sound a bit strange, but it felt like that cell had been sealed by my own magic. As you had made physical contact with me, you were able to suck up my magic."

"Suck up being the technical term?"

"Do you want me to continue or not?" he challenged.

Lacking a better idea, she stuck her tongue out at him.

"This door has been sealed by someone else, and apparently, you are not able to draw their magic out of it. I am not sure if it's lack of discipline or just an inherent limitation in your ability." The way he said it made either option sound like an insult.

"Shall I just give up then? Maybe I'll find my way back out the way I came in, and you can stay here with all this useless finery." As she waved her arm around, she realised she should probably take a few pieces with her.

"Give me a moment to reflect on it. I hadn't anticipated your magic being so deficient that I needed a contingency. Here, take the basket while I think. It's your turn to carry it anyway."

"I do apologise, Lord So and So." She would not usually stoop this low, but he was *really* trying her patience.

"Catacombs," he declared erratically a few minutes later.

"I'm sorry, can you repeat that, please?"

"We will exit through the catacombs."

"Other than the logistical difficulty of navigating through what I'm assuming is an unmapped maze of tunnels, how do you know *they* won't be sealed, too?"

"No, I doubt they are."

She put her hand on her hip. "Is that... a *hunch*?"

"I don't think anyone would even know they were there. Don't worry, I built them."

"Oh yes, of course. *Of course,* you did. I completely believe you dug up and fashioned an entire underground labyrinth yourself." He ignored her. "Besides. That's not at all a contradiction to the fact you have no memories. Allegedly." He clearly knew his way around Lucis; something wasn't adding up.

Varick still didn't bother to answer, and instead marched away with a determined expression on his face. She had to decide quickly whether or not to follow him.

Curiosity got the better of her. Although she now found it very difficult to believe anything he said, she was genuinely tempted by the idea of the adventure. She also – as he seemed to be enjoying pointing out – had nothing to go back to.

Varick attempted to walk briskly, and she could only assume he wanted to leave her behind. Amusingly, however, she had to intentionally slow her strides to stop herself from overtaking him. Months of climbing Tenebrae Mountain had left her easily able to keep up, whereas it had been a long while since he had been able to properly stretch his legs.

She assumed, based on his physique, that he had maintained some level of activity during his years of isolation, but this was obviously no comparison to the extreme conditioning she herself had endured.

For a moment she felt sympathy for him, but then she noticed his swagger and her annoyance returned.

A benefit to their slow pace was it enabled her to continue surveying her surroundings. The importance of remembering her way around wasn't lost on her. Despite her willingness to follow him for now, she couldn't imagine a situation whereby she didn't want to return the way she'd come in.

Having been led up a grand staircase, then into what looked like it must have been one of the master bedrooms, Adria was slightly perturbed at first.

While she was still lingering in the doorway, he walked straight across the room, ostensibly with a clear purpose. She had been expecting him to show her a trap door behind a tapestry, but it was actually a large, heavy rug that he lifted to one side.

Impatient and unable to wait for him to share his thoughts, she blurted out, "There's nothing there."

As could have been predicted, he ignored her. She was left to simply watch as he pressed the fingerprints on his right hand into the floor like he was playing an imaginary piano.

After a brief wait, she heard a clicking sound, indicating a catch was being released. He turned and winked at her before pulling open a hatch, which had been hidden seamlessly in the floor.

"Wait a second. Did you use magic to open that? Do you have magic?" *Deep breath. He won't care that I'm angry, so there's no point losing my temper.* "But if you had sealed yourself in that cell with your own magic, why could you not just use magic to open it again?"

"Questions, questions. At least you're demonstrating you do have an ounce of intelligence in you, after all."

She glared at him. What a strange impact he was having on her usually calm and polite demeanour.

"I did not use any magic to open this trap door. Not *exactly*. It is conditioned to open only when it recognises my magical imprint. As suspected, no one had sealed it – most likely because nobody else knew it was here. Or possibly, whatever magic I used to create this was not able to be overridden by whatever sealing magic was used on the door."

Adria scratched her head. *He… what?*

"Secondly," he continued before she could get a word in, "Yes, I *did* have magic, but apparently, I have fully expended it. Almost certainly I used the last of it in sealing that cell."

"I'm amazed – you actually deigned to answer my

questions again. Anyone would think you might enjoy talking to me after all." Even if what he'd said sounded like a half-truth. Not a lie, but there was clearly much of the story he'd omitted, and not just for the sake of expediency.

"Whenever you ask me something sensible, it's much harder to garner my disdain. Besides, it's such a long time since I have spoken to anyone worth talking to, and I have a lot worth saying; I am forced to make do with the only option I have."

Wrinkling her nose, she considered holding back her reply, then said it anyway. "How did I ever think you were anything *other* than revolting?"

"I'm not revolting; you are just uncultured and have no taste. You should learn to be less disrespectful towards me – I may not continue to tolerate it. Now, stay here a moment." He disappeared off into a side room.

It turned out to be a very long moment. After a few minutes, she moved over to peer down the hatch. The top of a staircase was visible, but otherwise she saw only that it was a little darker down there than it was in the dusky bedroom.

When the stranger... *Varick* emerged, he was dressed in a black shirt and trousers. Not only that, but he had trimmed his hair and had a wash. He looked – and smelt – like an actual person.

Having had plenty of time to prepare what she wanted to say to him, Adria needed to speak before she lost her nerve. She could react to the change in his appearance later. As an added bonus, there was a small amount of pleasure she could take in not giving him the satisfaction of her admiration. "I have been respectful to people all my life. To people who have *earned* my respect. You seem to have some sort of presumption that you are just *entitled* to respect... and you have given me no reason to believe you are my better, other than your own inflated sense of self."

"That's nice. Do you feel better for that outburst? I agree with you, but you're missing the point. The crucial thing being that, yes, I do consider myself better than everyone else, and consequently, I don't actually care what your opinion is."

Adria decided he was right, although possibly not quite in the way he intended. She needed to toughen up.

Mentally readying herself, she climbed through the trapdoor behind him.

CHAPTER 13 – CRYPT

He felt unsettled.

He'd become very much aware that he had sealed himself *in that room.*

He had done it… to… himself.

To say it had been out of choice was misleading; a more accurate description would have been that it was done out of necessity – but the result was the same; he had intentionally drained his own magic dry.

After everyone had fled Lucis palace – the intention being that they locked the doors after themselves, with him still trapped inside – he'd started to go slightly delirious.

He'd known he could not remain alone in that huge fortress. He'd known there was a risk to the world if he escaped through the tunnels.

For someone who'd long since tipped past the brink of logical thought, he'd chosen wisely. The magic he'd performed had excluded his cell from the passage of time, rendering him impervious to aging or bodily degradation. It had been the safest way to shut off his own awareness of being. He had wanted to forget. He had needed to calm the storm inside his mind.

He'd woken up refreshed, but… perhaps not quite enough time had passed to render his release safe. A happy and an unhappy accident both at once.

Hearing the pattern of Varick's footsteps change alerted her to the fact she was nearing the bottom step. Even so, she stumbled a little as she stepped forward to find the floor had now become level. The stone wall she steadied herself against was rough, and unnaturally cold, beneath her hand.

A sound akin to rummaging through a pile of objects reached her ears, and she turned towards it expectantly.

"It's quite dark down here, isn't it? I'm sure I would have left a lantern around somewhere."

She didn't respond – he was almost certainly talking to himself. When he did, however, quite triumphantly declare he'd pulled a lantern out from its resting place, she found she couldn't resist. "How are you planning to light it then, if you don't have magic?"

"With a match."

"If you used to have so much magic you were able to create this place, why would you have bothered to store matches?"

"For my manservants, who did not have magic. Are you quite finished with this pointless game of 'trying to catch me out'?" As soon as he had filled and lit the lantern, stowing the spare matches in his pocket for later, he returned to the top of the stone stairs, pulled the rug back over the hole, and closed the trapdoor. It was a slightly tricky manoeuvre, but one he appeared to be quite practised at.

Finally, she could see something of her surroundings. They were inside a crypt – empty of bodies, it instead contained two full bookcases and a desk, each littered with books and papers.

Although this area was reasonably spacious, the corridors running away from it – all five of them – looked disconcertingly narrow. Worse, there didn't appear to be anything demarcating one passageway from another.

Adria regretted having asked about the matches now because the more pertinent question seemed to be how well he actually remembered the route. She shivered, consoling herself with the fact that if she was going to be stuck down here – which apparently, she was – then perhaps it was better not to know.

Even so, she wished he wasn't deliberating *quite* so obviously.

From the way the Steward had described it, it had to have been an awfully long time since he could have last been down here, and five different routes to choose between seemed like a lot.

In an attempt to distract herself, she wandered over to the bookcase and read the titles. Even with the preservation enchantment laying over the palace, the spines were well worn as if, even centuries ago, they'd been read over and over. They looked to cover a good mix of topics – physics, alchemy, magic, and there was even a shelf with several adventure stories.

Without warning, the light started to fade. *Of course.* Varick had wandered off down one of the paths without having bothered to say anything. She had to make a quick decision, but with the trapdoor closed above her and likely needing magic to re-open it, she was forced to hurry after him.

He *almost* definitely meant her to follow, given he'd left the basket behind too. She grabbed and pocketed one of the more interesting-looking books before she did. He was still walking amusingly slowly, so she didn't overly have to hurry to catch up.

Unlike the crypt, these walls were dirt-packed and appeared unfinished. Whilst the width wasn't so limited as to be uncomfortable, there wasn't sufficient space for her to walk next to him, and she was left with no choice but to trail behind.

The roof of the tunnel was low, too; Varick had only a thumb's length of room above him and she wondered how it was he didn't feel the need to bow his head.

Even with the slightly larger headroom she had available, Adria had to keep reminding herself to stop hunching over.

"What are you muttering to yourself?" Varick's deep voice echoed slightly. Disconcertingly, she hadn't even realised she'd been speaking aloud.

"I was wondering how stable the ceiling is. This place is rather… *crudely* assembled. Are we safe? Maybe don't answer unless you're going to tell me we're fine."

"I've decided you worry too much."

Adria waited for him to say something else – anything really – that might sound vaguely comforting. He didn't. *But he's probably, intentionally, trying to scare me.* She coughed slightly, which set her off on another train of erratic thought, questioning whether there was enough air down there. Especially as they moved deeper through the mountain – *how would that even work?*

"Could you try and quieten your thoughts down a bit? I can hear you panicking in a hundred different ways. It's like a cacophony of competing anxieties."

Easy for him to say; he had obviously been down here before.

"Look, I have been through this network more times than I can count. Yes, it's been, what, nearly a century since the last time, but these sorts of things come back to you as soon as you see them. I'm sure I'll remember which way to go. The place is securely built, and I'm almost certain nothing new will have moved into residence here."

She had been feeling reassured until those last few words. Taking a deep breath, she asked, "How long is it actually going to take us to get through this warren?"

"Oh, the things we'll be contending with are much bigger than rabbits."

She knew he was winding her up, as he struggled to stifle a laugh.

"Maybe three days if we keep moving and do not stop to sleep for more than a couple of hours a night."

"Three days!" she exclaimed. "Three whole days? That makes no sense. It takes me less than a few hours to climb the top third of the mountain. It can't possibly be longer than a day – and I'm not including the night – to make our way back down!"

He turned to face her, and the lantern-glow revealed up his amusement. She'd fallen foul of his flippancy *again*. "You really need to pause for breath before you speak. You probably ought to wait until you've thought through what you're about to say as well. Didn't your mother ever explain that to you?"

Judging by his expression, Varick realised he'd put his foot in it. It was ironic, given the subject matter of his lecture. She almost began to feel sorry for him, as the silence extended until it became slightly awkward. Whilst she was tempted to say something to relieve the tension, she managed to resist.

They walked without speaking again for a while. The floor was uneven, and the break in conversation enabled Adria to concentrate more fully on her footing. It was fortunate she had been provided with sturdy footwear.

The paths declined only gradually, and she could tell they had been sculpted with the gentle gradient taking priority rather than how quickly they took one to their destination. No wonder it was going to take them so long to descend.

After several occasions on which he'd had to pick a route, she let out the question she'd been trying to stop herself asking. "Why are there so many different divergences?"

"So that no one, other than myself, would be able to find their way." He tutted disdainfully, clearly disappointed that she had not figured out something he considered obvious. "Think about it, Adria. What's the point of having an escape route from a *palace* if somebody could easily follow you out? Or find their way in. That would be at least as bad – if someone found the mountainside entrance, and they were able to simply sneak in and murder the inhabitants during the night."

"It still seems like a lot of effort to have created each of these different routes. You'd already sealed the entrance such that you were the only person who could open it; could you not just do the same magic at the exit, too?"

"You're assuming nobody is able to override my magic, or overpower me then prevent me from closing the trapdoor. There are numerous possibilities that make my precautions sensible. There's no need to make me sound unbalanced."

"And no need to be so sensitive about it. Anyone would think I'd touched a nerve. And I notice you didn't contradict my assertion you'd used magic."

"I could just abandon you in these tunnels, you know."

"Sure." There was no way he would be able to run fast enough to leave her behind.

Although, if he thought to put out the lantern... he'd probably still be able to find his way in the dark, and she would presumably struggle to follow. It was not a particularly pleasant speculation, but perhaps it was an important one, as it led her to the realisation that she needed to stay on his good side. "In that case, I appreciate your genius. Where do the decoy paths lead?"

"A lot of them link back up, sending the intruder in endless loops. Some of them do culminate in actual chambers. I found it useful to have remote places to practice certain elements of my magic." Circling back to her earlier comment, he added, "I didn't have any magic, but perhaps when my memory began to come back, so did a small spark. I'm unsure as yet."

Adria was determined to test the limits of what Varick could remember, but now didn't feel like the right time. She wanted to keep him talking, though; it helped provide a distraction from the growing sense of claustrophobia creeping up on her. "How far through do you think we are? Have we made it halfway?"

"It's possible."

"Are you hungry? Shall we stop for water?"

"Quiet," he commanded. It was harshly spoken, even for him.

What's happening?

I think he heard a noise.

What had caused it, she couldn't guess – Adria still couldn't hear anything.

At last, her ears picked up a simple scuffling sound.

"It's probably just rats," she whispered. Varick shook his head and put his finger to his lips to silence her.

CHAPTER 14 – DHARJIGS

He'd forgotten all about the dangers of the other creatures which roamed these walkways. They could be a considerable threat to those unable to repel them.

To him, this was novel; he couldn't remember ever having felt afraid. Once upon a time, he'd had enough magic to be their King.

There was something exhilarating about being under threat.

It brought the layout back to the forefront of his mind. He knew exactly which way they would flee... and yet, the room they would utilise brought up emotions of a different kind.

Unpleasant ones.

Unsettled by Varick's behaviour, Adria could feel the beginning of an adrenaline surge, readying her for a fight or flight response. He'd picked up his pace in front, switching to a light jog, and she took large strides to keep up.

At the next fork, he chose a path that led uphill.

When they reached a small room, he gestured for her to stand on one of the chairs while he did likewise, then smothered the flame in his lantern.

The only upside of being plunged into darkness was

there was no way for Varick to see how much she was trembling. He clearly had an advantage, as he knew what they were facing.

Although... did she really want to know?

"Don't... make... any... sound..."

By now, Adria's imagination was inevitably running wild. She tried to remember any creatures she'd read about which might live underground. Nothing she recalled had been frightening enough to draw this reaction from Varick, but she appreciated they may have made less of an impact on her at the time, given she'd never anticipated she would actually meet any of them.

Only a short time earlier, she had thought *Varick* was the thing she needed to be most afraid of. Now he was a reassuring presence.

The more she tried to quieten her breathing, the louder it seemed.

Her legs complained about carrying her weight. They'd walked for a long time without a break – why had her body chosen *this* of all moments to feel the effects of it?

The scuffling noise moved towards them, closer and closer, until she was certain they were almost in the room.

Turn back. Don't come in here. She felt herself tensing.

Then, all too quickly, they were no longer alone.

Whatever the creatures were – insects, presumably – they were numerous. The basket she carried weighed heavily in her arms as she attempted to remain still. She was cold, too. It was a struggle not to shiver; yet beads of sweat formed on her forehead. *Don't drip. Please...* There wasn't anything she could do but pray nothing fell.

Surely, they'd soon recede. How much longer could it be?

She wanted to ask Varick what was going to happen.

Whether they were safe. How long they might be standing here. The questions clamoured for attention inside her head, pressing her to seek their answers.

As time slowly passed, her attitude shifted. Instead of expecting relief would come soon, she began to believe this would never be over.

She'd stand on the stool until she no longer could, and then… then they'd crawl across her.

Were there as many of them as it sounded like – a whole floor full of them?

She closed her eyes, hoping to escape even if it was solely in her mind – only to find herself conjuring pictures of what might lie below her; imagining how big they might be. It didn't even matter. They'd swarm across her just the same regardless.

Her throat was scratchy and dry. The more she thought about holding back a cough, the more it tickled. She scrunched up her face.

It was just as well the ceiling was higher in here. She wondered what the room had been used for.

Her head began to pound from all the unasked questions.

There was an itch on her arm, but she couldn't move to scratch it.

If they could smell, they would have reached her by now… so they'd been drawn towards their movement. No, Varick had told her to be quiet, so it must have been the sound of their footsteps.

Did that mean they were likely to have recurring encounters with these bugs until they found their way out?

When the intruders eventually retreated, the relief was immense, and a spark of hope grew within her; they might survive this journey after all. Her whole body relaxed with such an intensity that Adria thought she might collapse and fall to the ground – but she couldn't, not yet.

Adria hadn't needed Varick's instruction to know they should continue to wait a while before dismounting, so as to be completely sure they didn't attract their attention once again.

After all, what was a few more minutes after almost an hour of waiting…

"Okay, talk. What were those?" she asked as he re-lit the lantern.

"A type of scuttling bug. They are unpleasant little critters. A mix between a cockroach and a spider."

"Dharjigs? They were Dharjigs? You have *got* to be joking! Surely they could have just climbed up the chair legs?" She'd read all about Dharjigs – albeit, at the time, she had not been quite certain whether or not they were truly real. Adria shuddered. A bite from one of those would leave your skin swollen for days, and this had been a whole convoy of them.

"Dharjigs – if you say so. I don't recall them having a name. And yes, of course they could have climbed up. That's why I told you to be quiet." He then had the audacity to laugh in the face of her horror. "It's just as well you thought we were safe on the chairs then, or who knows how you'd have managed to stand still while they explored the room."

She was about to let it go when another thought occurred to her. "Roaches and spiders have a better sense of smell than us, so surely these do too?"

"Yes, I did rather worry they might go for the food – and then, of course, they'd reach you and, developing a taste for flesh, they'd almost certainly have come for me next. No one's been below this mountain for almost a century. They wouldn't have remembered what humans smell like. I wasn't overly keen to remind them."

"Okay, I'm feeling a bit faint."

"If it helps, I think being in such a large pack prevented them from smelling anything bar each other. Or perhaps, having been underground so long, they've developed other, preferred ways of identifying their prey, like sound."

"Either way, we don't actually know if we're safe now. Are we going to be at risk of encountering them again the whole time until we're back outside?" There, the question she had been most afraid to ask had been said. She pretended to look around the room, hoping to avoid letting him see her reaction when he gave his answer.

"Absolutely. We'd be very unlucky to encounter them a second time, however." Was that... the first time he'd said something reassuring? "I suppose it's not implausible they would have multiplied rather drastically since I was last down here."

"I... I..." It was pointless prolonging this topic of conversation. Rubbing her hand on her forehead she said, "I think we should stop and eat something." Making their way through the last of the fresh food, Adria was even more glad of the sustenance than she'd anticipated. It helped her feel back in control – of herself, at least. It had been a long while since she'd been in control of her own circumstances.

"What was this room for, Varick? I was sceptical about their existence, but we were lucky you'd built the side routes after all."

"This is where I kept some of the bodies."

"Very funny. Don't tell me then." She hoped if she feigned disinterest he might elaborate, but he simply raised his eyebrows in response and plucked another bread roll from the basket.

Backtracking downhill for a short distance, they rejoined the main route.

The Dharjigs had left the paths filled with cobwebs and

insect husks, an unpleasant and constant reminder of what had passed through ahead of them. At first, she hesitated. Going slowly, she tried to brush against the walls as little as possible, albeit with limited success. Her need to leave the catacombs soon encouraged her to pick up speed; besides, she was already filthy.

However far they walked, she didn't think she'd ever get used to the feeling of the strands clinging to her. She tried to pick the larger ones from her hair, but they were too sticky and there were too many of them to continue fighting what was quickly becoming a losing battle.

As well as the discomfort of being coated in insect mesh, her body had become so thoroughly chilled that she struggled to get warm again. She was forced to resign herself to feeling cold until they eventually found their way outside again – if she was lucky, they'd emerge during the day.

If she wasn't…

Don't think like that, Adria. He knows his way out; you will be free of this place.

And then what?

She found she was no longer inclined towards conversation. All she desired was to escape from the oppression of the mountain. It had been far too long since she had last slept, but there was no question of stopping until they were outside.

She'd experienced more in the last couple of days than she had in her whole life at Ember House leading up to that point.

CHAPTER 15 – BREEZE

He had spent a lifetime roaming these tunnels. Every wall, floor, and path was familiar to him, reassuring.

Nevertheless, some of his memories of this place weren't entirely positive. It was probably for the best she hadn't asked why he had referred to them as catacombs... was it an oversight, or did she simply accept some truths without questioning them?

The girl was a burden, but perhaps she could be a lesson to him in patience. She wasn't complaining nearly as much as she could have been; as much as he might have expected. It was a new experience. He was used to women throwing themselves at his feet – whether to gain his attention or his mercy.

More than two generations had passed since he had last seen the outside world. He had learnt everything he could from his companion in preparation for this moment... without asking those things he was too proud to admit he yearned to know.

As much as the tunnels gave him safety and security, he itched to leave them. To once again feel the breeze on his face.

His situation was frustrating. He lacked power, both through his inability to use his magic and *his absence of any status or position in the world.*

He needed to regain control.

Something in Varick's demeanour led Adria to suspect they were finally nearing the end of these dark passageways.

This was all but confirmed by the natural light, which began to seep through from somewhere ahead.

When they finally approached the large wooden door, Adria's sense of relief was stronger than anticipated. The enclosed space had clearly had a greater effect on her wellbeing than she'd perceived.

A tiny voice told her she'd been strengthened by the experience. She knew she never wanted to be as reliant on anyone, as she had just been on Varick, *ever* again.

The three deadbolts were old, and he visibly strained to force them open. She experienced a brief moment of panic – her imagination running away from her – when he tugged the first one and nothing happened, but with a little persistence, Varick successfully wrenched each of them free.

Next, he tapped his fingers lightly on the wall. To release the seal, if she'd been following correctly. He really seemed to be taking his time over getting it open, and she had a funny feeling it was mostly intentional. Adria found she struggled to tell whether he was laughing at her or merely despised her.

A waft of air hit her forcefully in the face, signalling he had it open at last.

They emerged into the world outside of Ember House.

It was mid-morning, and the light was intense, hurting her eyes. Varick was similarly scrunching up his own. He appeared to be sporting a genuine smile, and it made her uncomfortable to note quite how odd the expression looked on him.

When they both acclimatised, Adria finally saw him in daylight for the first time. She was struck by the marked glowering in his eyes. A certainty washed over her – this man was evil.

Yet, when she blinked, that look she thought she'd witnessed had passed. She was left uncertain whether she had glimpsed into his depths, or if she'd seen a premonition of what could be. Either way, Adria reminded herself to be on her guard. She hadn't yet made her mind up how dangerous he was.

Why was he imprisoned? I still can't even hazard a guess.

Their burgeoning friendship now seemed forgotten, but he'd done nothing to threaten her as yet. Or had he? Subconsciously, she'd begun rubbing her wrist. There was a thumbprint-sized bruise where he had grabbed her to pull her inside his prison.

She understood why he'd acted in such a way, and could empathise with someone who'd only wanted to be free. That didn't mean he was a good choice of companion. Having grown a little used to him in the days they'd spent in each other's company so far, she had relaxed her guard more than she perhaps ought to have. Although his appearance was unassuming, his reactions were impulsive. Volatile, even.

Whilst she didn't want to believe he might have killed people, it was undeniably a possibility. There were plenty of murderers who'd been locked away... but who among them would have warranted a whole palace for their crimes? Plus, there was the matter of why all the secrecy had been required. Nothing made sense.

"Varick, what bodies were you talking about?"

"Context?"

"After the Dharjigs retreated." Adria shuddered. "You said it was the room in which you kept the bodies." *Then I pretended it was a joke because I was too concerned about getting out of there.*

"Oh right. I used to practice science."

With his back to her, she couldn't see his expression, but it was as much of an answer as she could have hoped for.

It irked her that she had no choice but to follow him. Adria had no knowledge of the area, or the way things worked in the wider world – it was why she'd never had the courage to leave Ember House. She needed to find a town where she might be able to settle, and it was easier to travel alongside Varick until they reached one.

It was the wrong time of day, yet they agreed to rest for a few hours; their legs would not carry them much further without doing so. Given how long they'd persisted, it was a wonder Varick was still standing. Not having walked anywhere for... *some time*, he must have been pushing his body to go further than was natural. Only desperation to be free could have spurred him to keep going. The moment he stopped, would it hit him? Might he collapse from exhaustion?

He wasn't showing any sign of suffering, and Adria reminded herself to close off any feelings of sympathy towards this unpleasant man. For all she knew, he was using magic to keep going and *she* was the only one who'd had their endurance pushed to the limit.

With nothing to be seen around them but grass and rocks, they set themselves up close to the mountain. Adria used the opportunity to catch up on sleep, the relief at being free of the mountain far outweighing her excitement over being released into the unknown.

When she woke up, Varick was sitting on the ground, seemingly deep in thought. He was concentrating so intently that he didn't immediately notice she had stirred. Giving herself a couple of minutes to shake off the sleep, she signalled for his attention.

"We do not have horses," he remarked, stating the obvious. "So we have a long walk ahead of us. We have no choice but to make for the nearest village and hope that, for now, nobody is looking for me."

"Is anybody *likely* to come looking for you?" Adria

mused, thinking him awfully self-important. It was a relief to hear he was heading for a neighbouring village – confirming in her mind that her best course of action was to stay with him for the time being.

"I suspect so, Adria. Yes, it seems rather inevitable."

"They will still remember you?" she inquired innocently, but one stern look from Varick silenced her on the matter.

As they walked, she recalled Alis's warnings and knew he had spoken the truth; the man hidden in the mountain had not been forgotten.

☆ ☆ ☆ ☆ ☆

After walking for around half an hour, they passed through an invisible, yet perceptible, barrier. Whilst Adria had detected a slight amount of physical resistance, it was the air having instantly turned dry and harsh that alerted her to the fact they'd moved outside the boundary of Ember House's glamour.

The countryside's colours, which had previously seemed so rich and warm, had faded to dirty, shabby versions of themselves.

The grass, which had been green, healthy, and alive, now appeared tan and parched. Whole swathes of the land comprised only muddy earth, where nothing grew.

Craggy hills were dotted all around them, more obvious, and stark, now they no longer blended in with their surroundings.

Adria found herself rooted to the spot in shock.

"Not what you were expecting?" he taunted.

Varick seemed reinvigorated for being outside in the fresh air – and was unaffected by the sudden increase in aridity. She wasn't sure why she hadn't noticed the change in him from the moment they'd left the mountain; it was more than apparent. "I know you're goading me. I'm not *that* naïve. No, it is not what I expected, as you know full well. How could I have been anticipating *this*?"

"Are you not educated? Have you never read a book?"

Adria was too shocked to be irritated by his condescension. "Of course I have, but... I just thought there would be... I don't know... fewer flowers? And the grass would be parched, the trees slightly withered. This... it's like a screen has been removed from in front of my eyes, and now everything looks not quite real. Or maybe it was the other that was fake. I can't wrap my mind around it." She inhaled sharply. "*Nothing* I could have heard or read would have prepared me for this. Even the *air* is unpleasant – it's worse than it was in those muddy passages." Light-headed from the confusion, Adria misstepped, regaining her balance awkwardly.

"Talking of mud. I'm almost embarrassed to be seen with you. How is it that I still look pristine whilst you look as though you've been rolling around on the ground like a pig?"

"Perhaps, Varick, it's because *you* were the one with the lantern, and *you* could actually see the walls of those passages. I am well aware of how filthy I am. I was hoping we would pass a river... but I suppose I may as well give up any expectation of that. In this changed world, I imagine the rivers run brown not blue."

Varick agreed he had no choice but to put up with her state of dress and thankfully, dropped the matter. When they reached the village, she would be able to find some water to clean herself up with.

Her state of dress bothered her less than her surroundings, and for the entire rest of the day, her astonishment lingered. No matter how far they walked, she couldn't shake her distress. Adria couldn't help but think that, until now, she had been living apart from reality. She imagined Ember House's grounds as the fey land from a book of fairy tales. *This* was the real world, starved of love.

She was an expert at indulging in her own fantasies.

At least Varick had sped up. Still keeping up with him comfortably, she expected he might continue to increase his pace, and was optimistic they'd reach civilisation soon. Hopefully, she'd find some better company and could send this ill-mannered lout on his way.

I can always dream.

"We're almost at Freeway," he told her – naming a habitation familiar because of its weekly market. Often, a couple of members of the kitchen help would take a cart there, but it hadn't ever sounded as far away as it now felt.

Today was *not* market day, Adria was relieved but slightly disappointed to note.

The streets were quiet, with only a few people here and there, but still feeling displaced, she was happy to let Varick lead the way. Even if, regrettably, it meant she appeared to be his subordinate.

It was odd to see the numerous wooden shacks the people here lived in; so in contrast with the living arrangements she had been used to. She cringed at the thought this might be her future.

It most likely will be.

The pang of regret surprised her; the veracity of the luxury she had walked away from suddenly all too clear. When she reminded herself she would have been resigned to climbing up and down Tenebrae ad infinitum – the lure of the occupant no longer a factor in staving off boredom – her spirits lifted a little. The resentment she felt over having been selected for the duty in the first place, however, remained.

When she snapped out of her daydream, Varick was no longer close, and she was forced to hurry after him. By the time she'd caught up, he was already engaged in conversation with one of the village's occupants. At her arrival, the uncouth gentleman very evidently looked down his nose at her, much to Adria's great embarrassment.

She had been judging *him* for his dishevelled appearance, forgetting her own was currently far worse. She bowed her head. She was well and truly ashamed of herself.

Varick reached towards her, and acting on instinct, she recoiled. Raising his eyebrows, he leaned forward and pulled some coins out of the basket.

Adria frowned. No wonder it had felt heavier than it ought, given how much of its contents they had eaten.

Belatedly, she realised he'd just acquired two horses. Perhaps it should have been a nice feeling, to realise he hadn't forgotten her and wasn't planning to abandon her now he was free, but instead, all she could focus on was how he'd effectively made her obligated to him in return. *She* may have been the sole reason he had escaped his prison, but Adria was so unused to anyone doing anything for her that his purchase made her uneasy.

How frustrating it was that all the wages she had earned of her own accord remained in her old room, and entirely inaccessible.

"Great!" Varick at least seemed pleased with himself. It did not escape Adria's attention that he'd waited for the vendor to leave before addressing her. "Now we have two horses, I can ride, *and* there's another to carry supplies."

Charming. How had she momentarily forgotten the severity of his arrogance?

"No need to look so aghast, I'm only teasing you. Although, I am now starting to wonder whether you even *have* a sense of humour."

She slapped her palm to her forehead. This man was infuriating. He never said what he meant. Or meant what he said. It was so unlike anything she was used to. "Please. Just find me somewhere to get clean."

Adria had seen enough of that particular day to know nothing was going to be handed to her on a plate. Despite this, it was still a grave disappointment to discover there was a distinct shortage of water. Unluckily – given Varick likely could have afforded whatever sum was required – it wasn't the 'it requires a lot of money' kind of scarcity; rather, it simply wasn't available in the quantities she needed.

They managed to procure a small bowl she could use to wash her face and arms, and then Varick had to track down a change of clothes for her instead. He also found a linen pack they could use in place of the cumbersome wicker basket, and Adria, having been doing most of the carrying, was unable to hide her gratitude.

It was lucky Varick could so easily call upon his exaggerated charm, as not only had he been required to approach the villagers' houses to obtain what they needed – with Adria remaining comfortably out of sight – but the sun had already begun to set, and her instincts told her it was an unusual time to be knocking on people's doors.

Although they were both quite tired, the short rest that morning having not been enough to combat a full day of missed sleep, neither Varick nor Adria wanted to linger in Freeway. Their welcome hadn't been unfriendly, but it was a small place with no inns, and it had been made plain their stay was expected to be one of short duration.

They agreed to continue travelling for another hour before finding somewhere to camp.

Whilst they had yet to find a tent, Varick had managed

to get his hands on a second sleeping bag. The villagers really *had* gone out of their way to accommodate him.

"Varick, I hope you don't mind me asking, but how did those coins end up in the basket?"

"Do you hear how accusatory you sound?" He tutted. "I picked them up while we were in my bedroom at the palace. I assumed you had noticed."

Adria felt a little foolish, but not because she'd missed him taking the coins. She had always thought herself reasonably switched on when it came to her surroundings; somehow, she had failed to realise it had been *his* room. Despite him having picked out a change of clothes and the trap door being synchronised specifically to him.

It was difficult not to question her own judgment. She was truly out of her depth.

Even when they lay down to sleep, a multitude of thoughts continued swirling around her head. Varick had insisted he was somebody important. Lucis Palace was huge, so she'd figured there'd been lots of people who lived there. Why hadn't she put the pieces together before now – to reach the obvious conclusion that Varick was a member of the sovereign family.

All of her original curiosity about why this man had been imprisoned came flooding back to her. The ruling family seemed to have imposed this treatment on one of their own.

Was that why he hadn't been in an ordinary jail? And why Alis was aware of his existence? The pieces fit together, but her awareness of just how little she really knew about Varick was heightened.

When she finally drifted off, it was not into a peaceful sleep.

CHAPTER 16 – RESPITE

Adria was back at Lucis Palace. Its appearance was mostly the same as she remembered, but currently, there were people everywhere. She had yet to move from where she stood in the foyer when a small puppy ran between her feet. A child of perhaps ten years chased after it, slipping on the polished tiles before he had chance to catch up.

"Are you okay?" she asked him. He didn't respond, or even acknowledge she was there.

A man approached the youngster as he picked himself up from the floor. "Master Varick, the rest of the family are already seated at the dining table, along with their guests. Once again, you are both late and an embarrassment." The man escorted a chastened young Varick to his room to change for the midday meal. Adria followed unseen – she now knew she wasn't really there, and this was some form of dream.

Whilst she recognised the room, in this setting it was untidy, and the belongings were strewn all over the bed and floor in disarray. It was nothing like the sparse, empty space that she and adult Varick had passed through.

The wardrobe was opened to reveal two sets of formal attire, which the boy was invited to select from, but he made no rush to change out of his breeches and smarten up.

When Varick finally arrived at the table, there was no place set for him – instead, he was sent into a side room and told he'd missed the first course. Adria lingered, fascinated by seeing the table she had admired being put to actual use. Guests were sitting on those beautiful chairs, the rows of candlesticks were lit, and numerous platters held food stacked in ornate towers.

She didn't recognise any of the people around the table, but it was clear – even without the addresses of 'Your Majesty' being directed towards them – which couple held the place of honour.

Varick's side room was not quite so lavish and only contained a table large enough for one. She guessed his banishment had been a reasonably commonplace occurrence.

After the meal, the guests retired to their rooms to change, and the family gathered in a sitting room. Varick, she learnt, had two older brothers. She had not realised their relationship at first, as they both appeared to be almost twice his age.

While he sat on the floor, playing with a small ball, his parents congratulated their other two sons.

"Princes," their father addressed them, "You have done well this day. I truly believe our neighbours will begin to accept the advantages of a monarchy in their own regions. Please continue as you are. You are dismissed."

Once the two boys had bowed to their father and left the room, he turned his attention towards his youngest. "Whatever am I going to do with you, child? Attending a luncheon is a simple request, is it not? I do not think I am asking anything difficult of you. Why do you continue to thwart me?" Varick's mother looked uncomfortable, but she remained silent.

"I'm sorry, Father. I wanted to play. I don't think those men at the meal would have liked my company very much. I don't know what to say to them."

"Then you sit there in silence and act like you are the

obedient child that you consistently fail to be." His tone was strong and left no room for argument.

After his father left the room, his mother put her arms around his shoulders and kissed him on the head. "I'm sorry, son. I know this is not how you'd like to be spending your days. You must try to make him happy, and maybe if you play along, he will indulge your request for a friend your own age." She followed after her husband, leaving Varick alone to sulk.

He bounced his ball until he threw it at an angle, and it rolled outside of his reach. Instead of searching for a way to get it back, he folded his arms and pouted. Adria went to retrieve it for him, discovering it felt solid in her hand. With this realisation, the perspective of the room shifted. The boy who became Varick looked up at her.

"What are you doing in my memories, Adria?"

She found herself cast out.

CHAPTER 17 – COMPLICATIONS

Adria and Varick sat upright in their respective sleeping bags.

"What did you do to me?" Varick shouted. Seeing how angry he was, she cowered.

"I have no idea. I'm sorry, I don't even know how that happened." Severely disoriented by the experience, she wasn't yet ready to deal with his ire.

"You must have done something! You do not just *accidentally* fall into someone's mind."

Adria had no idea what to say. She hoped her dismay was obvious. She tried to think of anything she could have done wrong, but everything before falling asleep had seemed normal – so far as anything in their circumstances, which included sleeping in the middle of nowhere and being unable to return home, could be considered normal.

While she was still thinking, Varick stormed off. He had left his sleeping bag, and she could still see their horses tied to the tree where they had left them the evening before, so she figured he was probably going to come back at some point. Whatever had happened, it had been intrusive and, worse, incredibly personal. She felt awful about it.

"I can only apologise," she told him when he returned a short while later. "I really mean it. I don't know what to tell you other than how sorry I am." She shrugged, attempting to convey her regret. "I still don't know how it happened, though."

"It's fine. Can we please not discuss it any further."

"Of course." *But what if it happens again… Best leave that question for another time.* "Did you have any thoughts on our destination? Where do you think the safest place will be?" She had been waiting for an opportunity to broach this particular concern with him anyway.

He looked at her as though he were weighing up how to break some bad news. She frowned. "Adria, our destination is and always will be Lucis Palace. It's my home."

"I don't understand."

"I know. You will though. Like it or not, we're a team now, and we have a long journey ahead of us."

Despite her typically placid temperament, his response riled her. "Varick, I am not taking one more step with you unless you tell me exactly what you are planning and where we are going." He stared at her. He was clearly taken aback at no longer being the only one of them that was angry. "I mean it, Varick, I do. Just because you used to be a person of unspecified importance does not mean you are currently in a position to lord it over me."

"Have you finished? Quite done? Is that out of your system now? I am only bringing you along with me because I am eternally grateful for your assistance in breaking me out of that place, and I am starting to enjoy your lovely, albeit simple, company." He didn't half lay it on thick when he decided he needed her to comply. Adria wanted to be suspicious, but sadly, she had no idea what he was up to. "Come on, let's get moving. There are two towns equidistant from here; I plan to pay my respects at each of them."

Luckily, Adria was learning how to dish out the flattery,

too. "I know you think I can't keep up with you, and it's probably true. I'm sorry for all the questions. You always seem to be one step ahead of me. I had merely thought we were going to try and work our way as far from here as possible – escaping detection of whoever wants to keep you in confinement."

"Nobody will be able to return me to confinement. According to the residents of Freeway, there is no new magic creation anywhere in the entire world. I may only have confirmed this with one town so far, but my gut feeling is they spoke the truth. I can sense its absence. Something is amiss. It would be unfortunate if anyone tracked us down, but more so for them than it would be for us."

"If you were part of the ruling family, you must be related to Alis," she foolishly mumbled, in an attempt to keep him talking while she figured things out.

"In a way. After my middle brother died, his widow re-married. I believe the Jhardi family are an offshoot from someone in my ex-sister-in-law's line. Technically, they do not have any claim to rulership, although I doubt there is anyone around who would remember as such." She looked towards him, puzzled. "That memory you saw was three hundred years ago."

It was evident he was *purposefully* trying to shock her now.

Yet unexpectedly, he proceeded to explain what he'd meant. It was difficult to take him seriously when he alleged that he considered himself to be the 'Rightful' king of the Azeileah province, but judging he wouldn't appreciate her mockery, Adria kept quiet.

He claimed to have lived a terribly long life before he had been interred. His magic had been strong enough for him to have maintained his youthful form, meaning he had barely aged, appearance-wise, since he had come into his full power. After he had been sequestered away, the seal's nature had been such as to lock the room in a type of stasis, thereby giving him the perception that no time had passed at all.

Until she'd disturbed his slumber. *It was like sleeping beauty but without the romance.*

Any clarifications she requested were conveniently greeted by the 'memory-loss' excuse. She wasn't sure exactly *when* he had regained his memories, but she was fairly sure they *were* there, in the same way she had believed they were missing before. He was acting differently. He'd always been calculated, but at some point, his actions had gained a subtlety they'd previously been lacking.

"You had two older brothers, though?" *What would have made* you *the rightful sovereign, other than vanity?*

"Neither Dayne nor Ghian had magic anywhere near as strong as mine. I was the favoured child and easily the best choice for heir. I was a little disappointed, I admit, when you didn't react to my name. I used to be quite infamous throughout the country. I was hoping there would be many who remembered the stories of my two-hundred-year campaign, if not the full details behind the man himself."

Adria tactfully placated him, "I led a very sheltered life at Ember House. We had little, if any, contact with the Sovereign family. I only met Lady Jhardi twice in all my years there. Remember my reaction to the land? I suppose some important details were kept from us – intentionally, perhaps. You could hardly expect the Jhardis to indulge their staff by providing details of how they came to power. Especially if it was not quite as... *proper*... as they had led us to believe." He appeared satisfied with her explanation, so she added, "That would also explain why there are hardly any books on that period of history in their library."

Atop fine horses, they travelled quickly, but they were both reluctant to approach anywhere during the night. As such, they had no choice but to spend a second night camped out in the wild.

Varick seemed stronger than he had been, and it was obvious freedom suited him. Adria, conversely, felt her desire for adventure had already been satiated and would have happily settled in one place for a while.

With no need for them to keep watch – between them, they had little worth stealing – they slept as well as the coarse ground would allow.

Adria had become used to the bleakness of their surroundings, but it continued to sadden her. It didn't seem like the world wanted, or *ought*, to be that way; there was a palpable sense of wrongness she couldn't shake. Twice now, she had attempted to discuss it with Varick, who had very decidedly shut down the possibility of any conversation on the subject.

She was finding him increasingly difficult as a travelling companion. Sometimes, they would hit upon a subject of mutual interest and end up chatting incessantly. More often, however, he would become critical of the most innocent thing she'd said, then withdraw.

There was something below his surface, and increasingly, this unsettled her. Adria tried to quieten the voice whispering of unnatural horrors, suggesting his persona was warped, even twisted in some way. She tried to convince herself it was inevitable that someone who had lived as long as he had would have hidden depths and the occasional strange secret. She was not worldly; he had seen and experienced more than she could ever imagine. But the whispers wouldn't relent.

Come morning, Adria's outlook was slightly more positive. Approaching another village, this time she felt far more presentable, and less meek as a result.

Varick wandered off – not wholly unexpectedly – leaving her to roam the streets alone. Whilst, in a way, she was glad of the space, there were a number of curious glances being cast in her direction.

At Ember House, they had always given a warm, friendly welcome to outsiders, but now she wondered whether her own view of this had been skewed and perhaps the visitors had not felt the same way.

This being only a small hamlet, there was not much to do or see. The settlement boasted a single meeting room for town gatherings, two outdoor stalls for selling produce, and all other structures appeared to be accommodations.

The muddy, wooden shanties, with two to three rooms apiece, had already ceased to surprise her. It would have been pleasant to enter into conversation with some of the residents, but nobody made the move to approach her, and she did not want to encroach.

Having walked around its entirety twice, Adria decided to make her way back to the horses. Varick wasn't there yet, so she whiled away the time by brushing down their coats. There was no question of this being somewhere she could see herself settling; if nothing else, it was clear she wasn't wanted.

Despite her attempts not to agonise over the matter, it was difficult not to worry that she might find the same everywhere.

Surely, they would encounter bigger towns where people were more used to strangers.

When he did return, Varick was annoyingly vague about how he had spent his time. Adria was used to his manner by now, so teased him for trying to be mysterious, confident in the knowledge there was nothing interesting he could possibly have been doing in that tiny place anyway.

It was lunchtime when they departed, and early evening when they reached their subsequent destination. Instead of waiting until daylight, Varick informed her that this town,

Lilliard Downs, was large enough to have a tavern – and therefore, not only would nobody take issue with them arriving at a strange hour, but they would not need to sleep outside for the night.

Although she did not express her concerns aloud, Adria spent their approach worrying they'd be forced to share a room, under the pretence of them being a married couple travelling together. She felt too uncomfortable to broach the topic with her travelling companion, who was unlikely to give her a straightforward answer even if she did ask.

Varick, one step ahead of her as always, introduced them as an engaged couple making their way to a relative's to be wed, and as such requiring separate rooms. Only then was she able to feel thankful for the opportunity to sleep in a real bed.

She was relieved, and not at all surprised, when he deposited her outside a room, then promptly disappeared.

A knock at the door informed her dinner was available and would presently be brought up to her, assuming she was ready. Enquiring further, she learnt this was something Varick had requested, and they were bringing a meal to his room too, albeit not for another couple of hours. On a whim, she asked for her own food to be served in the main hall, where the other guests were seated, instead.

As interesting as the general chatter was to Adria, she overheard two things which particularly piqued her curiosity. The first was the discovery, much to her disappointment, that there was a shortage of work. This came alongside a number of complaints about the residents' current hardship. It wasn't a huge revelation, she supposed, but it sounded unlikely she would be able to find work and thereby remain here in Lilliard Downs.

The other thing which intrigued her was the suggestion a cloaked stranger had recently passed through the town. At first, she had assumed they were talking about Varick and even rolled her eyes at the amount of interest they were showing in him. However, as the conversation developed, she picked up that they were talking about a female; from thereon, she began listening more intently.

This lady had only stayed a short while but had been travelling on her own, a fact that, in and of itself, was apparently quite remarkable to these people. She had remained hooded, and no one had fully seen her face. Every description of her seemed to vary wildly.

When she overheard this individual had claimed to be hunting down an outlaw of some kind, Adria squirmed in her seat. Not wanting to appear affected, she stayed where she was – and having no idea of Varick's whereabouts, she would have been unable to find and warn him anyway.

As a result of this unusual occurrence, the residents were muttering warnings to be wary of strangers. Adria presumed the reason they paid her little heed was not down to her unassuming appearance, but rather due to the fact this lady had claimed to be looking for a gentleman.

On reflection, she thought it strange this huntress was not *also* looking for her, given she'd directly aided Varick's machinations, but it was quite consistent amongst the rumours and chatter throughout the room that this man was considered to be alone. She wondered if it may have been an oversight or misunderstanding. Or perhaps Adria was thought to be of such little threat or import she'd not been considered worth mentioning.

It was unlikely this person was not aware of her existence – they clearly had knowledge of Varick's escape – and surely it would have been helpful to alert people he was not necessarily travelling alone.

Whatever had caused the mistake, it had certainly been helpful in throwing these men off their trail; Varick was likely to escape suspicion purely by virtue of her company.

It did briefly occur to Adria that perhaps it was a coincidence, and it was not Varick being tracked at all. The thought was fleeting. It *had* to be him.

When Varick knocked on her door the next morning to retrieve her for their departure, she updated him on what she'd heard. Whilst not altogether surprising, there was something chilling about the fact he seemed entirely unperturbed.

CHAPTER 18 – PORTHOLES

He was unsure how much longer he could continue lying to the girl.

She seemed content with his vague non-explanations of what he was doing... the innocence instilled by her upbringing had been a blessing... but surely *she wouldn't continue blindly following him. Not indefinitely.*

His preference would be for her to stay with him out of choice; it would be easier and so much cleaner that way.

The more places he visited, the more he came back to himself, but he increasingly struggled to contain his folly.

Her magic was soothing to the overpowering demands of his own, despite how much her presence irritated him. He tried to ignore the latter, as he needed to put up with it regardless. It was unlikely he would come across another siphon until magic, and the island's equilibrium, returned.

Adria couldn't bear trotting in silence for much longer. "Redmonde, Water-Rise, and then Waterfjord?" There was no response. "Well?"

He ground his teeth. "Is there a question in there somewhere?"

"Oh, for goodness' sake, Varick. Can you please tell me

what is going on? If someone is tracking you, then we should be visiting as few places as possible, not as many." They'd already passed through three different places in the week since leaving Lilliard Downs.

"Perhaps."

"You are the most infuriating man I have ever met. What could possibly be your purpose in stopping by any and every excuse for civilisation we come across?"

"I was sure I'd explained this to you already."

Adria rolled her eyes at him.

"I need to remind them to whom they owe their allegiance."

She floundered for a moment, wanting to say something quickly, before his engagement faltered… as was so regularly the case. "You think the villages will rise up in support of your claim to sovereignty?"

"No, do not be ridiculous, Adria."

"I wasn't, I just… I don't understand why it matters."

"It's a metaphor."

Had she not been clinging tightly to her mare, her head would have been in her hands. "What does that even mean?"

"A metaphor is when you use irregular words to describe something, but don't explain that's what you're doing… so you avoid using 'like' or 'as'." He frowned and scratched his forehead. "It's actually quite a difficult term to explain. Anyway, it's when something is not literal."

"I *know* what a metaphor is." *Deep breaths.* "What is it a metaphor *for*?" She turned back to him, but he'd kicked the side of his horse and cantered on ahead. Clearly, he was being obtuse on purpose.

At least she'd begun to learn how to tell when he was

being flippant. She understood, now, how much of her life she had spent being naïve – and quite embarrassingly so.

Adria determined she would follow him closely at their next stop; she had no better ideas. He had gained the habit of sending her on pointless errands, which always *sounded* important until she ultimately realised they had been a wild goose chase.

Last time, he'd asked her to procure a map, which, of course, was not something widely available. He'd pretended not to have known this, but Adria felt certain he must have done. Worse, *she* should have known. After all, she was more than familiar with Ember House's library, and surely if anywhere had managed to lay claim to a map, it would have been there.

She'd attempted to determine *why* there weren't any maps, but the best theory any of the townsfolk had proffered was that the lands were too 'dark' to encourage travel. She was fascinated to learn there *had* been maps but, at some unspecified point, around a hundred-plus years ago, the lands had shifted unrecognisably. This cataclysm had rendered all previous cartography obsolete.

Varick had obviously been no help at all, unshakably insisting he had no idea.

Now she was even more certain he was lying – that it had been a false errand – on the basis he had no need for a map. He knew the land inside out.

She had been distracted, tempted by the idea of having one for her own use. So much so that she decided she'd buy some paper in order to begin creating her own. It would be crude but better than the alternative.

Adria had been distinctly lacking in purpose of late. Perked up by her idea of sketching their route, it was now apparent she'd been feeling more miserable than she'd appreciated. Something about her travelling companion was weighing heavily on her spirits. The more she reflected on their previous conversations, the stranger she felt about them.

Varick had told everyone he'd met that he believed he was the rightful king – she certainly hadn't anticipated that. The truth made her cringe, and she wasn't sure whether she wanted to laugh at him or feel embarrassed for him.

She also fretted at the revelation he'd been announcing his presence to all and sundry. It could only increase the likelihood this hunter would soon cross their path in earnest.

As they approached the boundaries of Redmonde, Adria prayed they would not encountered her here.

Another village too small to have an inn, they were planning a quick respite for the horses before re-embarking, enabling them to reach their subsequent destination of Water-Rise by nightfall.

Adria was beyond frustrated when Varick commanded her to feed and brush down the horses.

Apparently, she hadn't hidden this very well. "There are no stables here. They're too poor for horses. You will need to watch them anyway, so you may as well give them some decent attention while you do."

Forced to wait alone, she was not only unable to trail Varick, but also entirely out of sight of the village.

At least paper, unlike almost everything else in this forsaken land, seemed not to be such a luxury item, and Varick promised he would keep a lookout for some while she waited. He was strangely keen on her idea of drawing a map, and she wondered why – although Adria noticed she was starting to become suspicious of literally everything Varick said or did.

Maybe I'm *the problem, not him.* It was an unpleasant thought. *No, he's just trying to keep me distracted and thinks a map will help.*

When Varick returned, Adria had only brushed down her own mare. Having been desperate to stave off boredom, she'd made a concerted effort to elongate her task as much as possible. Without chastising her – without saying anything at all – Varick climbed back up on his saddle. She quickly gathered their pack and made to do likewise so he didn't get too far ahead.

Fumbling in her haste to be ready to depart, she couldn't get the strap to tie… but much to her amazement, he was waiting for her. "Are you upset I didn't brush him down? I'm sorry. I thought you'd be gone for longer."

"It's fine. I'll get it done properly in Water-Rise anyway."

"Why did you ask me to do it now if it would be done this evening anyway?" she asked indignantly.

"I didn't want you to be too bored waiting." His logic did make an annoying sort of sense. "Oh, and here you go." He removed something from his jacket and waved it in the air – allowing her to determine he held a notebook and some charcoal – before moving beside her and placing them in the pack.

"How do you have such good control over that horse?" she mumbled. Varick didn't respond, and she didn't bother repeating it, certain he wouldn't answer with anything helpful.

Adria wondered why *she* was now the grumpy one while he seemed perfectly cheery. Selfishly, she had almost begun to wish someone *would* be able to track them down, as at least it might be an interesting distraction.

Great, now I'm grumpy and *selfish. Aren't those supposed to be Varick's traits, not my own? This whole situation is bringing out the absolute worst in me.*

Adria barely noticed the time pass on this leg of their travels. Now overly familiar with the boredom of travelling, everything had become rather samey.

At least she was out seeing new places rather than making the same trip up and down Tenebrae each day.

Her clothes, which had been clean only several days earlier, now scratched at her skin, adding discomfort to her ennui. They still hadn't happened across any streams or lakes in which she could wash.

Varick explained some of the strange pits scattered around the outskirts of residential areas were actually man-made holes, intended to catch water, but even they were devoid of much moisture. Just thinking about it made her thirsty. She really missed having baths.

Luckily for Varick, he had been correct that Water-Rise was large enough to have an inn. He checked them in with the same aliases as last time.

As soon as she had seen her room, Adria returned to the hallway and lingered outside her door. Although she had to wait a while, Varick did eventually emerge.

"Fine," he declared on seeing her, although he rolled his eyes, making it clear he wasn't exactly thrilled. "I'm sure you'd have followed me eventually. Well, let's go then." She hung back, maybe a pace or two behind him as they left the inn, intending to continue doing so. She wanted to be as much out of his way as possible. Not for the first time, she was rewarded by being laughed at. "You're not exactly helping the impression we're supposed to be giving of enamoured lovers here, Adria."

Reluctantly, she moved to stand next to him as he paced the streets. It seemed like he was working his way around the town semi-methodically, but his purpose was far from clear. He ignored the few people they passed, but most of those around seemed to be inebriated, so it was unclear whether that was why.

They were one courtyard away from the central square when Varick stopped beside a circular stone about shoulder-width in diameter. She probably would have walked over it without noticing anything was there, but now she saw it, the distinction from the other paving stones was quite apparent. There was a pattern carved into the centre, although it looked more like several random lines than anything you might consider visually pleasing.

Varick squinted at her. "I'm not going to be able to do this without you asking questions, am I?" He sighed. "I tell you what. If you let me do this without breaking my concentration until I say I'm done, I'll explain anything you want me to about it afterwards. Deal?"

She nodded. Partly to show him she could be silent when needed, but also because she was afraid saying the wrong thing might jeopardise his offer.

Moreover, even if he reneged on his word, at least she would have had the chance to watch him in action.

Bending down, Varick put his hand to the ground, splaying his fingers over a couple of the lines. He remained in that position for several minutes. Nothing else happened. Or, in any event, nothing she could see. She got the impression that Varick, at least, thought he was achieving something through the process. Perhaps his eyes worked better in the dark than hers did.

A bat fluttered past them and she worried he might stir, but he showed no signs of having noticed the distraction. Adria, conversely, could not keep her steady resolve; for some reason, the winged mammal brought back memories of the Dharjigs, and she was forced to stifle a shudder.

At last, Varick righted himself. "Okay, go ahead then." He sounded less than enthused. She examined him for a few moments, trying to gauge his mood, before deciding it was not favourable to providing in-depth answers.

"Don't worry, I won't ask loads of questions right now. If you prefer, you can cover the headlines, and we'll discuss more later – over dinner or next time we're travelling?"

"Not really something to discuss over dinner, but sure. You can ask me more when we move to Waterfjord. Knowing what you're like, I'm confident you won't be satisfied with whatever I tell you anyway. There will be plenty of things you want to know once I begin."

"A summary for now, then?" she pushed.

"A summary. Right. That stone is the town's source of magic."

"There isn't any magic left, though. Are you still able to get magic out of it?" She crouched down, before cautiously running her hand over the circle. There was nothing out of place about its texture, nor did any noticeable sensation reach her fingertips.

"Hold on, let me finish. You are constantly interrupting me. Sometimes I need time to think while I'm explaining things."

Adria blushed, feeling suitably castigated.

"Okay. When there *was* magic, this is where it originated from. It was a bit like the power source, in that it was a reserve ready for them to use, should there not be any magic wielders nearby. In an emergency, that sort of thing… although this particular one had a large capacity, so they would have had plenty to use day to day, without needing to save it for emergencies."

Adria waited, unsure whether he was going to continue of his own accord.

"My magic was trapped inside. So, I put my hands on it, then drew it back out and into myself."

He was right; she had a lot more questions than she'd

anticipated.

CHAPTER 19 – ONWARDS

He could finally feel an increase in his abilities. It was slight – there was still a long way to go – but it was there.

The largest towns, those which would make the biggest difference, were to the east. Nonetheless, he was intentionally charting a course through the central-west side of Azeileah. He needed to be certain he was strong enough before he entered any place where he might be challenged on approaching the portholes. The larger towns, which had two or three each, would be more likely to remember their purpose.

He could have metamorphosed far more quickly if he had gone there first, and their situations would have been easier for him to remember – he had paid far more attention to the positioning of the ones in important locations – but he'd made his decision and had to have faith in himself. Hadn't he always?

He wondered whether those towns would be as ruined as the ones they'd passed so far.

He had tried to call up some emotion, to feel any kind of sadness at their dereliction, or regret at the decay of his country.

So far, nothing.

They retired to their individual rooms to eat, and that was fine by her; after their evening excursion, she was desperate to warm up. It was one thing sleeping outside at night, wrapped up in a sleeping bag beside a fire; it was another standing around dawdling out in the cold.

With the remainder of her evening, Adria did her best to sketch what she could remember of their journey so far. It was slower going than she'd anticipated, and she didn't get much past the very early stages. However, she was encouraged by the notion that, if she made an effort to update her map daily, once she caught up, she'd be able to add more detail.

Her progress had been hindered further by her numb fingertips, which remained uncomfortable even after the rest of her body had begun to thaw.

She slept well.

While the days remained temperate, she'd detected the weather cooling slightly as they moved northwards and wondered if the trend would continue, dreading the day she'd be forced to ask Varick to buy her a cloak.

Unfortunately, her pleas to spend a second night in Water-Rise proved pointless. She had even threatened to stay without him, to which he'd laughed and simply said that was fine. She didn't have any money, so they both knew it had been nothing but a last-ditch attempt to get him to change his mind. Apparently, she wasn't allowed any say in… well, anything.

At least the road would be a good chance to ask some of the questions currently buzzing around in her mind. There was certainly nothing of interest to look at, and she didn't even have to direct her mount, as it simply followed wherever Varick's led.

It was a struggle, but she managed to hold in her first question until they'd crossed the town's boundary. "So, did you basically just take all of the town's magic?"

"Sort of." Helpful as always.

"Please could you elaborate on that?"

"I suppose I did say I'd answer your questions. I tell you what – anything you ask between here and Waterfjord in relation to last night, I'll do my best to explain."

Sometimes, Adria thought this was all a game to Varick. He didn't always seem quite *human*. "Thank you. I appreciate that."

"I did take their magic, yes, but as observant as you are, you cannot have failed to realise they were not using it. Before you start moralising, this is because they were entirely unable to. Those portholes are designed to hold magic in several forms – such as a bit of healing magic, a bit of construction magic. You may have noticed the ring around the circle designated various quadrants. My magic was neither a type they could use, nor one they were designed to hold. In truth, my magic was *preventing* the use of the porthole as it had filled all of the quadrants to the brim."

"Portholes?" *Or did he say potholes?*

"The circular stone thing."

"Yes, but why are they called portholes – does it mean anything in particular?

"Oh, right. No, they just look a bit like the windows on a ship, I guess."

Adria blushed a little. She'd never seen any type of boat in the flesh, but she had seen some pictures of fishing boats and couldn't imagine them having windows. "And you said they are split into four quadrants, for four types of magic – healing, construction, and which others?"

"Quadrant was a poor word choice. There are actually five. Healing and construction, as you said, two connected to cultivation and light, and then there was a general one." He waved his hand, signalling there was more he could have said but perhaps wasn't sure how exactly to explain. "In theory, a flicker of magical ability would be enough to allow someone to pull from the general one and shape it in the way they needed. The advantage of it being pre-conditioned to a certain type was that anyone from the wider population could use it, even if they had no magical inclination whatsoever." Varick scratched the side of his head. "Actually, in a practical sense that's not quite true as some of them have covers, so the town administrator could control usage."

"Why was your magic not in the 'general' bit then?"

"Even general magic is usually… already formed. Think of it as partial conditioning if that helps. Mine is a bit different. *Raw*. Anyway, those categories are not the limit of the way magic can be shaped, just the most useful ways it can be stored."

Adria frowned, wondering whether she'd understood correctly. "But there was nothing stopping the wrong magic being put in the wrong quadrant?"

"The quadrants are specific to magic types – you would not be able to mix them up accidentally, say by putting light magic in the construction quadrant."

"Then how did your magic fill all five quadrants?"

"To put it quite bluntly, because it was far stronger than the seal placed on the porthole." He didn't seem particularly modest about it. Whether true or not, it was clear to Adria that Varick at least believed this to be the case.

She was, once again, all too aware of the mess she might have created by releasing Varick into the world. If he, and he alone, had access to all the magic in Azeileah…

No. He wasn't the only person with magic; *she* was a siphon.

Maybe she was the only person who could prevent him from doing anything drastic. It was a heavy weight to place upon herself, but one she could not deny she deserved.

Unfortunately, she had no idea how her magic worked. She cast her mind towards the book in her pack – she'd picked it up when they'd entered the catacombs then forgotten all about it.

Determination struck her. She would read it as soon as she could... but something told her *not* to do so while in Varick's presence.

To begin with, she needed to find out whether she had to wait for him to expend his magic before she could siphon it. Her next priority was to understand what actually happened to the magic once siphoned. It would be of no use to release it back into the environment if Varick could simply gather it up and use it all over again. What she knew so far made little sense, and made siphoning seem worthless, but instinctively, she felt there *must* be some purpose to the ability.

If there was a whole book on the subject, there had to have been something worth writing about. Admittedly, it might simply have been a case of getting her hopes up, but she questioned whether Varick had been right in saying it was such a useless skill after all.

"Our 'expedition' next, then. We're visiting these portholes so you can reclaim your magic." *Or what you're pretending is your magic. I can't think of a way to prove it was ever yours to begin with and that you aren't stealing it.* "Is that why you look different?"

"I *look* different, do I? Funnily enough, I don't have a mirror handy."

Must he make a jest of everything? "Yes, you look healthier. At first, I thought it was the fresh air, and being free from your prison, then from the mountain. That isn't it, though, is it. As you gain magic, you're changing."

"It is certainly possible. I was only part of myself without my magic. I am starting to become my full self once again." Adria ignored the palpitations she was starting to feel. There wasn't much she could do to resolve anything just now. Her only real option, until she knew more, was to stay close to him and see what happened.

"Next question. Will you teach me to use a dagger? I know we haven't passed anyone on the roads." Was that strange? Adria wasn't sure. It was not how she'd pictured the world would be, but she was struggling to recall any good reason she'd expected otherwise. "When we're in towns, though, I always feel a bit exposed and vulnerable."

"No. Your question was not related to the portholes, and my magic will protect us now."

Adria determined it was best to let the matter lie and try again another time. It was entirely possible he appreciated that *he* was the thing she wanted to be able to protect herself from. Trust was something severely lacking from their current... *not friendship*... acquaintanceship?

"Understood. Last question, then. How did your magic end up trapped in the portholes in the first place?" Adria thought this would provide her some insight as to whether it really was Varick's magic, or he was merely able to harvest it.

"That, my dear, is a long story, and we have just arrived at Waterfjord."

CHAPTER 20 – WATERFJORD

He was confident nothing could stop him now, so what did it matter if he shared some knowledge with the girl? He knew his only motive was enjoying the feeling of superiority, but equally, he saw no need to deny himself the small pleasure.

This Jhardi tracking them was an unnecessary irritation, which would have to be dealt with once he was given the appropriate chance.

His path was not yet clear to him, but a cold-blooded murder at this moment would do nothing for his ambitions. He needed circumstances to arise in which he could make it appear an accident. Or if needs must, it would have to be self-defence.

Unfortunately, unless an opportunity presented itself imminently, the latter was more likely.

Waterfjord was the largest place they'd stopped at so far.

They arrived shortly after midday, and the streets were bustling with people who seemed to be either hard at work or hurrying from one place to another. Despite the hour, the sky was dark, the grey-black clouds blocking the sun and shrouding the town in unbroken shadows. Between the weather, and the general mood of its populace, the town had a miserable atmosphere.

Adria felt a pang of empathy when she saw women with

huge baskets full of linens on their backs – something which seemed commonplace here. Their daily routine was likely as repetitive as the arduous trips she'd taken up and down Tenebrae.

Dismounting, they led the horses on foot, while Varick explained some of the area's history. "Water-Rise and Waterfjord used to be along the same river. They were linked towns, with only one administrator for both – that being all they could afford. The river was fundamental for fishing and transportation."

He went on to speculate that when the river had dried up, the once prosperous towns had struggled. Adria did her best to listen, while also surveying the area as they passed through.

"A quintant," Varick exclaimed out of nowhere.

"Sorry, come again?" She scratched her head in puzzlement, then regretted it, as her hair felt matted and clumpy, reminding her how much she needed a wash.

"That's what it's called. I've just remembered. When you have quadrants but there are five."

"Oh. Are you still having issues with your memory loss?"

"No, of course not. Everyone forgets things sometimes, do they not?"

"Ha! So, you admit you remember everything?" She felt rather proud of herself for setting him up to reveal this, until she remembered he'd technically done it to himself.

"Yes, of course – my mind became whole the moment you siphoned my magic from the cell."

Infuriating. She wished she'd never even asked.

"So why *were* you locked away?" Adria cocked her head, throwing him the obvious question, despite the fact she'd have stood on her head if he'd actually deigned to answer. She squirmed slightly as a passerby, who must have overheard, gave them an odd look.

"I was just too good-looking for this world."

She didn't bother faking a laugh. Nor did she satisfy him with an eye roll; he'd only be happy to know how annoying she found him.

"You can actually use pentant, too, I believe. Quintant *or* pentant. Both are correct. Consider yourself enlightened."

They dropped their horses at the place they intended to rent rooms – from the outside, it looked clean and comfortable enough – picked up some hot pastries for lunch, and made their way across town to the porthole.

Adria couldn't shake the feeling someone was following them, even though she hadn't actually managed to spot anyone. Repeatedly looking back over her shoulder, she nearly lost sight of Varick.

He wasn't moving slowly anymore.

A rather strange sight greeted them as they approached their destination; the street was blocked with people waiting. Unable to pass through, they joined the queue.

Varick was predictably impatient, "This is ridiculous. I should not have to wait in line for this!" They were shuffling forward at a reasonable pace, but it quickly became apparent to Adria that he had never queued for anything in his life before – despite his alleged centuries of experience.

Once they were only three or four people from the front, she finally saw what they'd been waiting for – and couldn't help but laugh, despite garnering angry looks from not only Varick but many of the people around them.

The residents were taking it in turns to spit on the porthole.

She had no idea why, and at that moment she didn't care.

Varick was angry, and her reaction wasn't helping, but now she'd got the giggles she couldn't stop.

Meanwhile, her travelling companion was becoming increasingly unhappy with the situation. "I'm going to have to come back this evening when it's less crowded. There's no way this rabble will manage to keep quiet and allow me my concentration. Even if I only need a few minutes."

As if to back up his reasoning, someone shouted, "Hurry up, some of us have been working all day and need to get home. You take your turn and leave, it's not a tourist attraction!" This earned Varick's irate glare, but apparently he wasn't being particularly intimidating, as the heckler took no notice.

"It's okay," she told him, deciding it was probably best to soothe his temper rather than enrage it any further. "You can come back later. We were planning to stay overnight anyway."

"Fine, but if there's a line at our next calling point, I am not standing for it! Oh, for heaven's sake, Adria, would you get a grip? What are you laughing at now?"

"Pun," she managed to spurt out. "Standing in line. Not standing for it."

"Okay. Very good." Turning towards each other, for once they actually seemed to be in agreement. They both spat onto the porthole. It was distasteful, but they would have looked strange otherwise.

"What does heaven's sake mean?"

"Heaven – you know, where *good* people go when they die."

She shrugged her shoulders at him, nonchalantly.

"How peculiar. Everyone had heard of it in my day. That is, in my original days. Before I spent ninety years as a recluse."

"Yes, I got what you meant. I've never heard of anything like that."

True to his word, on reaching the assembly office Varick ignored the handful of people waiting outside and marched straight in. The queue had been for the reception desk, which he also bypassed entirely, walking straight into the office of the administrator.

Interestingly enough, the office was only occupied by one gentleman, who sat at a large desk sifting through paperwork. He was somewhat perturbed at the incursion, and without so much as an acknowledgement, he marched through into the reception room. He could quite clearly be heard shouting at his receptionist. Apparently, he'd been quite explicit no one was to be permitted an appointment with him that day.

When he returned, he rather plainly attempted to usher them towards the door, suggesting they made a request at the desk to see him on another day. Varick took this as his cue to turn on the charm.

"Good afternoon to you, kind sir. I apologise for our intrusion, but I am afraid we are an envoy from the Palace by Ember House and are only passing through your lovely town for a very short time. I felt it would be rude of myself not to stop by and wish you my regards." Seeing his efforts so obviously faked while directed towards someone else, Adria felt a bit sickened they had worked so well on herself previously.

The man looked taken aback, and Adria could only assume he was surprised by Varick's manner of speech and affectations. It was obvious he also hailed from a wealthy background, and was now looking at her cohort in a renewed light. She saw him take in Varick's clothing, clearly expensive despite its travel-worn appearance, and likewise noted Varick's smile upturn slightly – involuntarily, she assumed – at having made the same observation himself.

As usual, she found herself ignored.

"Forgive me, though. I have not provided you with my name." He reached for a handshake. "Lord General Varick Azeileah at your service."

Adria couldn't help but roll her eyes at the theatrics.

A frown crossed the man's face, as though he couldn't quite pull the information he was looking for from his mind. He took Varick's hand. "Ted Digby. Administrator for this town and Water-Rise. I hope you haven't got expectations too high for this place. There aren't many new people passing through these days, and those that do I can't do much to help."

Ah, so that was why he seemed unnerved. He was expecting some kind of arduous request to be made of him, and perhaps even thought his job was somehow at risk, since he'd decided Varick appeared to be a person of some importance.

"Do not fret. I bring you a message with good tidings, I hope. I have returned, and better times are ahead of us. I suggest you find my details in the records if you are not familiar with my past reputation – and ask that you kindly disseminate my name and optimism amongst your subjects."

Knowing how calculated Varick was, Adria had watched the exchange intently. There was now a stark contrast in Ted Digby's manner, which had shifted from nervousness to genuine relief.

She was only marginally disappointed Varick hadn't included the words 'rightful king' in his speech, as the childish side of her had fancied a laugh at his expense. As things were, both men seemed appeased by the interaction, and it was only Adria who'd wound up disappointed.

How had she become embroiled in this nonsense that saw two grown men meeting to have pointless, daft conversations while she was made to feel like the child, merely there to observe?

Doing her best to put the exchange out of her mind as they walked back, she began to grow excited at the thought of eating a large meal – and if she was lucky, having some time away from Varick.

Based on her earlier glimpse of its exterior, the inside of the inn was much as Adria had imagined. Once the arrangements had been dealt with, she was shown to a single room and given a key for the door.

It was small and sparse, and the bed was tidy albeit a little hard. There was no desk or dresser, but a small basin of water – the size akin to a bowl one might put their porridge in – had been left so she could refresh herself. She wondered whether Varick had paid extra for this, and determined she'd save most of it for the morning, as based on her experience in other places, this was unlikely to be refilled.

Varick was unusually nervous about returning to the porthole, and she found it easier than she otherwise might have to persuade him to let her come with. She wanted to watch more closely this time, now she knew what he was doing.

They agreed to wait until shortly before midnight, so as to have the best chance of remaining unobserved. While Varick retired to his room immediately after they checked in, Adria took her meal in the tavern. She felt a little guilty for preferring this to updating her map, but this was the first place they'd been that seemed used to travellers, and she didn't want to be alone.

She was also on the lookout for the individual following them – whom she'd now convinced herself was the mysterious lady she'd heard was hunting Varick, while in Lilliard Downs.

There were a few people in the eating area, but it was not overcrowded, and she didn't feel guilty about taking a table to herself in preference to sitting on one of the communal benches. Rather than the usual stew, she was served potatoes with leeks, but they'd been generous enough with the salt that the meal both filled her up and tasted good too.

At first, she received a number of stares – she figured she'd been wrong, and there weren't a lot of people passing through this place after all – but before long, people started to ignore her.

Growing braver, she stopped the barmaid and asked her a few questions. A couple of patrons who overheard her came and seated themselves at her table.

She supposed people were curious about her in return. Maybe they had even been waiting for an opportunity themselves.

Adria hadn't prepared a story, so had to clumsily make something up on the spot. It was an inept oversight, and although she stuck to the line about being engaged to Varick, she stupidly mentioned she had worked at Ember House.

Anyone asking questions would know for certain they had passed through here now.

In fact, she was lucky the person tracking them hadn't already been asking around Waterfjord, as otherwise, she would have just put a huge target on her head. On reflection, she'd probably also raised suspicions by sitting alone, having not been joined by her fiancé.

Still, she'd made her decision and now she intended to make the most of the opportunity to do some fact-finding. "When we passed through town today, there was a huge queue over by the…" Luckily, she was interrupted as she had no idea how she was going to explain the location.

"Never realised it was so specific to our town, but perhaps things are different at Ember House, with it being such an *important* place. We are not superstitious people otherwise, but I'm not ashamed to tell you that this one particular superstition has served us all well. You came by on the right day of the week to join in; it's always done on Fridays as work closes. Otherwise, it's Sunday lunchtime."

"Is the belief that bad luck will fall if it isn't observed? Any idea how it arose?"

He leaned in until his voice was a whisper, "I should've warned you people don't like to talk about these things." His whisper actually carried more loudly than his speaking voice had. Having drawn the attention of those around them, they paused for a few seconds, drinking their ales, until the moment had passed. "It's not just about luck. There's a bad feeling around that stone. Most everyone senses it. Something not right, something *otherworldly*. What with the plague lying over the land, it's only natural for people to assume the two are related."

"Plague." It wasn't a question as such, but the man took it as encouragement to continue – which had been Adria's intention.

"Curse, plague, whatever you want to call it. The endless drought, the barren land and resultant famine. Life is harsh, but we don't know any other way except from stories. I'd have called it pure misfortune, 'cept everyone feels the same – a weight is hanging over us. Everyone senses the curse. Just not all will be admitting to it, mind."

This viewpoint gave Adria a lot to think about. She pressed him further, but only in relation to the hardships facing daily life – such as which crops they had managed to grow and how they rationed water.

She 'forgot' to mention anything to Varick when she met him later.

Luckily, the area around the porthole was deserted on their return.

Watching his rite for a second time, she'd thought it would look different now she knew what to expect. Much to her disappointment, Adria still couldn't see or feel anything happening. He just looked like he was kneeling on the floor.

As she was wont to do, Adria lost herself in thought on the walk back. Not fully paying attention, the back of her fingers brushed against Varick's wrist. He quickly withdrew his hand and shook it out slightly, but didn't say anything.

Adria, however, became very aware she was newly buzzing with magic. It was a higher level of alertness. She felt more awake, but not in any way she had before.

Why hadn't she felt like this after siphoning the magic from Varick's cell? The only reasons she could come up with were that it was either because she had taken it from the walls rather than directly from him... or that Varick really had amassed that much more power than a mere three weeks earlier. Worryingly, the latter explanation felt like it was more probable.

It was a struggle to sleep that night. Unable to get used to the sensation of being charged with power, she writhed around like there was an itch just beneath her skin; but rubbing against the sheets did little to relieve it.

The magic was trying to escape.

She would have let it out, if she could, but she didn't know how.

The uncertainties swimming around her mind only served to make things worse, and she now had a new worry to add to the list – that she was ill-equipped to handle her magical talent.

No matter how much she told herself the issue was a lack of familiarity with her siphoning skill – that maybe she had just taken on too much and needed to practice more – the doubts, like the physical discomfort, wouldn't shift.

CHAPTER 21 – ABEYANCE

Unlike the first time she'd found herself in one of Varick's memories, Adria knew what had happened immediately. She supposed she had finally fallen asleep after all.

The magic crawling through her must have found a way to burn itself out. Had it... could it have simply thrown her into the mind of the person nearest? Was this the only way her body had known to expel the excess reserves which had been running through her?

Her questions would have to wait until morning. For now, she had two choices. She could find a way out... or see more of what was in this troubled man's mind.

Whilst she could have – perhaps *should have* – walked out of the palace through the front door, she was too tempted by whatever was about to be revealed; she wanted to learn what she could about how he'd been moulded into such a *unique* character.

Any information I discover might well be useful should I need to stop him.

She was careful to stay out of sight, not wanting Varick to become angry and throw her out of his head again.

This Varick was in his late teens and did not look greatly dissimilar to the Varick she knew. He had stopped ageing sometime in his mid-twenties, so this was still a few years before he'd fully grown into his magic. The scene unfolding before her was back in the sitting room, where the king and queen were addressing their three sons.

"There are a large number of people coming with the delegation; please take care to treat each and every one with respect." The king seemed to be directing that particular sentiment entirely at Varick. "Dayne, we all wish you the best of luck in gaining the attentions of Lord Drew's daughter. Remember, you have one week to secure the alliance."

"Would he not be better off marrying someone outside the country?" Varick asked lazily, lacking the formality of his father. It was clear he thought he knew best and was trying not to rub this in their faces. "We could do with better relations with our neighbours."

"We have been through this before." Dayne, despite his even temper, clearly did not have a great deal of patience for his brother. "Firstly, the wealth is more important than an army. We are not under any threat of conflict. Secondly, I find it quite distasteful that you cannot even pretend to hide your desire to see me relocated far away."

Varick shrugged noncommittally, not bothering to make eye contact with his older brother.

Ghian also had something to add. "Lady Jezebel is closer to my age than Dayne's. Would she not be a better match for myself?"

Varick's mother raised herself from her seated position. "Children," she called them – even though Dayne had to be at least twenty-four, and Ghian perhaps only a year younger. When Varick had been around six, they had seemed far older than him; now, the age gap was evident only in their demeanour.

"Enough of this silliness," she continued as their father

sat in silent contemplation. "Dayne has already met Lady Jezebel at several social functions, and he will be in a far better position to gain her trust. You will give him three days to see how he progresses, without interference. I have a good feeling they desire this engagement as much as we do."

As Adria watched, their movements sped up, and the scene began to fade. She felt herself pulled away and physically displaced into another memory. This one was after the delegation had arrived.

They were in a large entertaining room, and a number of guests were present. It had been decorated with holly and ivy, and many of the ladies wore silk shrugs about their shoulders, suggesting it was approaching Yuletide.

Dayne was in confidence with a girl about the same age as herself, whom Adria assumed must be his target. Varick watched from an inlet, appearing to have gone unnoticed. He was pretending to read, but it was very clear his attention wasn't on the book. Dayne, however, only had eyes for the young lady – his affections were obvious.

Adria began to experience a slight embarrassment at intruding on such a private moment. It was obvious no one had taught Dayne about subtlety. She was amused, thinking that, as a prince, he'd have had far more experience with women, but perhaps it was a sign times had moved on in the last three hundred years.

Still, his target was doing a much better job at playing hard to get. She was being polite but certainly not giving Dayne any encouragement in his advances.

Once again, the scene changed around Adria, and she was swiftly relocated to the main hall. There didn't appear to be anyone around, so she took a moment to shake off the disorientation brought on by being displaced twice in short succession.

She was beginning to wonder why the memory had brought her there when she heard faint noises coming from one of the alcoves. Adria had to stifle a laugh when she realised Lady Jezebel was seated inside, making out with her prince.

She was a little surprised she had that much passion in her after what she'd observed earlier.

A door opened, making her turn, but the lovers seemed not to have noticed. Dayne and Ghian walked into the hall. *Hold on a second… then who is she kissing?*

Dayne, who had evidently heard the same sounds she had, approached the alcove. When they finally broke apart, and Adria saw Varick had been the recipient of Lady Jezebel's affections, she had no idea how to react. She had never considered him in that way, and the idea that anyone else might have done so was a revelation to her. *That poor girl.*

Too proud or too well-mannered to confront Varick, Dayne strode off without saying anything. He clearly wanted to run away but managed to control himself – at least, until he left the room, at which point she could no longer see him.

As much as she felt sympathy for Dayne's plight, she knew this was all long in the past, and Adria's attention was on something else. It would be helpful to figure out *why* Varick found this memory important. It was obviously something which had stuck in his mind.

She wondered if maybe he *was* capable of feeling guilt after all. As she pondered this, she was swept back into the sitting room.

Another family meeting.

Apparently having given up on the situation, the king sat with his head in his hands. It was the most emotion Adria had seen him show. Although she'd only seen him a few times… and maybe he was different when not in public.

The queen, Varick's mother, addressed him, while her

other two boys stood to one side of the room. Only Varick was seated. "Son, seeing as what your father is saying is clearly not having any effect on you, let me state this plainly. You have put us in this situation. It is fully of your own making. You are not a child anymore; you knew what you were doing."

"I understand the sentiments, Mother, but I'm far too powerful to be wasted in marriage to this nothing girl."

"You should have thought about that before you got involved! There was no need for you to marry her, but your actions have left us with no other choice. You will ask for her hand. Immediately."

Adria's eyes widened. The king was incredibly angry. Dayne's silence also said a lot to Adria.

"She had no interest in Dayne. It's not my fault she preferred me." Varick remained as nonchalant as ever.

"Varick. There was no need for you to act on this. Quite the opposite – you were directly instructed not to have any involvement. If nothing else, you should have brought it to your family for discussion. By acting of your own accord, you have taken away all other options. Lord Drew has made it quite clear he will consider it an insult to the family if you do not make things right with his daughter."

"I apologise, I do, but you will not convince me to do something I have no intention of doing. So you may as well not waste your breath. Now, if we're quite finished…" Varick stood.

"That's it. I've had enough now. You are disowned. You are no longer one of my heirs. You are no longer my son." The king spoke as if the mere act of doing so exhausted him.

Adria gasped. Not guilt or regret, after all. It was now far clearer why he considered this to have been a defining moment.

Her reaction disturbed Varick, who turned to face Adria directly. "Devil girl! Get out of my sight."

CHAPTER 22 – LOST

Her touch was harsh, untrained. It was lucky, as he would not have perceived her actions had she been more skilful. Although... it had been a relief to feel some of his magic being siphoned away. Even if she'd only skimmed the tiniest amount from the surface.

Had he truly already been approaching his limit so quickly? It was difficult to judge where the line lay between sense and lack of.

Having finally started to appreciate her usefulness, she'd decided it was acceptable to be poking around in his memories... and that was a wholly different kind of line to have crossed.

He could not accept this level of impropriety.

He'd manage without her. He had before.

Adria woke feeling strange. She'd slept for almost ten hours and it was already late morning, but for some reason, she didn't feel refreshed. Rubbing her eyes, she realised it was actually a knock at the door that had disturbed her.

She debated whether to open it, or rush to pull her things together first. Having overslept, she could imagine Varick was itching to leave – it was surprising he hadn't knocked earlier – and she didn't want him to see her in this state. "I'll just be a second," she called while she made herself decent.

The door opened to reveal a man she didn't recognise. "Miss, you've overstayed what's been paid for." At least he sounded apologetic. "We need you to vacate the room so we can get the linens cleaned."

"I'm so sorry. My fiancé usually wakes me before the sun is even up." He looked slightly embarrassed but didn't say anything further before taking his leave.

She quickly washed her face, made the bed, then gathered her shawl and left. She knocked on Varick's room, which was next to hers, but he didn't answer.

Instead, she was forced to locate the innkeeper, "Do you know where the gentleman I arrived with might be?"

"I'm afraid when I opened up the inn this morning, he'd already left."

Her eyes widened. "No, you must be mistaken."

"Perhaps, ma'am. I have not seen him since last night, though. That much I can confirm."

The truth dawned on Adria. He'd actually left her. *The dream last night, was it because of that?* He hadn't seemed as angry as the first time, but with hindsight, he must have been.

Her current outlook was not great; she'd got herself into quite the predicament.

In desperation, she made a final plea to the innkeeper. "This may sound unbidden, but you don't know of anyone looking for some help, do you? I find myself unexpectedly in need of work." She wanted to crawl back into the bed upstairs and hide under the covers. This felt like begging. "I've got plenty of experience."

"Afraid not, ma'am." He fidgeted awkwardly with his hands. "Times aren't easy around here. Plenty looking for a bit of luck. I think you'd be best trying another place – anyone with spare coin around here would likely take on local first.

Maybe times aren't as hard elsewhere." His eyes gave away the lie – he didn't really believe things would be better anywhere else. Adria appreciated his patience, however, and thanked him genuinely.

Varick had the bag with all her supplies in it. Varick held all the coin. She had nothing but the clothes she was wearing. Running outside and across the street, she no longer cared whether she appeared dignified.

The mare was gone, as was Varick's horse; he must have taken both of them. Her last hope had come to nothing.

Dejected, she had no idea what to do. She wished she'd been paying more attention to Varick's plans. Maybe then, she'd have been able to chase after him and... then what? Apologise? It was hardly her fault, but she knew he wouldn't accept anything less than a well-thought-through grovel.

Did she even *want* to rejoin him?

With no option to stay in Waterfjord, she was going to have to gather some information on where the next town might be... assuming the innkeeper was right, and there was no chance of work here. It might be worth her time to make a few inquiries and confirm his assertion first. Even if it felt like a lost cause before she'd begun.

Left to wander the streets, she found herself meandering aimlessly, hoping to find some inspiration.

Approaching a market stall, she attempted to introduce herself, intending to ask about work, or for directions. She would even have settled for a simple, friendly conversation.

Adria had barely spoken a few words of greeting before she was sent away for having no coinage.

Everyone had always been friendly when Varick was around, but it seemed they were not going to extend her the same courtesy.

Too ashamed to approach any other stall owners – there were only three others and they all seemed to know each other – she slunk off, feeling dejected. *What next?* Finding some steps to sit on, she whiled away her time, hoping Varick might yet return, and her worrying could cease.

Her stomach rumbled, but there wasn't much she could do about it.

Adria tried her utmost to remain stalwart as dark fell. She had spent many nights outside – and whilst she'd had Varick for company, he had hardly been a reassuring presence. No. She could do this. She would not be broken.

By morning, she felt less resolute. She was dirty, thirsty, and alone. Nowhere would consider employing her in this state, even if there *had* been work to go around. She was entirely out of options.

There was nothing left to do but head back to Ember House and see if they might take pity on her.

That was, if she managed to find her way.

It would be a long return journey, and take far longer on foot than it had on horseback, which was how they'd travelled for the majority of the outbound journey. Weak from lack of food and having been awake all night, her pace was even slower than a normal walking speed. Nevertheless, her stamina was impressive. Her legs would not soon fail her.

She trudged onwards for hours, barely feeling. Her mind was blank of all but her shallowest thoughts; anything else simmered somewhere beneath where she could reach them.

She hadn't meant to enter Varick's memories, and it was ridiculous of him to be so angry at her for something she hadn't been able to control, but he was just the sort of obstinate person who would refuse to listen to reason.

If anyone could have taught her how to deal with the magic, it would have been him. It *should* have been him. He could have helped her to release it safely, and then it wouldn't have run rampant while she was asleep. So, really, it was his fault, and she was practically blameless.

To think, she'd actually considered he would come back for her. She'd waited in Waterfjord as long as she could, but by this morning she'd far overstayed her welcome. If *welcome* was any way to describe it.

When she came across a stream, it took her a moment to work out what she was seeing.

Could she have gone the wrong way? Adria was sure she hadn't, though. She'd been following the same path they'd taken from Water-Rise to Waterfjord, but in reverse.

Desperate for a drink, she rushed to its bank, not caring how fresh the water might be. Only once she'd taken her fill, did she stop to consider the matter – it hadn't been there before, and there'd been no rain, so there must have been a spring underground which had recently been uncovered.

It hasn't rained since… since before I left Ember House.

Hope. A fleeting sentiment, gone as quickly as it had arrived… but once she'd felt it, she was sure she could conjure it again in the future, should the opportunity ever arise.

Having already stopped to quench her thirst, Adria treated herself to a break. Even this close to the water, the ground was still dry, and her clothes were quickly covered in dust.

They'll probably never be clean again.

After only a handful of minutes, she re-embarked. It was difficult to get going again now she'd relaxed, but after a while her legs settled back into a rhythm. In this direction, it was predominantly downhill, and although she wasn't sure she'd have managed the climb had she been travelling in the opposite direction, she was forced to devote most of her concentration to the placement of her feet.

It was almost nightfall the following day when she finally reached Water-Rise, and she did not think it would work in her favour to approach the town at such an hour… should she decide to approach it at all. Luckily, she could delay making such a decision.

For the second night in a row, she lay on the hard ground. Having walked a considerable distance, she was tired enough to sleep, despite the dried grass prickling her whichever way she turned.

Come morning, she found herself uninclined to enter. The sun's light highlighted her atrocious state, and appearing this way was less than desirable. The dark would have better hidden her flaws. She very almost passed the town entirely.

Except, she couldn't.

If there was any chance she might receive a better reception here than she had in Waterfjord, then it was a risk she had to take.

However humiliating it might be.

CHAPTER 23 – HUNTED

Free.

Alone with his thoughts. Which had turned so petty. He'd left her because he enjoyed the idea of her suffering more than he wanted her assistance.

It wasn't logical, which only implied he needed the siphoning more.

Yet, he didn't turn back. The thought of her desperation filled him with a pleasure such as he hadn't felt in a long while.

Perhaps he'd even bed someone at his next stopover. But no, waking up to a world where no one washed had put somewhat of a damper on any proclivities of that kind.

Steeling herself, Adria approached the wide, sombre streets. Finding the reception unfriendly did not brook disappointment, as she had not expected otherwise. She remained proud of herself for having made the attempt.

Having hoped she could gain some favour by informing them of the new stream, it transpired there was no one willing to hear her out. Wherever she went, she was quickly shooed away. It was time to continue her long journey.

Worried she might not leave via the right path, Adria lingered for a moment, attempting to call to mind the way they'd entered Water-Rise a few days ago. It seemed like such a long time ago now.

While she was deep in thought, an arm reached out and grabbed her wrist, before pulling her, roughly, into an alleyway.

A hand clamped over her mouth, preventing her from making any sound. Adria struggled, but she was held firmly, by someone very much stronger than herself, and made no leeway in her attempts to free herself.

Having ascertained her efforts were futile, she gave up. Her body slumped. She would have whimpered, had she been allowed.

Once she'd ceased to fight, her attacker also relaxed slightly, and Adria was spun around to face her assailant. Her eyes widened. She may have been wearing a covering over most of her face, but Adria would have known those cool, green eyes anywhere.

Never had she been so happy to see someone.

Lady Jhardi put her finger to her lips, indicating Adria should remain silent. It was superfluous – she wasn't sure *why* there was a need for secrecy, but she had already understood.

They remained in the narrow passageway for a while – Alis was watching for something, or more likely, someone. Unable to assist, Adria paced back and forth, anxiously waiting to see what would be said, and trying to quash the voice in her mind worrying she'd been wrong to rejoice.

A stern look told her she needed to stay still. Her steps must have been making too much noise. Staying hidden, away from the street, there was nothing for her to look at but the wooden planks to either side of them; the minutes passed slowly.

Eventually, Adria was taken by the hand and led out of town.

"At last!" she exclaimed, seemingly to the Lady's amusement. "Were you here looking for me?"

"In a manner of speaking."

Adria frowned. "I am very thankful you found me, either way. But what was the reason for your discretion, might I ask?"

"Of course. I did not want that man to know I had found you, as I would have lost the element of surprise. Tell me, though, where is he staying? I could find no trace of him at the inn."

Oh. Lady Jhardi was looking for *Varick*. Why did she feel quite so... disappointed? "I... I'm sorry. He isn't here. I lost him. That is to say, I angered him, and he abandoned me."

A flicker of consternation crossed Alis's face. Casting her eyes across Adria, she took in her unkempt state. "Am I to understand you do not know his location then?"

Adria looked down at her feet. She felt horrible to be letting Alis down, and had always hoped for the Lady to hold her in high regard. "We passed from here to Waterfjord, but where he went from there, I could not say. We were... I mean, *he* will be on horseback."

Removing her hood and the scarf from around her face, Alis sat on the ground, so Adria sat down next to her. *She must have been wearing it as a disguise then, as it's dustier here than it was along the streets.*

"Don't be disheartened. Besides, that is more helpful than I had expected. There are only a few places he could have headed to from there – Redmonde or Bridleway are the most likely. How many days is it since you were in Waterfjord?"

"It's been three now, although he left very early in the morning on the first."

"So," she rested her hand gracefully against her chin. Her fingers were long and slender, much like the rest of her. "He will likely have already made it to the next town and possibly left again too. We must choose carefully."

"We passed through Redmonde before we came to Water-Rise. So, we should head to Bridleway." Adria spoke confidently, but immediately worried she had overstepped.

"Yes, I believe you are correct. We must move quickly. The two of us can share my mount, though he will not carry us as surely with his load doubled, so we will have to alternate between riding and progressing on foot."

"Yes, of course." Adria was thrilled. "I can come with you then?"

"I don't see why not. Or, if you want to return to Ember House, I could provide you with some coins. By the look of you, I'm guessing you have none of your own. I'm afraid I cannot spare Cotton, my horse, but you may find one you could purchase."

Adria was embarrassed all over again, wishing she could have somehow prevented the grand Lady from seeing her in this state. She was effectively destitute, and clearly, this was obvious from simply looking at her. "I would certainly like to stay with you. If you are willing to have me, that is."

"I've just told you I am, silly, hesitant girl." It was a fair description, but she said it affectionately. "In return, you can tell me the whole story behind the man you released. Maybe it will even help us find him." Alis looked at Adria anew. "When did you last eat, Adria?" Seeing her hesitation, Alis instantly began rummaging around in one of her packs for some food, which she promptly thrust into Adria's hands. "I'm afraid we will need to set off imminently. It's the peak of day, and we must make the most of these sunlight hours."

They agreed to head north. Once they'd passed Bridleway, they would try to guess where Varick might be journeying next – for they both felt sure, based on his previous pattern, that he would soon not be staying in any one place for long.

Riding double was a new experience for Adria. Try as she might, she could not feel comfortable, nor stop being conscious of the way her arms encircled Alis.

It was different to travelling with Varick, but *good* different. They made conversation, and she didn't feel judged. Alis understood her humanity and her flaws; she wasn't angry at her failures. Perhaps she was reading too much into nothing, but Adria felt something she had not for a long time – safe.

When they began to walk on foot, she felt less on edge, and relaxed even further as she began to tell Alis about Varick. It helped to talk about a subject she was familiar with, but in a way, she was beginning to feel absolved. She hadn't realised quite how much the guilt had been clawing at her.

Despite doing her best to paint herself in a favourable light – where possible – Adria was decidedly honest.

Alis did not give her a single unkind word in response. She nodded and looked serious at times, but she did not shame Adria at all.

"I'm sorry. I made a mess of things, I know that. Thank you for being so understanding and not condemning me, however much I deserve it."

"The guilt you feel yourself is more than sufficient. If it helps, it sounds like he manipulated you. He has been around for enough lifetimes to have the experience to do so; it is not your fault – not entirely – that he succeeded."

It was immature of her to continue to seek reassurance, but the truth was she felt better than she had in weeks. "In a way, yes, but you warned me, and my judgment was poor. If I had the chance to go back... well, I would do things so very differently."

"I'm sure you would." With Alis having shut conversation down, they walked in silence for a while. Adria replayed the conversation in her mind, hoping she had said the right things, and waiting for her companion to say something to indicate how *she* might be feeling. Nothing of her thoughts had been revealed on her face.

The only time Alis had reacted was when she'd mentioned siphoning away the magic, but her expression had been difficult to interpret. A frown, but not an angry one – more like her words had triggered a thought. Or helped her understand something. Yes, that had to be it; Alis must have been wondering how she'd reanimated Varick and her mentioning of siphoning had now explained it.

As night fell, Adria was pleased to find Alis had a tent, and while she did not offer to share her bedroll, she allowed Adria to lie down beside her.

Despite being glad to have shelter, and her situation having been much improved, it took Adria longer to fall asleep than usual. She cared far too much about whether Alis held her in a positive regard.

CHAPTER 24 – KINDNESS

Free of responsibility, and free of cares. It mattered not as long as he could return to himself.

He knew he had reached, perhaps crossed, the line. It wasn't like he hadn't done so before. It came as a necessary side-effect of having access to more magic than any other person ever born.

He was a glitch, a beautiful mistake that never should have been.

And there was still more, far, far more magic, that was his and his alone.

He had finally taken enough to become free. Liberated from a different kind of prison. The magicless self he'd been trapped in.

And his storage capacity had barely been touched.

Something fell from Alis's pocket as she rose. It clunked down into her blanket, and Adria, still lying on the ground, picked it up and chuckled. "I remember you holding this stone when we first met. Does it mean anything? It just looks like an oval to me."

"Not at all. It's smooth and feels nice in my hand. Sometimes holding it helps me think."

"Oh, I see how that would work." She smiled and quickly passed it back to Alis. "I'll get packed up before we eat?"

"Thank you. When we get chance, we must get you a bedroll, too." Once again, Adria was taken aback by Alis's kindness. Fumbling over the tent poles, she tried to say thank you, but barely any sound left her mouth.

The morning was grey and bleak. If the wind picked up, she was going to be freezing, but she'd manage as long as she was able without complaining. At least when they were walking, she'd be okay – and when they rode together, she'd have some body heat for extra warmth, too.

"I'm surprised he kept you around as long as he did," Alis admitted as they sat on logs to take a small breakfast, souring the mood. The comment had seemed to come out of nowhere – she must have been mulling over it during the night.

"Varick? I suppose I was confused about that, too. Especially since he made it incredibly clear he could barely stand my company. At least, when he forgot to pretend otherwise." They both laughed in the sharing of a joke. Not necessarily because it was funny, but in companionship.

It seemed to imply that Alis did not resent her.

For the first stretch of the day, they travelled on horseback, and Adria had to keep reminding herself to pay attention to their surroundings. Just in case. She was no longer on her guard like she had been before, but having learnt the horrors of being alone – of having *nothing* – she did not want to be at such a loss ever again.

Mentally, she tweaked her map whenever they stopped, focusing on its accuracy in addition to increasing the area it covered. She wasn't sure how much of it she'd remember, but her paper had been left in her pack.

Adria had tied her hair in a ponytail to prevent it blowing everywhere, but Alis's seemed to hold in place, inexplicably unaffected by the wind. She couldn't help but stare, finding it strange. It had to be the thickness of it, weighing it down. As tempting as it was to touch it, to see if she was correct, she managed to resist.

Almost no time seemed to have passed when Alis declared they should switch, and travel on foot to rest Cotton. Once they'd walked off their stiffness, they talked of books they'd read.

The Jhardis' private area had held its own small library, which Alis described in some detail. While Adria had read more widely, Alis had been privy to some unique, specialised books on similar topics, so they had plenty of information to compare. Adria was secretly quite pleased to find she was able to comfortably match Alis's pace, even while chatting.

Soon they had fallen into a routine.

Despite having been of a mind not to, they found themselves forced to stop in Bridleway. Adria's clothes were close to ruin, and her boots were beginning to show holes.

Happily, Alis also used the opportunity to deliver on her promise of a bedroll. It was of some comfort to know the shopkeeper had seen a man matching Varick's description. He had not long since passed through the area.

Much like Varick, Alis radiated confidence wherever she went – in large part, a gift from her high upbringing. Adria did her best to emulate the way she spoke and moved but it didn't come naturally. If Alis noticed her vain efforts, she said nothing of it.

With Adria more suitably attired, and both of them keen to try and catch Varick, they chose not to linger in Bridleway.

"Might I ask you to explain your part in this?" Adria asked hesitantly, hoping Lady Jhardi did not mind. Having become so used to Varick's constant snapping, she now worried about causing upset every time she opened her mouth – or at least, when her words related to any matters of the personal kind. "I cannot help but wonder how you find yourself in the position of chasing after him. Do you enjoy the freedom? I guess… if it wasn't obvious… Varick told me very little about how or why he was imprisoned."

"I suppose it will pass the time while we travel." Alis's tone was always serious, and Adria didn't think she really meant things quite as they sounded. "I have never met this man, Varick. Indeed, it is only from yourself I know his forename. He was shut away for around ninety years. To be precise, he was locked in the palace itself, and everyone else vacated it hastily. I'm not sure how he ended up in the cell you described."

"I think he must have done it to himself. When I tried to siphon things… Hmmm, it only worked when I tried to siphon Varick's own magic. I couldn't take the lock off the palace door, so that must have been someone else's magic. Yes. It stands to reason he must have locked himself in that dark place. Almost as if he wished to hibernate." She scratched her eyebrow. "Except he obviously did it in a way which prevented himself from leaving again. How curious."

"I understand he was quite power-mad at the time, which led him to make rash decisions. Perhaps he regained his sensibilities enough to shut himself away from the world."

"Yes, it is plausible, I think. He certainly showed moments of recklessness and folly. Even if on the whole he seemed to be quite in control of his actions," Adria reflected. "And what came next?"

"After Lucis palace was abandoned, the family moved into Ember House."

"I wondered about that. I hope you don't find it impertinent for me to ask, but Varick was rather of the opinion the throne should have been his, so to speak. I wasn't sure… how did the Jhardis become the sovereign family in place of the Azeileahs?" She watched Alis's reaction carefully. She did not seem offended.

"The *then* Lady Jhardi was married to one of Varick's older brothers. As they didn't have children, and there were no other heirs, the rulership passed to her younger sister. The Azeileah family was all but gone. Unfortunately, Varick remained. Or the shell of him did. We were left with no choice but to become his guardians – a role which included tracking him down should he ever escape."

"Oh yes, he said something about a sister-in-law. But wait… he is really *that* dangerous?"

"What have you seen of him thus far? He is without the majority of his magic still, and you already know he is cruel. Can you imagine how capable he might be at his full power? He is the most accomplished mage ever seen. He, quite literally, took the magic out of the world."

Adria was dumbstruck, trying to digest what Alis had described. "It's his fault there's no more magic?" It wasn't really a question, she was merely processing what Alis had just said, but the implications were immense. "He's really *that* powerful?"

"He will be when he's back at full strength. The whole story is a bit darker, but the amount of magic he had eventually drove him to devastating measures. As long as he expended or stored enough of it, he was able to successfully moderate himself, but at some point, he stopped being careful."

Alis took a deep breath and kicked a stone. It was unlike her to be discomfited. Adria wasn't sure what to say, but Alis continued, regardless.

"Or maybe he did it intentionally. He released a huge burst of magic across the entire country. I do not know if there was a name for it, but I would say 'blighted, shadow magic' would accurately describe it. It wreaked widespread destruction. The aftermath was a very desolate time – most of what you see around you is the result of rebuilding."

"I've heard people talking about a curse lying over the land." Adria appreciated she sounded superstitious, but she really wanted to keep Alis talking.

"Yes, they are correct. That curse is quite literally Varick's magic. When he unleashed it all at once, it needed to go somewhere. It attached itself to the land, using the portholes as its focal points, given they were already configured to contain magic. I am not sure whether the effect was altogether intentional on Varick's part."

"Does that mean that when he gathers it up, the land will start to heal? If you're saying that's why all the grass is dead and the lakes are depleted, then might not it actually be a good thing that he has been released? If he is the only person able to fix it." Adria gasped. "I saw a stream regenerate. It had previously been dried up!"

"Perhaps. It is a risk that, so far, we have been unwilling to take. I guess my hand has now been forced." Adria felt her cheeks heat and thought they had probably gone red. "Obviously, the healing of the land would be beneficial; the ultimate question is at what cost. Varick is unpredictable and cannot be controlled. If he was – *when* he *is* – the most powerful person in the world… Who is to say whether we would have been better to have desisted from upsetting the status quo."

"I see." Adria had now made that decision on the world's behalf. The fact she'd done so unknowingly was little consolation. "Why is it that Ember House isn't ravaged like the terrain here? We had rain, and flowers could grow there. It was the complete reverse of everywhere else."

"When Varick released his curse, the land immediately around where he was standing – atop Tenebrae Mountain – remained protected. Due to the huge radius of his spell, this area was larger than you might have anticipated, and therefore some of the land around the mountain's foot was sheltered from his outburst too." Alis seemed to anticipate the question she was about to ask, as she added, "At the cost of the glamour, that is, which came about because immediately prior to casting out the devastating blow, he hid himself from view, to prevent anyone guessing what he was up to; to stop his subjects from seeking shelter."

"He really is as awful as I'd thought. I'd begun to wonder if I was simply over-sensitive." She pursed her lips. "How is it that he became so powerful though? Why do you think he was gifted more magic than anyone else?"

"Why does anything happen?" Alis kept her voice free of emotion. "I'd call it an unhappy accident."

As Adria was nodding in agreement, a thought struck her. "Are we going about this in the wrong way? I could probably siphon his magic from the portholes instead. Then he would never gain enough power again?"

"Ah. Yes, you did mention that before. It's an interesting theory. Are you sufficiently confident in how your magic works – knowing everything that's at stake? I have little learning in anything magical." Alis frowned. "I will think more on this. I cannot help but feel my preference would be to stop him first. Already, he has gained enough magic to be of great concern. You may still be able to remove the curse over the land later."

Adria thought the most logical conclusion was for them to split up, but for purely selfish reasons, she did not want to say as such. If Lady Jhardi suggested it herself... well, she'd worry about it then. Instead, she said possibly the most stupid thing she could have done in the circumstances, "You're not just trying to stop Varick so your family can stay in power, though?"

"Your naivety astounds me sometimes, Adria. Women are deprioritised in the line of succession, and I am not the heir. Nor am I particularly close to my brother, who is. Ruling is a great burden. Can you honestly tell me, irrespective of Dann's flaws, you would want Varick to rule in my brother's stead?"

"It was a dumb thing to ask. I'm so sorry, Alis, I spoke without thinking. You've been nothing but kind to me, and I really haven't deserved it." Adria was ashamed of how thoughtless she could be sometimes.

Alis put her arm around Adria's shoulder, "You need to gain more confidence in yourself. Come, I believe our horse will now be refreshed enough to carry us again."

CHAPTER 25 – WITCH HUNT

With her new understanding, Adria found plenty to occupy her as they travelled. The more she searched for them, the more she noticed subtle improvements in the health of the land. Occasionally, she spotted beetles or clusters of aphids. Weeds were newly growing amongst the grass, which in places was even returning from its dull tan colour to a healthier green.

The layers of Alis were becoming increasingly visible, and her glowing eyes no longer instilled fear whenever she met them with her own; she was beginning to see the feelings behind her companion's rigid demeanour.

Evidently, the Lady's upbringing had included being trained to hide her real self.

Adria thought she was likely the first person outside of her own family to have spent this much time with Alis. Other than perhaps her tutors. It was incredible really, given they'd only spent a handful of days together… and a little sad.

Her own confidence had increased measurably, and Adria was sure it would not have gone unnoticed.

She wondered whether Alis would still have described her as a meek girl, who had never before had encouragement from anyone other than a man she hadn't realised was manipulating her. She didn't like to be so harsh on herself, but after all, she had, on some level, *known* Varick had wanted his freedom at any cost – she'd simply thought some of his attentions and flatteries were genuine as well.

Regardless, right now, she felt like a different person. She finally understood she was something more than simply an immature girl whose only purpose was to please others – and it was solely Alis she had to thank for that.

As if she could sense her thoughts – or, more likely, she had sensed that Adria's thoughts were pointed in her direction – Alis turned to her and smiled. It wasn't that she had softened as such, more that Adria was now able to see through her demeanour and appreciate her warmer side.

"Do I seem different to you?" Adria continued her pondering by asking aloud.

"In what sense?"

"I *feel* different. For the first time, I don't have anywhere to be, or anyone to please."

Alis let out a deep, melodic but hearty laugh. "You certainly do have somewhere to be. We need to find Varick. Or have I distracted you so much you've forgotten about him?"

"Oh, that's not what I meant, and you know it."

"I certainly hope not."

"No, I just meant you're treating me as an equal. I'm not saying I *am* your equal, just that you don't make a point of telling me what to do, and you act like you actually value my opinion."

"Adria, one thing you have yet to learn, is not to care what people think. Merely being lucky enough to be born in a higher position than you doesn't give me any right to order you about. The fact you were integral in Varick's escape on the other hand... well, that does give me some right to demand your help." Alis always sounded overly serious, so Adria had to impute some humour into her tone. "Besides it's not about equals or otherwise. I enjoy your company and therefore welcome your presence more than that of many others."

"I suppose I've never actually felt worthwhile before... felt like I was worth someone else's time," she said, seeking praise again – her insecurities would not quieten.

Alis stopped abruptly before walking back towards her and placing a hand on each of her shoulders. For a while, she didn't speak, and Adria became a little nervous. "It's okay to feel like that sometimes; that doesn't mean it's true. You've got me to talk some confidence into you now, but I might not always be around. Ultimately, *you* are the only person you can rely on. You need to look out for yourself."

Adria knew her friend was making sense. She also fully appreciated that, before now, she'd never *had* any confidence to draw upon.

She couldn't have grown in perception and insight without Alis's regard.

It was all too easy to relax into these light-hearted, effortless days and ignore the serious nature of their journey. Most of the time, she wanted to simply forget about Varick, and magic, and enjoy her present company without any concerns about the future. It was a selfish wish, and she supposed she'd learnt at least one thing from her time with Varick after all.

As recent others had been before it, the night was strangely warm, and Adria found it difficult to settle. Alis seemed able to fall asleep relatively quickly wherever they lay, but for her, it never worked that way. She would try to clear her mind, then count the stars, and listen to Alis's gentle breathing, but she would always end up feeling agitated. There would be a stone in an awkward place below her, or the lack of humidity would make her feel uncomfortable in her own skin.

Tonight, she knew something was bothering her but

couldn't quite put her finger on what.

She had been in a light daze when Alis nudged her to say it was time to start moving again. At first, Adria thought she hadn't been asleep at all, but on reflection, figured she'd probably dozed off at some point. It hadn't been enough. Being up and on her feet again, she felt groggy.

Luckily, their first stint was atop Cotton, so all she had to do was avoid falling off. Despite her best efforts – which included falling asleep against Alis's back – she somehow managed to stay mounted.

When she admitted as such, Alis promptly informed her she'd had to hold Cotton's reins with one hand, and Adria's hands – which had been clutched together around her waist – with her other, to make sure she didn't slip.

"How did your parents feel about you leaving Ember House to seek out Varick? I got the impression you were specifically chosen as the guardian, rather than your brother?" Adria asked as they climbed down from their seat. They always chatted more when walking than riding.

"They were more distressed about the situation than any danger to me. Dann is the heir, and I am the expendable one."

"Surely…" Adria flailed about for the right words, "He might be important as the heir – well, of course, he would be – but that can't mean their hopes for your future were that you'd be a hunter."

"I don't suppose they had many… *hopes for my future,* as you put it. As their *other* child, I am forbidden from marrying." When she saw Adria's confusion, she added, "So as not to create any conflict in the line for the throne."

"That's… but that's ridiculous!" *I wonder what caused the Jhardis to decide such a thing. It certainly wasn't that way in Varick's time.*

"Perhaps. I have never been too concerned by it; marriage is not exactly something I'm interested in. However, I do find myself surprised you weren't cognisant of this rule."

"I'm not sure if you're aware of this Alis, but there isn't much chatter or gossip about your family or anything related to them. You've always been completely secluded from the rest of us."

Regrettably, that seemed to put a halt to the conversation.

When Adria looked over, Alis was deep in thought. She wondered whether Alis had no interest in marriage because she'd always known she *couldn't* marry, or whether it was for a different reason. The way she'd said it had implied the latter.

Adria was starting to think *she* wasn't too fussed about that sort of thing, either. She was far more at ease in her present company than she'd ever felt before, and couldn't imagine how the dynamics of a relationship would work in a marriage.

Being dependent on Alis's experience to get by, she still didn't feel like her friend's equal. Things like rationing the food, and even geographical awareness, were not in her skillsets, and she fretted over the fact she wasn't pulling her weight.

In an effort to go a short way towards rectifying this, Adria had been doing her best to care for Cotton as often as possible. Try as she might, she hadn't quite managed to attain the feeling of connection she'd had with Velvet, but remained hopeful this would at some time develop.

☆☆ ☆ ☆☆

Having passed through several towns and villages without catching their quarry, Alis informed Adria they were faced with a choice. There was only one hamlet left on the westerly side of the Island. Situated significantly further north than where they were now – and any of the other settlements – the trip would take several days. Their other option was to head east and bypass it entirely.

As far as they could see, the only advantage of heading north was expediency, as Alis hoped they might meet Varick returning in the opposite direction. There was also every chance they might somehow miss him.

Travelling east seemed to make more sense; they would be ready and waiting when Varick approached.

There was also a risk he would not take the time to make the trip north anyway, in which case, journeying that way would be a significant setback. They both felt his immense vanity would ensure he did go that way, but the chance they might be wrong remained in both of their minds.

"I'm not sure why we're debating this – we have to head east. We're only torturing ourselves by prolonging the decision. Plus, if we finally arrive somewhere first, I may have the opportunity to drain the porthole myself, which would only be an advantage." Adria had been checking the portholes at every town they'd passed through and had yet to find a trace of magic. This could simply have been down to her inexperience, but she was convinced it was because Varick had already drained each one prior to their arrival.

"Everywhere we've been, the high cliffs have acted as a barrier to the sea. At North-Harbour, we would have been able to walk out onto the rocky promenade and touch the water."

"Oh."

"We could have taken a boat out together, into the middle of nowhere."

Adria laughed. "We're in the middle of nowhere now."

"It's not peaceful here. You have to experience it to

understand. We went once, when I was a child... It was a happy place." She let out a small sigh. "We've already come all this way. I should have liked to visit it once more." It was the first time Alis had shown any resentment towards her responsibilities, but Adria was not swayed.

"We'll go. If not now, then later. It's a long trip but we'll have plenty of time."

Alis perked up slightly.

"And we'll enjoy it even more, knowing Varick has been dealt with." Her stomach flipped slightly. Varick had brought her and Alis together; without his interference, Adria would have spent her life alone.

Although... before her daily trips to Tenebrae, she'd had friends. There would have been no Alis and no travelling, but the camaraderie itself wouldn't have been absent.

Except, if she was going to look at things that way, who knew where Adria would have ended up, if not for Varick. It may well not have been Ember House.

"Alis, I don't suppose... would there be any way to find out *how* I came to reside at Ember House? I've always assumed I'll never find out, but the Steward was not exactly open about these things. I thought you might know whether there are any records." Adria shuffled her feet awkwardly. "Seeing all these people living differently to the commune I grew up in has made me wonder afresh."

"You're asking me if we might be able to find your parents."

She nodded.

"I'm sorry, Adria. There was an orphanage. In the time before, there had been several, but the population reduced, and there was only one left. When they could no longer afford food – and the locals had nothing spare to contribute – it was forced to close. None of the toddlers or tweens who lived there had any family we could track down."

"Oh." Alis put an arm around her.

"Ember House doesn't require two hundred people to run it; there's only four of us. My parents wanted to give the lost children a home and a purpose."

At least now, she knew for certain – albeit she couldn't quite decide if it was a relief to finally know the truth, or whether she felt sad that any hope she'd held of finding them was gone forever.

CHAPTER 26 – UNITY

It had been a mistake to head to the coast without returning for the siphon. Yet, there was no way he would turn back now – his time was far too valuable to waste in such a way.

Her presence would only have made the murky seaside village more unbearable anyway. It was cold there, and the smells of fish merely served to remind him of how far he was from home… assuming nothing had changed since his last visit.

If anything, it had probably become more *miserable.*

Tempting as it was to skip the place entirely, he would not leave his magic lying around unattended. He needed to be whole.

For all her excitement, Alis remained a little dejected at their decision to head east, so Adria silently planned something that might cheer her friend up. In the middle of these empty, withered grasslands there were limited options, and yet it didn't take long for her to stumble across the perfect idea.

"You're unusually quiet, Adria. Not scheming to run off and leave me for Varick, I hope?"

"Don't even joke about such things." Adria shuddered.

Alis was holding her smooth, oval stone again – she only seemed to do so when she was worried. "Something is going on with you," she eventually said.

Adria smiled, pleased that her companion was paying

such close attention to her. "It's nothing, I'm just deep in thought."

"Care to share?"

"You described the coast so beautifully, I suppose I was trying to picture what it might be like." Alis nodded, as though she approved. "It's hard to imagine anything more spectacular than Ember House, although I don't suppose I appreciated it at the time. Not fully. In the real world, even the sunlight is hazy and distorted."

"Our home is a truly beautiful place. It's a shame about that ugly Palace casting its shadow over it. I wonder if things will ever go back to how they were."

Adria shrugged, thinking the land was still devoid of growth and they were the only people around for quite some distance, but not wanting to be so negative aloud. It would take more than their own lifetimes for Azeileah to recover. "Perhaps they may begin to."

"I meant for us, truth be told. Whether we might ever enjoy the luxuries of Ember House again."

"Surely *you* could Alis, even if I am no longer welcome?"

"You will always be welcome, Adria." Then what had she meant? Unless… Did she fear Varick was far stronger than they were? Was Alis afraid for their lives, while she lived in blissful ignorance?

I've been relying too much on her… feeling like I'm safe with her protecting me.

How did one apologise for being selfish? Even if it was unintentional. Words weren't enough, but perhaps if she attempted to lift Alis's spirits, it might go a little way towards showing she cared.

"You will let me know if there's anything I can do to help, won't you Alis?" she asked, jogging a couple of steps to catch up.

"Of course. Although, I don't imagine there will be. I'm quite self-sufficient." Adria frowned; Alis had answered too quickly, she could barely have given her question any thought.

There was no further discussion on the matter because, as if out of nowhere, the sky began to darken. Together they halted, and looked towards the clouds.

"We might need to light a fire tonight," was all Alis remarked.

Until now, the evening light had always faded from a pale yellow to a faint grey, before disintegrating into the gradual blackness of night. It was a far cry from the kaleidoscopic sunsets of their home, but today, something had shifted a little. Had Varick drained another porthole?

Let's hope it was the one on the northern coast.

The width of the country was around a third of its length, so even if they were forced to stop soon, it would not be long before they reached their destination. Tonight, they'd sleep in a tent, and the following night they would spend in Cent.

Then she'd have the chance to gain some magic of her own.

I'll be able to fight beside Alis, instead of behind her.

They persevered for another hour or two, but the visibility became too low to continue, and they made camp – although they both agreed it was still too early for dinner.

"In that case," Adria proudly declared, "I would like to tell you a story."

"What kind of story?" The flames reflected in Alis's eyes brought back that cat-like impression she'd seen the first time they'd met.

She'd made up countless stories over the last year, and

this one was her favourite. "I told Varick many tales, at his insistence, but there was one I never shared with him. He was a little sensitive when I mentioned the person who inspired it."

Standing behind the fire, she put her all into the performance. Adria began with a description of the melancholy portrait, that many people walked past each day, but never really noticed.

"Even when the spy edged out from the secret entrance behind it, her movements were so fluid that people mistook her for a feline." As she described the spy creeping around the castle unnoticed, she acted out the motions.

"Is that really how I walk?" Alis interrupted.

Determined not to break character, Adria tried to ignore the question, although was forced to bite her lip to hold in a laugh.

"Then one night, there was a great ball, and the spy wished to dance." Adria held out her arm for Alis to join her. "Though they twirled like empresses swathed in jewels, no one saw them. For they were alone in the world."

"That last part was a little much, don't you think?" Alis teased, taking a step backward to resume her role as the audience.

Persisting with the dramatics regardless, Adria held out her arm, as though grasping for something just out of reach. "She let go, and the spy was left wondering if it had ever happened at all."

"But it had?"

Smiling wistfully, she whispered, "Yes, it had all been real."

CHAPTER 27 – WAITING

At some point, sometime soon, he was going to have to retrieve the girl. Without a siphon, he was out of balance.

Hopefully, it wouldn't require much of a detour.

She would probably come easily. There'd been nothing combative in her nature. He'd have to threaten her a little, but he wasn't worried.

His main concern was whether he found her before he forgot he was even looking.

Despite her companion's initial disappointment, Adria was certain there would be some enjoyment to be found in Cent.

This community had a more upbeat atmosphere than they'd felt elsewhere, and the residents seemed easy-going. It was larger than the other towns they'd stopped by, with more options for amusement, which went some way towards explaining why the overall mood was lighter.

Plays were shown twice a week on an outdoor stage. Aromatic food stalls lined one side of the daily market, with trinkets, fabrics, pots, and small items of furniture sold along the other. There were open spaces, with large game boards drawn on the ground, and benches set out for the residents' enjoyment.

She couldn't believe her luck – that this place, in particular, was where they would have a few days to enjoy the amenities.

Before they could take up a room at the inn and make plans for the evening, they made for the centre of town to check Varick hadn't yet passed through. There was still a chance that he'd skipped the northern coast, and if so, they would be forced to move on first thing in the morning.

Her heart pounded as she held out her hands, but Adria knew immediately that this porthole felt different to the others.

Having identified that Varick was yet to collect his magic, Adria heaved a sigh of relief. They could finally stay in one place for a while, and Cent was the most magical town she'd visited.

Alis had previously declared that she would prefer to make enquiries around town than rely on magic, but when she saw Adria's joyous reaction to the porthole, her opinion was swayed. No longer seeing any reason to alert anyone as to the incoming fugitive – at least, not while they remained there, waiting for him – they let the town remain oblivious and free of disruption, at least for the time being.

The eating area was over-crowded, leading Adria to worry the inn might be full, but happily they did have sufficient space available, and Alis made a reservation for the entire week.

The room itself was pleasant enough, but nothing special, and they retired to the communal area in the tavern downstairs. As was typical of the settlements on the Eastern side of Azeileah, there were more people living here, and they paid very little attention to the newcomers. Adria was sure *she* observed *them* more than vice versa.

Alis had a pack of cards, and although they shared a few

games, they spent an equal amount of time talking.

"We ought to retire for the night," Alis declared as she swooped up the abandoned cards to place them back in their box.

Adria was about to protest, but then realised there was no one else around. "I hadn't realised how late it was."

"No, I'm not tired either, but the proprietor is waiting for us to leave before he locks up for the night."

Bidding him thanks, they made their way upstairs. Any disappointment that the evening had come to an end was outweighed by her excitement at the possibility she'd soon be able to match Varick's power.

Shortly after sunrise, Adria wound her way back through the streets towards each of the town's portholes and attempted to draw out Varick's magic. Finding no success, she repeated her attempts for three mornings in a row. The magic was there, calling to her, and she could feel it had been *his* – yet there seemed to be a knack to removing it, which so far, she'd been unable to determine.

Betwixt her attempts, something had shifted below the surface. Now, it was beginning to feel as though it was *herself* it belonged to – but she still could not break it free.

In the afternoons, she'd joined Alis in her patrols of the area. The rows of houses and businesses were a welcome distraction from the open, hilly, but otherwise empty ground she'd spent weeks traversing. Adria was fascinated by the winding streets and nooks you could stumble upon, with no idea where they might bring you out.

But her mind kept returning to the portholes.

The magic wouldn't come to her touch. Why wasn't it heeding her call?

They examined them for a catch, hoping they might

spring open, even though Adria knew she had never seen Varick do anything of the sort. She had tried to wait, sitting in contact with the seal, hoping with time it might weaken. There was no indication even the slightest drop had been shifted by her efforts.

Miffed by her lack of success, together they had returned during the night, and Alis had attempted to smash the seal over one of them.

Her frustration was mounting.

It didn't help that Alis seemed unbothered. Whether she doubted Adria's ability, mistrusted magic, or simply didn't see the need for Adria to gain the advantage was unclear, but it was causing the build-up of tension between them.

"We should go back and try again this afternoon."

"I am expecting Varick to be nearby; this may be our last day of relaxation."

"All the more reason for urgency. I must obtain his magic before he does!"

"Adria, you wouldn't even know what to do with it. Haven't you said as much to me? All you've managed to achieve so far is accidentally entering a couple of dreams. There isn't time for you to learn control of it now, and you're as likely to harm *yourself* as you are Varick." Alis scratched her chin. "With this many people around, I'd be loath to have a magic display, anyway."

Although the words were not said with any hostility, Adria was already sensitive to her own lack of utility. Feeling hurt – although admittedly, this was unjustified – she marched off towards the nearest porthole, leaving Alis to spend her time however she pleased.

The main thoroughfare was heaving, so instead she changed direction, and made towards the other porthole, which was situated in a quieter residential area. Reaching the spot, she sat on the ground and wondered what to do next. There wasn't anything she could think of that she hadn't already tried. Being close to the porthole didn't provide any new inspiration she'd lacked the previous few days.

Embarrassed, and not quite ready to apologise, she remained where she was and sulked. The sun bore down on her, and for the first time in a while, misery began to creep upon her.

She hadn't felt this way since…

Adria startled, jumping up – but it was too late.

Like a mirage clearing, the images around her fell into place just as Varick grabbed her from behind.

He was much stronger than he looked. She tried to cry out that he was hurting her, but with his arm crushing her neck she couldn't make the right sounds.

Somehow Alis was there too – she'd followed her or Varick, it didn't matter which; the important thing was she was there. Holding a bow and an arrow, she stood her ground. The arrow was nocked, and the string pulled back, ready.

She isn't going to let him take me.

Only Adria's position as Varick's human shield had prevented her from acting. The extreme concentration on Alis's face, alongside the way her hands trembled ever so slightly, revealed she'd been about to release it, only to have held the arrow back at the last second.

Because I'm in the way.

The restraint she'd shown… I can't believe she stopped herself. All to save my life.

"What do you want with her?" Alis shouted, from her position across the street.

Varick scoffed. "Nothing at all." For some reason those words felt like a lie – but in such a precarious position, there was no space to decipher his intentions. "Put that bow down and I'll let her go."

Alis hesitated – and Adria was sure she'd have done the same in her place.

If only I hadn't insisted on coming here.

Where Varick touched her, she felt chills. All the happiness she'd accumulated was being leached out of her. It was a relief when he removed his hands.

Then, too late, Adria realised he'd let go solely to make use of his magic.

She saw the rush as his blast displaced the air, and reached out her arms as if to hold it back – but she couldn't.

Varick's blow hit Alis in the middle of her chest. The resultant smoke obscured her vision of the impact – giving Adria hope, where none could exist.

Before, the moments had dragged out. Now everything happened so quickly her mind couldn't comprehend it was real.

She has to be okay.

Before Varick could catch her again, Adria ran towards her companion, falling straight to her knees on the uneven cobblestones.

She was still more beautiful than it was possible to be.

Her body shook with sobs. Unable to stop herself, she slumped over Alis's body, her friend supporting her even in death. Her fingers clutched at her tunic, now damp from tears, not ever wanting to release it.

In the distance, she registered Varick retrieving more of his magic. While he wasn't looking, she plucked Alis's black arrow from the floor – something small she could carry with her – and clutched it to her chest.

Mere moments later, Varick prised it from her grasp. "I'll take that. Only thing that could actually have killed me." He snapped it, and Adria felt as though it were her heart which had been broken in twain. "We need to get going."

"Get away from me." Adria doubted he could understand what she'd said through her tears. "Help! Please," she called out to someone passing. Finding herself ignored, she kept trying.

"We're going now. Or did you have some other option?" Varick rolled his eyes at her.

But she did. Ember House. How could she explain… Adria began to wail again. How could she even go back there now, without Alis? There was nothing for her there. Nothing anywhere.

Before Varick could drag her away, Adria managed to attract someone's attention. They assured her the town had a process for deaths and, on seeing the coins in Alis's purse, which thankfully Varick had not plundered, promised Adria they'd see her friend buried.

There was no question of blaming her, nor accusing her of murder. As far as the people of Cent were concerned, magic did not exist, and with no fire nearby, there was no way Adria could have caused those burns.

Varick seemed to have gone unnoticed, but she knew he was still there, waiting for her in the shadows.

Could she escape – would he give her the choice to leave?

Rage seethed within her, triumphing over the sadness. Why would she want to leave now? She'd kill him herself. The memory of power – magic her body had burnt through by entering his dreams – came to her, but there was no release. No spark left.

She'd have to use her hands instead, if she had no other choice. Casting a glance around her, she sought anything she could use as a weapon.

A steady hand wrapped itself around her bicep and there was nothing Adria could do to shake it free.

"Get off me," she shrieked. "What have you done! You murderer!"

He clasped his other hand around her mouth and whispered in her ear, in a deep, psychotic voice, "You might want to stop that or you're going to make me mad. Now, come on. It's time to leave this decrepit place."

And really, what choice did she have but to comply? The smell of his hand made her gag, but when she managed a subtle nod, he removed it.

Adria was only semi-conscious as she let him lead her away, unsure where they were going, but not caring. When he handed her the reins of Alis's horse, she choked back another sob, and forced herself to reach out to receive them. Her hand felt weak, her fingers too numb to grasp the rope, but she somehow managed to climb atop him. Presumably, Varick had supported her as she'd mounted.

She cared nothing for where they were going. Only two things consumed her mind – regret and shame. Her chest ached.

Alis hadn't wanted to spend the afternoon at the porthole, she'd wanted to go for a meal together; she was only there because she followed me.

Then she hadn't killed Varick, solely to avoid harming me.

Not only that, but I made some terrible mistakes... I could have reached for Varick's hand and siphoned his magic the moment he grabbed me. I could have moved out of the way as soon as he let go. Perhaps Alis might still have fired the arrow, had I only ducked quickly enough.

Despite her own unforgivable shortcomings, the one thing she couldn't face was how they had parted. Not only without kind words but mid-argument.

She refused to believe it was true.

Adria let her mind shut down. It didn't want to process her situation; it didn't care about her surroundings. She let herself be blindly led.

They'd probably already been travelling in silence for hours, but Varick's voice was what finally broke through to her. "Silly child. If you'd simply expended a little of my magic, you would have been able to use it to tease a hole in the seal. But you had wasted it all entering my dreams, hadn't you." Knowing he was only trying to goad her, she did her best not to show any reaction. "Perhaps I should now be thanking you for the violation. With hindsight."

She might have thought that was sufficient to pierce her, but he continued. "You led me right to that Jhardi hunter as well. Perhaps you are good luck after all."

Bile rose in her throat, and she swallowed it down. It was likely the only thing she'd be eating for some time.

CHAPTER 28– SENTENCED

Things had turned out most fortuitously.

He now had ample material with which to keep the girl browbeaten. He probably wouldn't have to put up with her chattering for some time, either.

It was strange she had reacted so strongly to the hunter's demise, but then again, hadn't he known she was weak of character?

"You lied to me."

"What do you want now, Varick?" She stroked Cotton's mane with the back of her hand, but it was of little comfort. Mara, the mare she'd ridden halfway across Azeileah, had been abandoned by Varick who knew where.

"You told me you'd had almost no contact with the Jhardis."

"I wasn't lying. Besides, I'm not in the mood. Spit out whatever it is you want to say and let's be done."

He was quiet for a moment before exclaiming, "You've never seen anyone die before. *That's* what's bothering you. It's only shock; it'll get easier."

"That's not... that isn't..." She clenched her fist and squeezed. As she did so, Cotton veered to avoid a stone, and

Adria was forced to make a quick grasp to avoid falling off.

"I can understand, you know. I do still remember what it's like to feel emotions. It's distressing the first time you witness a death, seeing that body once the life has left it. You'll feel better soon."

The frightening thing was, at least in this moment, he was trying to be kind. "Why did you do it, Varick?"

He shrugged, as though it had been nothing. "She would have killed me, so I killed her first."

"She never said anything about killing you!" Adria's voice came out high-pitched and broken – but it wasn't like she hadn't already let on that she cared.

"What do you think the arrow was for? When I sealed myself away, she couldn't get to me. But once I was out…" He sounded almost human.

But she didn't want to think of him as human. She *hated* him. He sucked all the joy out of her, a perpetual drain on her spirits – and now he had taken away the one thing…

He raised an eyebrow. "Were you two *more* than friends?" She ignored him, but instead of heeding her silent message, he continued, "I must say I'm impressed; I didn't think you had it in you."

She bit her lip and willed herself to stay silent, doing everything she could to shut out the sound of him chuckling to himself.

At night, she pulled her bedroll over her face and wept silent tears.

Puffy-eyed, she forced herself to get back on Alis's horse and follow him.

Morning after morning.

Her eyes glazed over, barely seeing their surroundings, and she let them stay like that. Making them focus took effort she didn't want to expend. Blurry was better; it hid the world. Hid the truth.

Her map remained incomplete and in Varick's possession. It was of no consequence. She wouldn't have been updating it anyway… could barely bring herself to care. Eyeing where her bag was attached to his horse, she wondered what he had made of her attempts at sketching, and whether he had found the small book tucked away in a back pocket.

If she wanted her possessions back, she was going to have to snap out of her fugue.

"Varick."

He started at the sound of her voice.

"You were right. I find I do feel more like myself again. I apologise for my state of… distraction the last few days. I'd like to try and be useful once again, if I can be."

Only now her anger had grown large enough to encompass her grief, was she able to be strong. One more time, Alis had affected her personality, making her into something *more*.

"You were never useful to begin with." The words were said callously but she could tell he was experiencing relief. It was clear that, for whatever reason, she was of value to him and therefore he preferred her to be alongside him. Even though he did not care one iota for her company.

"I wondered if I could attempt to update my map again. I found it to be a pleasant distraction from the travelling. I hope I haven't forgotten too much… it will be a lot of work, but it would keep my mind occupied."

"What consequence is it to me?"

"Only that you have it in your possession."

"Oh, right. I didn't touch this grimy thing; is it in here? You'll have to remove it from my saddle yourself when we stop.

We'll be reaching Kings'land this afternoon, so you should have a bit of time at the inn – but don't be staying up all night. Or rather, if you do, know you'll not be spared any of the travelling tomorrow."

Assuming he afforded her the luxury of her own room, this would give her ample opportunity to examine the book on siphoning with sufficient privacy. She didn't care much for the magic, although perhaps when she knew more about it, she might begin to; however, she was certain it held the key to her true objective. Revenge.

Although she had been faking the change in demeanour, for the first time in days, Adria truly felt her spirits begin to lift. It was a strange feeling and was accompanied immediately after by an overpowering thump in her chest, signalling her feelings of guilt returning in full.

A little voice said perhaps *she* would become the monster. In Varick's place. *And what if I do?* she hissed back, quietening it.

"There are four portholes in Kings'land. You may as well follow me around and keep a lookout."

"I've had a rough few days. I'd rather catch up on rest if you didn't mind."

"It wasn't optional. I thought you were planning to sketch, anyway?"

She gritted her teeth. "I meant that I would find working on the map restful."

"Well, the more quickly I regain my magic, the more time you'll have to pursue your frivolities." Somehow Varick's twisted logic always *sounded* like it made sense. He wasn't serious, like Alis had been, but he presented everything he said as though it was incredibly *reasonable*.

Adria was distracted from their conversation and couldn't help but gasp when Kings'land appeared on the horizon, revealing row after row of tents. Proximity showed them to be in varying states of disrepair – some had their holes patched with mismatched fabric; others simply had holes through which their contents were exposed to the elements.

It never rained, so perhaps these signs of wear hadn't caused much inconvenience for the occupants.

"I've no idea," Varick declared in response to her unspoken question. "It wasn't like this before. We should head for the city gates."

Between the tents, fires were placed at intervals, and large, clay pots were being heated over many of these. There were people everywhere. More than she'd ever seen in one place before. Some wandered around, but many were simply loitering.

"Gates? Is this not the city?"

"Not yet; we're still five hundred paces out. Probably more." Dismounting, they weaved their way through the area. Adria was relieved to find the people dwelling there ignored them as they passed. "Listen, if the inns are full, we'll still have some way to travel tonight, but my main concern is something is going on in the city. The more people, the more risk of us being separated, and there will be pickpockets everywhere."

Adria remained apprehensive as they approached the fence, which was around twice her own height and therefore revealed nothing of what lay beyond it.

Before they could enter, a toll was demanded, consisting of a gold for each of them and an extra gold for the two horses, coming to three in total. Varick seemed to deliberate over something before handing it over.

Only once the sentries had satisfied themselves that the coins were real did they open the gate.

The empty, residential street was the opposite of what Adria had been anticipating. Kings'land now looked like every other place they had visited. "Where is everyone?" Adria gasped, but Varick shushed her and pushed her onwards. The gate was closed behind them, ominously. For a second, Adria's mind returned to those passages under the mountain – but then she tilted her head upwards, took a deep breath of the fresh air, and banished her fear.

Passing through several rows of houses, it was clear Kings'land was much larger than Cent had been. It wasn't until they met the centre – with the stalls and public meeting areas – that they encountered many people at all. Even then, they had more than enough space to move around comfortably.

Having walked through the marketplace, they reached a street with several inns – Adria counted at least four. Varick chose the second, seemingly at random, and enquired within. When she asked him why that particular one, curious as to what he'd factored into his decision-making, he simply raised an eyebrow.

They had no difficulty in obtaining lodgings there, and Adria quickly unhooked her bag before the horses were led away to the adjoining stables.

When the innkeeper led them upstairs, he opened the door into a large, lavish room. The bed frame was grand, though the rustic gold paint was chipped and fading. Likewise, the blue velvet curtains were moth-eaten. With a pang, she thought of her pony; try as she might, she didn't have the same connection with Cotton.

He departed, having only shown them the one room. "Varick…!"

"There is a servants' room adjoining this. It's rather convenient as it happens, and will allow me to keep an eye on you. All inns used to be set up with side rooms such as this; it is rather sad that only the old capital has upheld the tradition. Although, from what Eirik said, I can't imagine they receive many visitors."

Varick, lost in thought, began muttering to himself about visiting diplomats and foreign princes.

"No," she replied, despite being unsure if he'd truly been addressing her, "I haven't heard of any such people coming to the island. We may have been secluded but it seems likely they would have come to Ember House as their first port of call." *Stay strong, Adria.*

"You've heard of the expression port of call, but you'd never heard of portholes being the windows on a ship?"

She shook her head in confusion. "It's just an expression." Trying to put it out of her mind, she ventured through the door at the back. Her own room was small and lacked windows. One-quarter of a candle had been allowed, the inn evidently worrying that if they provided any more, it might be stolen.

With Varick wishing for them to both get cleaned up before leaving the inn, it seemed unlikely they would return until shortly before dark. Tonight was not going to allow much opportunity for reading, but she would make of it what she could. Sadly, she would also have to spend some time updating the map, just in case Varick happened to ask to see it. She didn't sufficiently trust his word to be confident he was telling the truth when he claimed not to have taken a look at it.

When a housekeeper brought through her bath water, Adria took the chance to ask about the shanties which ringed the city. "They're just people who can't afford to enter Kings'land, madam. I suppose they come here thinking there might be work but can't afford the gate price. Then, rather than going back, they join the rest of the community as is gathered there. Mayhap they think one day the world will have need of them."

"But how do they live?"

"They pool their resources. Every three or four weeks

they can afford to send someone inside to buy food for all of them."

"Only once per month? Yet there's hundreds of them!" Adria couldn't quite believe they were made to pay the gate price just so they could come in and buy food.

It was a surprise to find she was still capable of feeling something other than the hatred and guilt; of lamenting anything other than her own loss.

"Sometimes travellers will help out. A couple of the local businesses will allow their scraps to go out there too – knowing that they'll then be in receipt of the spend next time they have the gold to do so."

"Why don't they move elsewhere? To a town with no fee to enter?"

"I guess they'd be moved on. Or it'd be too much upheaval. It's pretty much a permanent village out there now."

By the uncomfortable look on her face and the awkward shuffling, Adria sensed she'd pushed it too far. "Thank you…"

"Sarah." Her attendant smiled. "Don't worry, they're really quite happy apart from the hunger. And there's not many around here who don't go hungry, being honest. Most of us inside the city… if we left, we wouldn't be able to afford to come back in."

Adria did her best to force a smile and offer a thank you.

It was apparent the residents here did not appreciate their own comforts – and how would they know they ought to? Unless travellers such as herself had taken the time to make them aware they were the *only* place outside of Ember House that had access to such luxury.

If they had, Adria felt sure they would have charged her dearly for the bath water. It may have delayed their day's schedule, but she fully intended to use the opportunity to finally shed the dirt from her body.

Nevertheless, the bath was not so peaceful or relaxing as it might have been. The situation here irked her, and she wondered what she should – or could – do to rectify it.

CHAPTER 29 – SIMMER

It was a relief to see the girl had snapped out of her mourning. Whatever that had been about.

He'd never seen relationships quite in the way other people did, so it wasn't clear whether her reaction had been normal – but it had certainly dragged on far longer than he should have had to tolerate.

Hopefully, the comforts of the inn would leave her indebted to him. She clearly had a fear of being destitute, ever since he'd left her with nothing. Seeing the number who were homeless, living in tents, had drummed in how lucky she was, effectively doing all the work for him. The girl was as good as loyal.

He also now had a platform to stand on. There would never have been people living out in the open air when he'd been in charge.

Time was going too quickly now, even though everything continued to move slowly around her. Ever since… *Alis*… things had remained out of focus. She was barely in the world. Sometimes when she reached out to touch something, she thought her hand might pass right through it, but it never did. She was certainly alive, even if her mind had dissociated from her surroundings. It could be dizzying at times.

The detachment hit her strongly as they walked towards the portholes. She barely registered the faces around her, and she realised she could not have commented as to the warmth of their reception in Kings'land.

Adria was simply watching Varick's feet and forcing her own to take one step forward after another in his wake.

When drops of water began to fall from the sky, the sensation against her face was refreshing. They were tangible, real. Adria began to notice her surroundings, the people shrieking and running for cover… because, of course, she and Varick were the only ones who'd ever seen it rain.

It was almost a shame she was clean from her bath, as this might have washed away her sins more vigorously.

Varick's hair had curled, and his appearance struck her as that of a young boy. For a second, dream Varick overlaid the real one.

He grabbed her arm.

Shivers ran through her as he forced her to siphon, as though the rain had woken him up, too, to the need for release.

She understood, at last, that the dark feelings she had around him had not been imagined.

As his magic had begun to return, the sense of unpleasantness had been increasing, but it was nothing to the feeling of being used by him now. Something in their connection allowed her to pick up on his sensibilities and, although the feelings of hostility and superiority had never felt like they were her own, she had been suffering from his proximate negativity for months.

For an awful second, she wondered if that might have been why she had grown so attached to Alis, if perhaps the separation from Varick had, in truth, been the thing to lighten her spirits rather than her companion. She hated herself for having even thought it, though she couldn't shake the idea it might have been true.

Adria tried to remember Alis from before she'd released Varick. She had felt her allure, been enticed by her airs and sense of mystery – but she'd also been afraid. Enduring Varick had made her less aware of status; it was a little ironic, given his obvious superiority complex.

Varick released her wrist, allowing her to step away from him. "Next time you do that, I would appreciate it if you asked my permission."

"Had I taken the time to ask you, the moment might have passed. It would have been too late. I assumed your presence here meant you had consented to your role."

Adria gritted her teeth. "Why don't you just leave your damn magic in the ground if it's too much for you to control?" He smiled at her, and she nearly hissed at him – but somehow managed to restrain herself. "I'm serious, if all you're doing is taking the magic up and then sending it out into the ether – through me – then why not just leave it where it is?"

He cocked his head, as though assessing her motives. "Are you sure you're ready for this conversation, Adria?"

It was the first time he had used her name in ages. Or, if he'd said it before, this was the first time he'd been addressing her rather than mocking her. Perhaps using her as his conduit really did help calm him. She thought for a second, then nodded. The more information she had, the better. Why he was telling her, she didn't know – and would have no way of determining until he began.

"There's a few reasons, and I think all of them are good ones, but I assume you'll bestow me with your own opinion when I'm done." Definitely sarcasm. "Firstly, once I started the process of regaining my magic, the land began to heal. Whether the existing population will begin to redevelop magic or it will be relegated only to newborn babes, I do not know. However, the return of magic is inevitable. I don't want my magic lying about where any random person could make use of it."

"Sure. Think of the devastation they could wreak. It'd be awful, should such power fall into the wrong hands…"

"Very good, Adria. I do appreciate your little attempts at humour, you know."

She shuddered. He should have been annoyed by her comment; surely anybody else would have been?

"Secondly, I can't regenerate fully while some of my magic is trapped. It's like my body can sense part of me is out there and falsely contained. Most unpleasant; highly irritating."

"*Something* is irritating all right…"

"I hope I'm not wasting my breath here. Are you listening?"

Adria nodded.

"Thirdly, and perhaps most importantly, who do you think will be thanked when the land is once again free? Everywhere I've been, I've made sure to announce my presence. I do not worry about wresting control back from the Jhardis – indeed, the only threat has now passed – but surely you can see the whole thing will be much easier if I have the acceptance and support of the wider population? I'd like to see Azeileah be prosperous once again."

She'd lost him to a daydream; Adria would have to ask him why, and how, his magic was even trapped there another day. Alis had already explained most of it anyway. For now, he'd told her plenty, and she could only hope the information would prove useful in time.

The streets were deserted, and water ran down the middle in rivulets. The intermittent holes were filled with murky, brown water and, not paying sufficient attention to where they were going, Adria stepped in one. It was deeper than she would have anticipated, and her entire leg came out soaked and mud-splattered.

Letting out a sigh, she attempted to wring out the worst of it. She hoped the residents had enough foresight to catch some of the falling water, even if Kings'land were ostensibly lucky enough to have access to a spring or well. It seemed unlikely, given the way everyone around them had panicked.

The ground would be another colour when they next ventured outside, decades' worth of grime having been washed away in a matter of hours.

What had started as a few drips had quickly become torrential. Rather than a gradual reawakening, the clouds must have been begging for release.

It was only as they approached the inn that Adria realised she once again had magic bubbling inside her. The urgency required for her to find out how to safely use it was clear.

Yet, alone in her room, her anger rose to the surface. The distraction was too severe; she couldn't concentrate. Perhaps she'd explode during the night and take Varick with her – and it would serve him right if she did.

It was tempting to go downstairs and denounce Varick to the patrons there, but they were all highly sprung on account of the rain. It was not a good time to throw more surprises their way. Besides, it seemed sure to backfire and end with them all worshipping Varick for bringing the rain in the first place.

She wasn't wise when it came to these things. Alis would have known exactly what to say.

Trying to sketch some more of her map, she couldn't set her mind to it – and was determined not to allow herself a peek inside the book until she had a sufficient demonstration of her time spent on the map.

Her hand against her forehead, she closed her eyes and attempted to think back to the last place she'd updated, but her mental image was entirely blank.

It was a shame the magic wasn't going to help her out.

CHAPTER 30 – FLICKER

At first, she thought she'd entered Varick's dreams again; it certainly felt more real than it should have. Adria would have desperately tried to wake herself up, had that been the case – but he wasn't here.

Instead, a tall, lithe, raven-haired figure glided towards her, and something within her fluttered irregularly. "Alis? Alis, is that really you?"

Giving no response, she turned around and walked away. Was she leading her somewhere?

She followed Alis to the stables, where Velvet was mounted and waiting – although neither of the familiar stablehands were nearby. The sun bore down on them, and Adria felt a clammy sweat cover her upper body.

Having pointed towards Tenebrae Mountain, Alis from thereon remained frozen.

Adria reached out to touch her; she was corporeal, but Adria could feel no sensation where their hands met, as though the sense of touch did not exist in the dreamworld.

It didn't make sense. Why did Alis want her to travel back up to the mountain; was there some secret there to Varick's demise? There must be; why else would she have returned, only to show her this?

☆ ☆ ☆
 ☆   ☆

Adria had fallen asleep in the chair with her head on the desk.

The waking world brought with it a revelation, albeit not a particularly welcome one. She hadn't been with Alis, or even inside Alis's mind – it had been her own. There was no secret to be determined; her friend had not returned for her. A tear fell down her cheek, and she let it drip, revelling in the sensation of the wet bead against her skin.

The servants' dorm room, adjoining the luxurious chamber where Varick, presumably, slept peacefully, was cold. Grabbing the blanket from atop the mattress – so thin, it was more like a sheet – she doubled it over and wrapped it around her shoulders.

Adria was surprised the colours of Ember House had been so vibrant in her dream when her memory could now barely call them to mind. She tried for a moment to take herself back there, but she was wide awake.

Darkness may have shrouded her, but the candle remained unlit and ready to be used. It had been early evening when she'd fallen asleep, so she hadn't needed it. No longer tired, the thought of reading tempted her. It wasn't like she could save the stub for the following day…

Scrambling around on the desk, her fingers found a match, and she procured herself a flame. Her eyes flickered to the door, wondering whether Varick might see the light below the frame, before concluding it was worth the risk.

The book assumed a certain level of pre-existing knowledge, which wasn't a surprise, given it focused specifically on siphons. Even within the couple of pages of introduction, there was information which was wholly new to Adria.

All magic held balance. Those lucky enough to have

a well inside themselves to draw upon were born with pre-determined strands of power, limiting the ways in which they could shape it. Just like Varick had said, some types were more fully understood than others, but the study of magic had been continuously evolving.

Until… it hadn't been. There was no mention of anything which might have happened to prevent magic; likely Varick was the only person who would be able to shed light on why his cursed spell had caused it to die out.

Adria would have liked to read more about the archaic engineering and social wonders Varick had alluded to, but even the promise of such obscure knowledge wouldn't make it worth having to return to his underground library – so it was likely this book would have to suffice. Unless Alis' gesturing had been her subconscious mind trying to tell her something… but if it was, she had no idea as to what.

For now, there was plenty to keep her mind occupied, just within the one small tome.

The overall principles sat neatly with Adria; the need for equilibrium made sense when you thought about the suffering the land and people had undergone when something – *Varick* – had upset the status quo.

For siphons, their balance came from having no magic well of their own. They could access all types of magic, but only in conjunction with another person.

Siphons, therefore, made good teachers. They could, for example, guide a medic-in-training as to how to use their threads most effectively. Or, for delicate building work, having two people to guide and shape the more intricate parts of a structure made for superior craftsmanship.

As much as what she was reading made sense, it sat at complete odds with how Varick's magic worked, and how her own seemed to compliment it.

In an ideal scenario, she would have been able to follow the theory set out, and therefore learn to guide the magic she'd accumulated to its intended purpose. Each example and explanation she discovered detailed in these pages referred to the siphon being in physical contact with the individual and utilising it *as* it was drawn directly from them.

Varick's power was wild and unshaped. She could feel it thrumming inside her even now. It was an angry, bitter monster that thrived on her need for revenge, but it was also subtle. Rather than overpowering her emotions, it nudged them, gently. As though it were a voice whispering misdeeds in her ear.

There was no sign of the sun rising, but rather than attempt to lie in the small cot and enjoy a more restful sleep, she chose to continue reading. Around a chapter in, annotations had begun to appear in the margins, and she now flipped back to the beginning in order to study these.

It was little surprise to discover she was not the first siphon to have been acquainted with Varick – although it had taken her a few instances of it appearing before she realised 'PV' denoted 'Prince Varick'.

Some of the shorthand was a little difficult to follow, and the pen was slightly faded, making the conditions not ideal for reading. And yet, these scattered notes turned out to be far more enlightening than the intended text.

Not only that, but Adria was relieved she'd trusted her gut and hidden the book from Varick.

There were absolutely no instances in which Varick would have been comfortable with her reading this.

He was keeping the workings of magic from her, and it was impossible to say for certain why, but she suspected he wanted her to continue to be reliant on him.

Even if he someday changed his mind, this book went

far beyond anything he would be likely to tell her. It contained notes personal to his own, specific magic and its usage.

Something of an anomaly, Varick's power stuck to siphons in a way that no other person's magic did. The sole fact of his existence upset the balance not only through his own unique, raw power, but by affecting those around him.

His first siphon had become so powerful, his family had decided to have him executed.

Varick must have still been young when this had happened, if his parents were the ones to have made the decision.

So, had they been as bad-natured as he was? They had certainly seemed respectable in the dreams. The young man must have been threatening treason or similar; she couldn't believe they would have had him murdered simply for his potential.

Surprisingly, 'PV' continued to dwell on his first siphon, even after he'd gained the assistance of others. Some of these siphons had stayed by Varick's side long enough for him to study them; their exposure to his power prevented them from ageing, much in the same way that Varick had stayed indefinitely young.

It was an unpleasant thought, but at least it meant Adria could bide her time.

Except, *then* she read that the later siphons had been slaughtered by Varick himself.

At least at one time, the skill had been rather commonplace, and he'd been able to surround himself with them. *I assume this was through no choice of their own.*

It was curious that Adria had developed magic; perhaps it had something to do with the exclusion of Ember House from the curse. Did that mean there were likely others there, with talents they remained entirely unaware of?

It was a shame she would not be able to enlist their help; to do so would have meant committing time to seek them out and train them. Any activities of that sort would surely not go unnoticed by her intended target.

There was also too large a risk they'd defect, especially if Varick pronounced himself to be the King, which he'd made clear was his intention.

She skimmed through the pages, aware her time was running out. There was still no sign dawn was approaching, but the candle was beginning to run low. Adria needed to find a way to siphon magic from Varick without him being aware of it.

The flame flickered out.

Hopefully, it wouldn't be long until she had another chance to study his notes, to find a way to hold onto the magic and prevent it escaping; ensuring she could accumulate power… and avoid accidentally entering any more of Varick's dreams.

CHAPTER 31 – CULMINATION

Varick was unusually cheerful as he announced there were only two towns left to pass through on their circuit.

Adria was quiet, although that was nothing different to usual. It didn't appear as though Varick had picked up on the shift she was experiencing *internally*. On the previous days, there'd been nothing she was particularly bothered to say. Today, she was assessing how long it might be before Varick attempted to murder her.

He'd said she was helpful for now, but what about when other siphons began to be born; would he take them as children and attempt to mould them? It was horrifying to think she now had a new reason to stay on his good side – she couldn't let anyone else be subjected to his whims.

Cotton also seemed in good spirits, and presumably, the stable had treated her well. This city had evidently seen far easier times than any of the others, even if they were not as comfortable as they had been *before*.

They led their horses towards the city wall, leaving on foot to avoid trampling any of the surrounding shanties, but the opening of the gate revealed a scene of devastation.

The fields around Kings'land lay flooded.

The hard, dry grass had failed to sufficiently absorb the excess water.

Rain had entered the tents through the unpatched holes, and the puddles had seeped across the entrance flaps, leaving many of the makeshift homes destroyed. Some of the tents had even been washed away entirely.

Dejected faces looked upwards as they passed, too morose to make actual conversation as they begged for food or coins. Adria had nothing to give, but there was no reason for them to believe her.

She'd gained entrance to Kings'land, paying a steep price for a residence of only one night. They didn't know the coins had not been her own.

She was clean and atop a horse. They couldn't see her bag held only a sleeping bag, a map, and a secret book.

Not quite charitable enough to give away her sleeping bag when there were still several nights ahead of them, she looked at Varick pleadingly. He had already gone on ahead, and it was no surprise to see him ignoring those he passed. Her thin hope that he may still want to gather support slipped away. *These* were not the sort of people who would help his play for power.

Adria mentally added 'save the world' to the list of things she needed to learn to do with her magic – or, more accurately, Varick's magic – and hurried after him. Had she been allowed to carry any of the food, this would already have been divested. She wished she'd thought ahead and taken some fruit from the inn at breakfast, once again proving foresight wasn't her strong suit.

"Varick," she shouted, slightly out of breath from the exertion. "What happened to make you leave the world like this? Why did you do it?"

"I'm surprised it's taken you this long to ask."

"Does that mean you aren't going to answer?"

"Why shouldn't I? I suspect you've already worked out

most of it. We've got a couple of days of riding ahead of us. Shall I tell it as a story?"

When he didn't continue, Adria realised he was waiting for a response. "Yes, I would appreciate that." He slowed his horse to pull level with her, enabling her to hear him more clearly. This was the first windy day they'd experienced during their travels, and he was forced to speak loudly.

"A long time ago…. no, that's not right. Let me start again. There once was a boy all alone in a palace, surrounded by servants and family. His mother loved him dearly; his father too, and if anything, he was harshest on this youngest son precisely *because* he was his favourite. Regardless of whether it was best for Azeileah, his place in the line of succession meant he would never rule, and this was likely one of the reasons he lacked any inclination to learn.

"Or, I should say, learn what he was *supposed* to be learning. Etiquette, history, mathematics – whatever it was they had his brothers studying in order to prepare them. His father wanted to bring him to formal dinners, but instead, he hid in his personal tunnels, extending their network and playing with his magic.

"Whatever he did to disappoint those around him was forgiven. There were frequent times he was sent to his rooms without dinner – but restricting him to his own personal underground playground was hardly a punishment. Although… perhaps his parents never knew what he did. They were certainly never invited to join him." He let out a laugh, as though some forgotten memory had risen to his mind.

"He gathered his own books and supplies, and cared not for food. He had magic to sustain him. Whatever happened, whatever he did, there were never any lasting consequences; when he had done wrong and was chastised, he thought, 'so what?'"

He stopped, suddenly, but Adria was determined to keep

him talking. "Until the girl? The one your older brother was supposed to marry?"

"That was certainly one of the issues. Being disowned was not enough to provoke him into action."

Why was he talking as if it wasn't himself he was referring to?

"As long as he still had access to his catacombs and servants, he cared not whether he was in line for the throne – as he never had been to begin with.

"No, the biggest issue was the reaction of his siphon. He raged at the boy's treatment and insisted wrongs be put right. Even with the passing of several years, which saw the marriage of one of the boy's older brothers and the formal announcement of the other as heir, his grudge did not seem to lessen." Varick sighed.

"Having fed on the boy's power, he had become the second most powerful magic-user in existence. He wanted change and was prepared to take action. Stepping above his station, he approached the king and queen, demanding they reinstate the boy as prince and third in line.

"The king thoroughly put him in his place. He was the boy's tutor, not his equal, and should never have been allowed to take advantage of his pupil – to use his position to make himself more powerful. Dejected, he abandoned the boy. Whether the boy cared for his siphon or simply lost control for the lack of one, I could not say."

Varick, caring about someone? It wasn't enough to redeem him, but she did understand him a little more. Perhaps that was why he couldn't bring himself to say his tutor's name.

"When the boy set out in search of his siphon, he discovered a much darker truth. You see, the boy's strange magic had stayed with the siphon in a way that wouldn't normally be the case. Usually, magic would be shaped before it left an individual, but this boy had a well of pure, unrestricted power.

"Using their connection, he found the siphon buried in a grave only one pace deep, not far from the Palace. With his hands, he dug him up, not realising until he was almost done that his intention had been to see the cause of death. A deep, ragged cut across his throat told the boy everything he needed to know. Enraged, he returned to his home atop the mountain.

"First, he confronted his mother. Her only contribution was to say she was sure her husband had acted in the boy's best interests. Until then, his anger had been at that flighty suitor, Lord Drew's daughter. Had she merely been interested in Dayne, then none of this would have happened. He hadn't resented his own mother, and so didn't anticipate being quite so provoked by the Queen's answers. Consumed by anger, he lost control of himself." Varick gasped for breath.

"She was gone in moments. The blast which hit her was so powerful the entire wall behind her was charred.

"With his mother dead, the last person he'd really cared about was out of the picture. His rage only built. It was too late for him to turn back; there was no longer any reason to. He sought his brothers, Dayne, then Ghian, and lastly, his father – making sure the King was informed of *exactly* what he had done to the rest of his family before he put the man out of his misery.

"He hid away for a few days to calm his grief, then told the world there had been a plague, and only he had survived. His health was a testament to the strength of his powers. No one in the Palace dared challenge him – challenge his authority *or* challenge his lies – and so, he ruled. And that rule was peaceful, ironically, for a time."

Nope, her sympathy had evaporated. She rubbed her neck, attempting to stifle a cough. The last thing she wanted to do was draw attention to herself when he was like this; it was as though his mind was somewhere else.

She wondered again if there was a reason, other than pure showmanship, that he talked in the third person. If perhaps there were two Varicks in there, and when it became too much, the power quite literally took control of him. Nevertheless, he hadn't been a nice person to begin with, and therein laid the issue.

Adria, not for the first time, wondered why *he*, of all people, had been blessed with the gift of such unusual magic.

CHAPTER 32 – SCARS

"The boy read every book he could find, hoping to bring his siphon back."

She looked up in surprise, not having expected him to continue, despite her question remaining unanswered.

"For too long, he was a worthless ruler, as it was all he cared about. Things only changed when several siphons requested an audience and offered up their assistance. They helped bring him back to reality... but even then, many nights were spent attempting to reanimate spiders and frogs."

"That doesn't explain why everyone else's magic dried up? Wait... *what*?" A wave of dizziness passed over her. "Did he succeed?"

A wry smile spread across Varick's face. "In a way. The smaller arachnids, yes. The frogs he could bring into comas, but they would not wake – and he did not dare attempt it on a human until he knew there was a chance it would work. Lest he lose the opportunity forever."

"Wouldn't it have been too late anyway? There wouldn't have been a body to bring him back into by then. You... you weren't planning on using someone else's body, were you?"

"No. I think that would have caused all sorts of problems *for him*. The boy had kept the siphon's body in stasis. His mother's, too, just in case."

Adria cocked her head at him.

"They're in one of the side rooms of the catacombs – only I would ever be able to find them."

That hadn't been her exact question, but when he was in these chatty moods, she found the most interesting information came from letting him go off in whatever direction he wanted.

"If you recall, I reigned for two hundred or so years."

Adria nodded, noting that despite having corrected her only moments earlier, he was now talking as if he was referring to himself again.

"I always kept several siphons around me. By then, I was all too aware of what would happen if I was reliant on only one. And when they became too powerful…" He drew his hand across his throat and clicked. "It worked well, until one day they decided to walk out on me."

"Did they not appreciate how dangerous that could be?" When he didn't immediately respond, she grimaced, hoping that had been the right thing to say. He was staring into the shrubbery, which contained newly appeared, pale-pink blossoms.

"We had been at peace for a long time; perhaps they had forgotten. Like me, many of them had extended lives, wrought by the effects of my magic. I let them leave, and I was too proud to ask them to come back – I'm sure that doesn't surprise you."

"Not exactly, no." Curse his stubbornness. What might the world have been like without it?

"It isn't really my fault. I didn't ask to be gifted with magic far superior to any other's, although I can't say I'm sorry I was.

"Having grown used to the relief provided by my team of advisors, I was unaccustomed to containing it. I think as a child, I must have been more practiced.

"It wanted to burst out of me. I held it back for two days … but I was so *angry* at them for subjecting me to this. Any lesser man would have succumbed far earlier."

Adria nodded, because she was eager to hear what came next. She suspected most people would have been better able to control it, but she had no real way of knowing.

"That's an Adria flower."

"What?"

"Over there, those buds will bloom into an Adria flower."

She frowned. "Oh. Thank you for letting me know, I guess."

"Having let my guard slip, under the luxury of constant alleviation, I could no longer control my full well of power, and the anger made it feel stronger. Far, far stronger. I cast it outwards, draining myself of all but the tiniest morsel."

"And it attached itself to the land, filling the portholes." It was interesting hearing Varick's version of the history Alis had previously regaled.

"Yes, it was attracted to the portholes, which were set up with charges to contain magic, but that is not where I sent it, only where it ended up. First, it tore across the entire island; perhaps beyond, even. But no, it cannot have passed the sea, or I would feel it lingering there…" He let out a deep sigh. "Not only did I kill the majority of the population – a fact that is only now clear to me, having seen what remains – but I destroyed most of the country. The buildings were ripped apart, and the livestock also died."

Hearing him speak of death so casually was hurtful, and Adria, once again, had to temper her own anger. Unfortunately, it was *Varick's* magic inside her, and it bubbled to get out of her, too. She hated to feel anything kindred with this man, but the idea of his desperation to release it had become all too real. But to such devastating effect? Surely, *she* wouldn't be driven to such a measure.

"Having already done severe damage through the initial blow, it lingered, with ongoing effects. It continually drained the land of life until its vitality had been entirely sucked away. Until *all* magic had been drained from the world. I'm not sure how long it took… but I'd guess a matter of months.

"Magic is inextricably linked to the land; it was the land that gave birth to it, and my theory is the devastation of the land meant it could no longer be provided. The land, desperate for life, therefore sucked away anything it could. Why are you frowning, Adria? Why *specifically*, I should say."

"I was just wondering how you ended up locked in that palace. Especially if all the magic had gone." She shifted in her seat. It was long past the time they would usually have stopped for a rest and her muscles ached, but it would have been an awful place to break off.

"Weren't you listening? It took time for my spell to draw away the island's magic. That palace was… *is* my home, and I cast my spell from atop Tenebrae Mountain. The radius around me remained protected from the worst of the incursion."

"You weren't trying to hide yourself from sight?" That had been Alis's theory.

"I don't think so, but I can't say I fully recall everything in my head at that moment. I was being consumed by the power and not in my right mind. I thought I might even ascend to the heavens. I'd thrown out so much magic – far more than I could have expected – that the protected area spanned the mountain and all around its foot."

"The glamour was just a byproduct of where you were standing when you cast the spell." Adria repeated. *When magic had later resurfaced, it had only been for those living within the glamour.*

Varick nodded. "Seeing I was weak, all my invited

guests fled, and between them – the strongest magicians had preferred to remain by my side, waiting for their chance to gain favour or seize power – they sealed the doors. I suppose they couldn't believe their luck. Until then, I'd ruled autocratically, and now they finally had the chance to take me out of the equation. It seems as though the joke was on them, however, as their power faded away the second they left the glamour."

"How do you know that?" He always seemed to know more than he ought, but his provision of this particular piece of history was severely at odds with the knowledge of someone who had been shut away.

"It's the only logical explanation. How else would the non-magical line of my brother's widow's little sister's great-grandkids have been able to step up?"

Adria frowned at him, trying to work out whether this deduction was enough to justify his assertion.

"Okay, so I asked someone too. People do still remember, you know."

"But…"

"No, Adria, I don't mean they were there, I mean it has been passed down by word of mouth. Now would you like me to continue, or not?"

She nodded, wide-eyed.

"I wandered the halls for a time. My magic wasn't regenerating – a clever trick from the way they had performed the seal. Using my siphons for enhancement, they made it repel, like a magnet. Something I had invented and taught them myself. Any magic which did find its way home to me, was driven back out towards the glamour, weaving further layers across it. I believe that is why it has endured without faltering for almost a century.

"I could have left via the catacombs, but I felt remorse,

you see. With my magic all but stripped away, I had a conscience; I had sanity. Yes, Adria?"

It was obvious he was irritated by her interruption, but something was bothering her. "Couldn't your magic seep through from other places, not just the front door? Like in from the catacombs?"

"Their seal covered everything above ground. The catacombs, as you know, I'd sealed myself. Weren't you paying attention?" Yes… but he hadn't said that part. "There was no need for them to actively repel magic, but I'd made them *watertight* to prevent any magic being worked against me from getting through. Even if I'd left the top hatch open, I would have had to go through the mountain and open the other. Which I could have done but what I'm trying to tell you is I didn't!"

Adria rubbed her forehead, trying to ignore his mood swing.

"I did something *noble*. I used the very last drops of my magic to seal myself in that room in a perpetual stasis – which, if you were listening before, I had practiced doing, so knew it was safe to do to myself. Albeit at the time, I didn't really care whether I was ever resuscitated or not; I believe I even thought it best left to chance."

Adria's head began to throb. It was a lot of information to digest, and she was becoming overwhelmed. With her brain also being taxed, she could no longer push through the physical discomfort. "Might we stop and rest soon? I could use something to eat."

"I tell you something of such a scale, something no one else is privy to, and *that's* what you have to say?"

"What would you *like* me to say Varick? I get the feeling you want me to absolve you of your sins, or at least congratulate you for shutting yourself away, but I have no intention of doing either. And I'm getting a headache."

"If you learnt how to use my magic, you could relieve your own headache, you know. It's difficult, but I could show you."

"Right. Doesn't solve my immediate issue, though, does it? Just finish whatever it is you want to say." She sighed. "It sounds like you need to keep working through it. So why now, Varick?"

"Why am I not still shut away, you mean?" He raised his eyebrows. "Even the tiniest bit of my magic was incredibly strong, yet when I sealed that room, for the first time, I left myself without a drop – and there was no one able to reverse the effect. Until you. The mere presence of a siphon caused a distortion of the magic and began to weaken the stasis spell. When you siphoned the constraints from the room – that was my magic you were siphoning, because we'd made physical contact – you released me; but it wasn't my magic on the main doors."

That part, at least, she'd already figured out. "Then we had to go through the catacombs... I remember. I don't think the conversation made much sense to me at the time."

"Had I been at my full strength, I could have easily broken through that seal. In fact, when we return, I think I'll let you do it; it'll be good practice."

Even though she'd tired of this conversation – of his irritating voice – she couldn't help but ask one more question as she slumped down into a seat on the spiky grass. "Varick, why are you seeking your power again? You had enough sense to shut it away, once upon a time."

"I wanted some time to think, and I had it. Instead of dwelling on my guilt, after a while, other more pertinent obligations came to the forefront. The world needed me. I was given that power for a reason; I ought to be ruling the continent not wallowing in some dark hole. And, I suppose, I was bored."

"With your magic back, do you no longer feel–"

"Feel guilty? Yes – I do know what you're thinking, Adria." He sighed. "I understand the idea of a conscience, but simply don't feel concerned by it anymore. What good would come of worrying about such a thing?"

She opened her mouth as though to speak, but no sound came out.

"Besides, I don't need to care about whether something is morally acceptable or not. I've got you around to make those kinds of judgements for me."

CHAPTER 33 – OBSERVATION

The girl was not only expendable, but she was becoming a risk – and he couldn't deny this was partially of his own doing.

Had he not needed to cleanse himself of the story... but no. Surely, she would have guessed at most of it already. She was not as sharp-witted as others he had been used to, so it was difficult to say.

As soon as other siphons materialised, she would be replaced with those more suitable for the role. He did not expect it would take long, given how quickly nature had recovered.

She might be pliable but something about her irked him incessantly, and she had no other positive qualities of which to speak – her manners were lacking, along with her intellect and humour, and she was too plain to provide any diversion of another kind.

They did not stop for a rest until it was time to make camp, and by then, Adria was far too drained to pull out her map. All she cared about was sleep.

"Not happening. You can move your bedroll over there. You're not camping beside me. This habit you have picked up of intruding on my dreams is abhorrent."

"That's away from the fire!"

"Build your own, then."

Cold and uncomfortable, Adria lay awake despite her exhaustion. Although the heat didn't seem to be reaching her in the area she'd been relegated to, Varick's snores could be heard loudly.

Her head still throbbed.

With him so heavily asleep… she wondered whether she might be able to siphon his magic without his knowledge. Once the thought had occurred to her, it played on her mind, until Adria knew she had no chance of falling asleep.

Needing some light, she carried the book over to the fire. Being careful to keep the flames from touching the cover, she skimmed through the pages as efficiently as she could, hoping to find something which might help.

There was a chapter which explained how the siphon could control the pull of magic. Previously, the magic had been pushed into her.

Last time when they'd touched, she'd been clumsy, and Varick had felt it instantly; he had so much magic it had tried to jump across to her without conscious thought from either of them.

Luckily, it was possible to do it without detection. The book described the sensation of siphoning as distracting and therefore provided a method of avoiding it. Everything boiled down to how lightly she touched him, and how slowly she could take it from him.

It was going to be a risk even to attempt it.

Adria hovered over him for a few minutes, attempting to determine how lightly he was sleeping. At least twice, she reached out her hand but did not quite make contact. It was made more difficult by the requirement to touch his skin – only his face and one hand were currently accessible to her.

She went for his wrist.

Tugging at the feeling of wrongness she had come to identify with his magic, it slid towards her far more easily than she had anticipated. It was like a river flowing downhill. Scrunching up her eyes, she did her best to diminish its flow.

Afraid to take too much – she didn't yet have a gauge as to how deep his power went and didn't want to alert him to what she'd done – Adria closed the channel after only a handful of seconds.

Although, on reflection, she wasn't fully sure exactly how long she had been there. Somehow, her legs had begun to ache from crouching.

Varick had made it clear he could sense when his magic was displaced, but she'd already had some of his magic within her. It was a conscious gamble she had taken – that he wouldn't be able to tell the amount she held was now more than it had been.

As well as the possibility he'd sense an increase in the magic she held, Adria was concerned she might have taken a noticeable amount and he'd feel depleted.

It was a long wait until morning. She tried to concentrate on the book, wondering whether she could learn how to control the magic pulsating uncomfortably inside her, but her apprehension made it a struggle to take anything in.

The information she needed was there. Varick's footnotes to chapter seven set out a method for holding the magic, which he had described as building a container inside your body, on which you could then close the lid.

For individuals with their own magic, it came naturally, as they were born with the mechanism for storing it. The book's original text went no further than stating siphons did not have the means to keep hold of anything for later use. Varick had therefore added comments regarding how his own magic worked differently.

Adria could not help but wonder why Varick had encouraged their experimentation when it would only make them more powerful. Unable to ask him, she had to assume it was a mix of curiosity and prestige – having powerful advisors would have augmented his own pride.

Unfortunately, Varick was incredibly intelligent. She was not going to be able to outwit him easily. Her best – and only? – chance was going to be to encourage his overconfidence and hope he became less careful as a result. His over-esteemed opinion of himself was certainly one of his biggest vices.

Sadly, she didn't manage to relax until the morning, when, at last, she could determine that Varick hadn't noticed anything amiss. Although she'd been worried, his lack of detection wasn't a surprise. In her gut, she'd been *certain* she had only taken a small portion. But afterwards, when she'd realised how noticeable her own increase had been – when she'd felt the stolen power singing loudly inside her – she'd begun to doubt herself.

A small thing, but useful, nonetheless… in her hours spent awake, she had observed Varick's sleep stages. He went through periods where he laid still, and others where he shifted and mumbled. On future nights, it would be easier for Adria to choose her timing. There was no doubt in her mind – if she could, she would continue to take from him over and over again.

☆ ☆ ☆

"Something is wrong with you today."

Having been awake all night, Adria was tired and lacked focus. She couldn't really be bothered trying to pretend otherwise. "I guess."

Varick frowned. "You look uncomfortable and a bit peaky."

"Okay." She was going to leave it at that but then wondered if she could turn the situation to her advantage. "I think your magic is sitting funnily inside me. I didn't mean to use it before, when I entered your dreams – or memories? – so I don't know how I did it. Could you help me learn to control it? Maybe I could release it gradually."

"I guess any hope for peace and quiet while we were travelling was wishful thinking." Varick groaned, and Adria tried not to let him see she was just as fed up with him. Probably more so, although she had no doubt they *both* wanted rid of the other. "I'll think about it. For now, you'll have to deal with it."

Adria was disappointed but took advantage of the quiet to see if she could manage the creation of her container without him. She didn't seem to have a natural inclination towards the magic. It resisted her every attempt to touch it.

"Where are you going, girl?" Having been deep in thought, she looked up at the sound of his voice. Cotton had wandered away from the path and was heading for a patch of healthy-looking grass and white flowers. "Can't you control your horse?"

Those five words alone were enough to weaken Adria's resolve and reduce her to tears. Alis's death once again consumed her mind. Lack of sleep undoubtedly contributed to her reaction, but the underlying feelings had been there all along.

Dismounting from the steed, which she still did not think of as her own, she slumped down in the flowers – wishing Varick wasn't witnessing her meltdown but unable to do anything to stop herself.

"Leave me alone, Varick. Just give me half an hour. By

myself. I need some space to think. I can't... Please, just go."

"Eurgh. This drama is the last thing I want to deal with. I'll go slowly. Make sure you've caught up with me before the hour is done." Adria counted the seconds as he turned his horse and rode away from her.

The moment he was out of sight, Adria laid down and relaxed into her anguish. She knew she was feeling sorry for herself, but she wanted to – *needed* to.

Rolling onto her stomach, she burrowed her face in the soil, hiding herself from the world. She never wanting to move from this spot again.

Adria came to.

Disorientated, she had to remind herself where she was.

Having sobbed so hard, she must have worn herself so far down she'd fallen asleep. Whether that had been for a handful of seconds, minutes or even as much as an hour, she had no idea. The sun, at least, still bore down overhead – the rays every day a little less dull than they had been before.

Pulling herself up, she looked around for Cotton. He had found some nearby cornflowers and was happily munching on them, ignoring her entirely. Adria felt irked; how *dare* Alis's horse be happy without her. As her anger began to rise, she identified the stench of Varick's magic all over the feeling and quickly did her best to quash it.

Hoping Varick had not ventured too far, she ran over and mounted, before letting out a loud gasp. From her raised position, it was evident that the spot of earth she'd occupied was badly scorched. It was a shame to have destroyed the newly bloomed flowers, but it was also a worrying indictment as to her lack of control.

She now had more than one reason to stay by Varick's side.

Panicking, Adria raced to find him, leaving herself winded, despite Cotton having done most of the work.

She found him lingering by a stream. It was odd to see him lying on the grass, absorbing the sun; strange to think of him doing anything other than working single-mindedly towards his self-absorbed goal.

It was easier to focus on her intention of seeking revenge now she was angry at having rushed.

"You took your time."

"I destroyed the earth…"

"Thought you weren't too keen on that sort of thing."

"Did you have to interrupt me? Varick, I am trying to tell you I can't control your magic. It once again found a way to escape. I really think you should help me."

"Haven't we already wasted enough of today?"

She folded her arms and glared at him.

"Right, hold my hand then." Seeing her hesitation, he added, "Yes, you have to."

Climbing back down from her horse, she edged towards him before perching on the bank next to where he lay, while Cotton joined Varick's mount in taking a drink. The water made a pleasant swishing sound, and she focused on it to help her relax.

Overcoming her fear, she reached out and took his hand – hoping that initiating the contact would help her feel more in control.

At first, Varick's incursion felt like exactly that – intrusive and unwelcome. Only when she let go of her tension could she understand what he was trying to tell her. He was showing her how to shape his magic by manipulating the magic swilling around *inside* her.

His touch was incredibly delicate – this was no child poking around with a stick. He knew exactly what he was doing. She did her best to focus on the benefit of learning to use the magic and to avoid any thoughts of what she was subjecting herself to. As sweat broke out on her brow, she reminded herself that she had let him in – had begged him, even.

It was much easier to understand what the book had meant now she had the demonstration to go with it.

"Thank you, I understand now. Perhaps you could show me how to release it more gradually, too?"

"Yes, I'm getting to that."

Adria waited, but she couldn't feel Varick doing anything.

"It's funny; my magic feels different. It's like you've taken the heat and tempered it… and now it's sad instead of angry. It's unpleasant."

She waited a little longer, trying to be patient but desperate for it to be over.

"I can't expel the magic now it's inside you; it's rejecting me." Moments later, he threw her hand away in apparent disgust.

"Oh!" she exclaimed, surprised by the motion.

"I can't use magic while we're making contact." Had he not been worried, he surely would never have revealed that out loud.

"That makes no sense – isn't the whole point of a siphon that they assist the original magic wielder?"

Varick frowned at her, sitting up so his face was now level with hers. "Where did you get that idea from? I don't remember us discussing it."

"A… Alis mentioned it." Adria's heart raced despite her

relief at having quickly thought up the lie. Presumably, it was because the magic had adapted to her... as a result of having been stored instead of immediately used. *She* could access the magic inside *Varick* while they made contact, but *he* could no longer use his magic once it had left his body. The answer seemed obvious now, and she wished she hadn't spoken so rashly.

Except... he hadn't been able to use his *own* magic either. Could it be that the intensity of her thoughts, and the way in which she'd clung to him, had prevented it? Siphons and wielders had been intended to work together, and yet her actions had held him in a vice.

"What else did she tell you?" Varick's temperament continued to worsen. It had been a while since he'd been this bad.

"I'm not sure." She racked her brain, trying to think of something dull and insignificant. "That siphons used to be reasonably common? Do you think we could work out how I can get your magic out of me now?"

"Fine. This time I'll just attempt to guide you, but you'll have to do the actual movement of the magic."

Adria could feel Varick squirming, still making every attempt to push the power out. She tried, too, with no more success than he'd managed. Something was creating a block – as though she'd built her well of power with reinforced walls.

She attempted to lift the lid from her container, wondering if that might make a difference. It did. The magic, which she'd only recently managed to cow into submission such that it had become content to remain, was now rushing out.

Loosening her mental grip, she allowed Varick sufficient access to release a little, too. Once he'd established he *could*, she let go of his hand and quickly clamped down the lid lest any more escape.

Already, a plan was formulating in her mind. Could she create *two* containers? One she allowed Varick to see, and another to be kept hidden away, so that he'd never be aware it existed. Almost as soon as the idea occurred to her, she felt sure she could.

Equally, the idea she could stop Varick from using magic merely by making physical contact with him was appealing. Especially given she'd managed to convince him he'd imagined it.

"Hmm. That was strange. I thought I couldn't use the magic for a second. Maybe I was surprised; you seem to have more inside you than I was expecting." His relief was evident, and she tried not to look smug. "Anyway, was that lesson sufficient to stop you imploding?"

"Imploding? Is that a joke?" But he'd already remounted and ridden off. Adria, once again, hurried to follow.

CHAPTER 34 – QUANDARY

There was something odd about her. It was a small consolation, at least, that she did not seem to be aware of it.

The sooner he could be rid of her, the better.

Had his old advisors irked him so? They had mostly fed his whims... until they had deserted him. He ought to be thankful she was an open book, and not so educated in the ways of magic and nobility as they had been.

If he had been privileged to other company, it might not have been so bad.

Just one more town, and then he could return to a more comfortable lifestyle. He had deprived himself for long enough.

"So, what can I actually do with this magic?"

Varick didn't respond.

"I mean, if I release it, does it just disappear off into the ether? Can I do something productive with it like shape it into a tree or something?"

"Whyever would you want another tree?"

She shook her head. "I thought you were all for scientific advancement?"

"And a tree would factor into that, how?"

"Well, what would you recommend, then? You're the intelligent one here. Do I learn to shape it into a specific type of magic?"

"I don't see why you'd need to."

She took a deep breath. "Are we nearly at the next town?"

"The last town, and yes, that's it over there. You see those buildings ahead; they aren't a mirage." He scoffed as though he thought she was ridiculous. He probably did.

"So, I could use it to see further…"

He frowned at her, as though he hadn't realised there was nothing visible on the horizon. Only fuzz off in the distance. "I think you might need spectacles for that. It's quite far off yet, but you should still be able to see it. I'm sure I would be aware by now if I had enhanced eyesight."

Frustrated, Adria resigned herself to having to experiment with the magic on her own. Perhaps there was something in the book which might be of use, but learning from information written on pieces of paper wasn't her strong suit – if indeed, it was possible for *anyone* to learn to manipulate magic by such a means.

She wasn't sure where Varick thought she was going to get the money from to buy spectacles, and it annoyed her that he'd laughed at her.

Giving up on her failing attempts to use the magic, Adria refocused her energy on imagining all the ways she might exact revenge on him. Most were far-fetched and for her own entertainment, but several of them bordered on plausible… if anything, it made her realise she ought to start giving the matter some serious thought.

It wasn't just about him having killed Alis… at least, not solely about that. With her companion gone, Adria felt compelled to unofficially take on the mantel of guardian. Alis's brother was the heir, and she'd had no other siblings. There was no one else to assume her duties, and Adria wanted to see the unfinished business complete; personal satisfaction was simply an added incentive.

There were several problems to overcome. One was the lack of imprisonment options. She was fairly certain no cell would be able to hold him – a non-magical one wouldn't stand a chance, and there were no magicians she could ask to seal him in. Even back then, it had only been possible because he'd expended the entirety of his power. He was unlikely to do that again, given his past experience.

Which led her to the conclusion she was going to have to kill him. Or do her best to try.

Each time it had occurred to her, she'd done her best to put it out of her mind, but whenever she thought about it – *really* thought about it – Adria found herself in a moral quandary. It was wrong to kill someone. Any situation in which she did would make her as bad as him.

The problem was that *someone* had to take responsibility, and who better than her, having caused the issue in the first place.

At least, the second time around. It wasn't her fault he'd been born. She could try and make the argument it was inevitable he'd have escaped at some point. But it had been on *her* watch, and that was a difficult matter to avoid.

Why *had* nature blessed such a type of person with so much raw magic? Was it truly just an accident as Alis had implied? Or had someone, somewhere, hoped that as a member of the ruling family, he would use it – alongside his high intelligence – to benefit Azeileah?

No, she found it difficult to believe there had been any conscious decision involved; the idea of happenstance appealed to her far more.

The other thing playing on her mind related to his

experiments. If he could help her bring Alis back, did she really still want rid of him? It would have been better to only punish him. If he were to be imprisoned, she might still have a chance at extracting the relevant information.

As much as she hoped to become strong enough to magically confine him, it would still be his *own* magic she'd be using in the attempt. Which brought her back to the sorry realisation it would only work if he'd fully drained himself first.

She wished she was clever enough to scheme. She enjoyed reading, and had learnt a lot from books, but lacked the talent for coming up with new ideas or taking the initiative.

It had never bothered her before.

Around an hour later, the town finally came into view. Adria stopped dwelling on her problems and instead began to look forward to sleeping in an actual bed.

She was caught out entirely when Varick asked her to remain with the horses.

"It's mid-afternoon; aren't we going to stay here overnight? Can we not leave the horses at an inn?"

"It depends how long my business takes me. If I'm done quickly enough, we'll set off immediately for Ember House. We could manage another four hours travelling."

"Surely not." Adria was exhausted, and having already had the expectation of stopping, the thought of travelling any further was too much for her. "A few hours won't make much difference."

"Don't you want to get home?"

It was *his* home, not hers; not anymore. Another thought struck her. "Varick, how many days is it from here to Ember House?"

"It's three, but if we do a few hours today, we could likely make it by Tuesday." She could hear the excitement in his voice, the antithesis to her own panic.

Only two more days. That didn't give her enough time. If he was allowed to reach the Jhardis, he was likely to go directly for Lord Dann. Even one more night could make a big difference in how ready she was. "We're close, but I'm still not convinced we should rush. It'd be far more pleasant to arrive back there in the daytime, and well rested?"

"Like I said, I'll make that decision once I'm done here."

She folded her arms exaggeratedly, to make sure he knew she wasn't happy, but he was a difficult man to reason with. Adria resigned herself to trying again when he returned.

Chances were, she was going to have to make her move sometime in the next forty-eight hours.

While she waited, she considered putting a stone in his horse's hoof. If Varick was as bad as she thought him, he wouldn't take the time to see her cared for. He'd simply buy a new horse. Adria couldn't bring herself to attempt it.

Having fed each of her companions an apple, she considered taking a nap, but doing so this close to a town, alone with two horses, didn't seem safe.

Yet, once the thought of sleep had occurred to her, she had to fight to keep herself awake. The scent of the daisies and the cushioning of the long grass reminded her of many afternoons spent lazing in the sun on the lawn of Ember House.

She groaned as a loud bang disturbed her closing eyelids. When a second bang came, she realised something was going on within the town. *What's he done now?* She felt a sense of guilt at having brought him here, despite being conscious of the fact his movements had been almost entirely outside of her control.

Leaving Cotton tied up with Varick's unnamed horse – taking care they were away from the patch of daisies, which could be poisonous to them – she ran towards the commotion.

She reached the main street too late. A fight had led to whole portions of the ground being upheaved, and it was not hard to leap to a conclusion about who had instigated it. The sides of the buildings were charred, and one now leant to the side where a supporting wall had caved in.

A leg stuck out from beneath the rubble near the spot on which Varick loitered. Could there have been others he'd harmed, or had this man been his sole target?

The more intently she looked, the more she truly saw what he had wrought. The entire street had been destroyed, and there were at least four others dead by Varick's hand. In times past she would have been overcome by sadness but today it was anger which rose to the surface – perhaps even a little at herself; she knew what this man was and should have done more to prevent his presence around other people.

"How could you, Varick? How many... what were you even thinking? Why would you do this?" Seeing a lack of comprehension on his face, which instead displayed a lazy smile, she grabbed his hand and tore the magic away from him.

He threw her away, but she had already sufficiently relieved his madness.

He sighed angrily. "It was their own stupid fault."

"You sound like a petulant child."

"We need to leave." He began running, but not towards the horses. She hesitated for a second, then followed him, newly reluctant to let him out of her sight.

It only became clear where he had been heading when they reached a porthole. Adria looked around nervously as he stopped to drain it, wondering whether the bigger risk was being caught and accused of murder – in which case, he would surely kill more people – or the extra magic tipping Varick back over the edge.

There were plenty of people around, but there was no doubt they were giving them a wide berth. Presumably, there had been witnesses to Varick's tantrum.

She wondered what they thought of her, to be colluding with him, and felt ashamed – regardless of what her intentions might be.

There was no fight to stay at an inn. Instead, there was an attempt to extract details of the situation from him.

Time was ticking away from her.

"After visiting the first of the two portholes, I passed the mayor's office, so I went in and paid him a visit. To begin with, he humoured me, while telling me there was someone he wanted me to meet."

She nodded, knowing there would be no use hurrying him. He always seemed to be reliving his memories as he was relaying them; more in a daydream than fully awake.

"'See,' he said to me, 'We have our own magician in this town. The land is recovering, that much I agree with, but why should we believe *you* have anything to do with it? Winson here can work with the plants and help them bloom. Sounds t'me like magic has come back and now you're here trying to take credit for it. Wouldn't be surprised if you're asking us for payment next.'"

It was absolutely the wrong thing to have said to him, Adria could see that. She hated her lack of surprise that five men were now dead as a result.

"'Have you not heard of me?' I demanded, and they shook their heads, and then they *laughed*. Well, it took me all of a second to take out their mayor, so who's laughing now? They began to run instead of apologising, so I got rid of the others too. Shame to have found my first instance of magic having come back and then been forced to get rid of it."

He cared more about that than the deaths themselves, and that was exactly what she'd come to expect from him. "You don't sound terribly sorry about it."

"Don't pretend you are either – all *you* cared about was where you spent the night."

"That's not true." Or was it? She certainly hadn't given much thought to those men's deaths. Although… it wasn't like she'd known them. So, wasn't it normal that her predominant reaction was anger at Varick?

Had morals always been quite this difficult? As a concept, Adria had always thought they seemed rather straightforward. There were some blurred lines between wrong and right, but usually only when decisions had to be made on the spur of the moment.

Now she was struggling with things which ought to have been simple.

She wished he hadn't killed those people, but he was right: she was lamenting her own comfort. Was Varick's magic making her a bad person, or had she always been this way? She wanted to pretend she felt bad, but the lie wasn't enough to make her feel better.

"It's okay, you know. There's no reason you should be mourning."

"They didn't deserve to die." That much, at least, she could say confidently… without feeling like a fraud.

CHAPTER 35 – EMBERS

He had to get away, lest he bring the entire city to the ground. The relief of having some of the magic burnt away had helped... but it was temporary; always temporary.

It had seemed so logical at the time, but now he'd lost the support of the third-largest town in Azeileah.

He would bring them around through fear alone if nothing else, but it would take time.

He ought to go back... but he would not show regret, and wanted to distance himself from the memory.

And he was still so angry.

The killing itself had come all too easily; it was barely with conscious thought. As though the magic had a mind of its own.

Had he thought as such before? Was he merely the vessel...?

It seemed a familiar notion.

He had been a man of science. An inventor and a creator. Above all others.

Perhaps his objective superiority was part of the problem...

As though things were conspiring against her, she was forced to endure several hours more travelling before they stopped for the night. Varick was insistent they put sufficient distance between themselves and Southfern, and it was a difficult assertion to argue with.

Albeit, as to his own motives she was unsure, as he couldn't have been worried about being apprehended.

Concerns swelled within Adria. She *still* did not understand him. She'd thought... she'd thought she might have been *good* with people before all of this. Now she was confused and wondering whether she might have been mistaken.

If she'd had friends, wouldn't she have kept them, even after she'd been forced into catering for Varick?

Perhaps if she had, they wouldn't be in this situation now. It was a bitter thought.

No, she *had* to avoid going down the mindset of allocating blame. "It's getting dark now; we cannot go any further."

"We shall."

Cotton snickered as though he supported Adria in her desire for a rest. "I'm stopping, Varick. I'm so tired... the horses need to rest. Pushing ourselves like this is fruitless." She intended to give him a few minutes to reply, then give up and dismount, but realised she could not risk leaving him.

She'd hoped he'd see sense, but he ignored her and kept going.

Their return to Ember House drew closer... Adria wished it held appeal, but it didn't. She had nothing and nowhere she wanted to be. *Except asleep*. There was no point to anything, until she saw through her need for revenge.

It wouldn't be long now. Would it feel familiar or strange to be back in the same environs? She'd changed so much since she was last there.

Would she see any reminders of Alis when she came face to face with Lord Dann?

Another weight upon her shoulders. How would it be

best to break the news of her death? Adria had never met the Sovereign or his wife, but presumably, she would soon be forced to… and what would they think of her when she did?

Arriving beside Varick, their first impression of her would be as Varick's companion. How could she make them understand that she meant well? Might they simply have her struck down before she even made it to the entrance parlour…? "Varick, I'm feeling rather unwell; we must stop now, I beg of you."

"A little longer."

She persisted, though her body ached, and her mind was overwhelmed.

She'd begun to give up any expectation of relief when, at last, he announced, "We're here."

"It looks familiar." She frowned, though it was too dark for him to see. "I can't place it, though."

"We are in Lilliard Downs. It is much changed since our visit here several weeks ago. I won't tire myself by pointing out how, as I'm sure you can see." The path was still muddy and worn, but the vegetation had begun to grow on either side of it. The trees held newly forming leaves. "Now you can have the bed you've been waiting for, and I can finally receive the praise I'm deserving of."

"But you caused the issue in the first place!"

"I think you mean, thank you, Varick. Or should I let you sleep out here with the horses? Well? I'm waiting…"

"Thank you, Varick. I would like to please sleep in the inn. However, what I said remains true. Is it not my role to keep you in check?"

He didn't answer, instead turning his attention to demanding the stablehand immediately wake the innkeeper. Apparently, he'd been tempering himself around her, but that 'royal' tone was still there for him to call upon – and it was clear he had no qualms about doing so.

Having procured their rooms, Varick informed her they would be staying for two nights. He intended to visit the surrounding villages, ensuring his good work was made known. She was welcome to either join him or remain there and rest.

Had Varick realised the favour he had just done her? Adria certainly hoped he'd handed her the advantage she so desperately needed – an entire day to recover her strength and study his book. Which, of course, he still did not know she had.

Despite the exhaustion she'd felt on going to sleep, Adria woke early enough for breakfast. There was no choice of food, only oatmeal, but at least it would keep her going for the day. Knowing Varick was unlikely to leave her any coins for lunch, she even decided to help herself to a second bowl.

"How were the celebrations?"

Adria frowned, then remembered Varick had told the innkeeper they had been heading to a relative's wedding. "Yes, it was very good, thank you. They were able to hold a reception on the grass, now it has once again turned green." Or had he claimed it was their *own* wedding they'd been going to? Adria couldn't remember… but she'd need to be careful what she said.

"Once again? Was it green before?"

"Oh… well, at Ember House, from whence I came, it has always been so." She was surprised to find she didn't hold a grudge against the small town where their reception had previously been rather unwelcome.

"From whence you came, eh. Were you hoarding all the water up there? Sounds like, in your absence, they've decided to let the rest of us have a bit."

Oh. If she couldn't even convince the proprietor she

meant well, how could she ever hope to succeed elsewhere? Her worries about how the Jhardi family would receive her began anew.

She hadn't even realised she'd started repeating Varick's archaic language.

"Actually, the man I am travelling with has been..." She wondered how Varick had been describing his so-called miracles. "Absorbing the decay. It is nothing to do with Ember House, other than I suppose they could afford gardeners. I am simply an orphan who happened to have been employed there."

Out of nowhere, her origins began to bother her. She hadn't minded before, but she'd been distracted, too happy in Alis's company to bother dwelling on it.

A sadness fell over her.

The world had discarded her before she was old enough to speak.

Until the Jhardis had taken her in. Where would she have been without them? She rose abruptly from her stool. "Please excuse me. I must retire to my room."

☆ ☆ ☆

Adria read the main text of the book because it was interesting, but read the notes in the margins out of necessity. Everything about Varick's magic was unpredictable. Sometimes it obeyed the usual rules; more often, it was domineering and overrode them. Its raw nature meant it bypassed some of the usual natural restrictions and limits which other magicians were subjected to. Worse, it reacted differently depending on the specific circumstances.

Although she still hoped she could use some of its quirks to her advantage.

The writing was just like Varick himself – erratic, messy, and often went off on a tangent. In many places, it was difficult to read.

One thing she couldn't deny was that he'd been thorough with his research. His scientific mind and natural curiosity had pushed him to gain a greater understanding of the relationship between siphons and his unusual magic.

When her eyes began to blur over, she closed the book and checked on her containers. She had been forcing increasing amounts of magic into her hidden storage and after so much practice, she no longer struggled with it resisting her.

The volume she held had increased significantly, but she seemed to be coping, feeling mostly unaffected by it. Taking a deep breath, she stepped away from the desk she'd just spent several hours huddled over.

"I would know, wouldn't I?" she said aloud. "If it was proving too much for me or if I was beginning to act as Varick does, I would be able to tell…" The truth was she felt no different for the magic. Angrier, perhaps, but she had not perceived any cognitive change.

Other than talking to herself.

Adria decided it was time to go for a walk. She needed an open space where she could think… and maybe see if she could put some of the book's words into action.

Her path took her past the small stables, where Cotton was alone. He lifted his head on seeing her, and she patted it, but he would have to wait until tomorrow for some exercise.

Once she reached the town's border, she kept going a little longer until she was out of immediate sight.

Teasing open the lid she'd placed over the magic, she tried to concentrate on letting a small amount trickle out. Internally, her wish to practice was at war with her fears of using too much in one go. She'd spent months hoping to have some magic to store.

Was it concern about having enough left over to fight Varick, or was it the power itself she was beginning to covet?

It isn't really making me powerful, not if I have no idea how to wield it.

No. Adria was *sure* she could change her mentality. She'd merely been so focused on hoarding it that actually using it felt like a contradiction.

Even after she felt ready, her attempts produced no actual results. Her heart still wasn't in it. There was more to convince herself of than simply letting go. Now, she needed to reconcile herself with the magic's intent being hostile. It would be easier to use if her intentions aligned with its own.

It wanted to cause harm. She didn't.

There was nothing she'd read in books which told her this, but its desire to be released in a chaotic way told her enough.

Any attempt to use it gently was too much of a struggle. Perhaps once she'd managed to attain a feel for it, she'd be able to coax it into submitting to her.

Focusing on her hatred of Varick, she worked herself into a more appropriate mindset. Revenge was a formidable motivator.

She was under no illusions she could best him in strength. Her only chance was to catch him by surprise. Not only that, but she would need a strategy – to accost him in such a way he wouldn't see it coming. It made her angry that she should be on the back foot like this.

The burst of magic came easily. It was obvious now that it *wanted* to escape.

Free from her usual, controlled self, Adria began to feel its boundaries more clearly. She had so much of his magic, even just in the visible container – the one she would allow Varick to see, should he ask. More than enough for her to practice over and over again, until she could control it.

Had she been trying to shape it, to work it towards a specific goal, then she would have had to try harder. She wasn't sure yet whether she could manage it. For now, all she had accomplished was the release of an uncontained burst of pure, unrefined matter.

It was the way in which she had seen Varick use it previously, and she appreciated now that he wasn't necessarily even having to use any effort to do so. As soon as he thought of the destruction, it would erupt out of him.

It was so *natural*. It should have been the opposite… but using it according to its own nature felt… right? It was incredible to see what she could achieve.

If her goal had been utter devastation.

Adria found herself becoming frightened of him in a way she never had been before, understanding now that when he said the expulsion of his entire reservoir of magic had happened on a whim, he'd been telling the truth.

A frightening truth.

He did not *seem* to have a propensity for lying, but there was a difference between an exaggeration, or misremembering something, and an outright lie. She had assumed it to be a case of one of the former rather than the latter. It was a horrible thing to grasp – that he'd meant it exactly as he'd said it – and she detested the thought of what was now running through her own body.

The magic chose her moment of revulsion to try and burst free, and she quickly clamped it back. She needed to be strong in order to overpower it; she could not let it sense any weakness.

Having now gained the feel for using the magic, she was

confident releasing it, but only in its current state. That did not satisfy her. She wanted to know whether she could *change* the magic. If so, Adria felt sure it would be sufficiently subjugated.

It might've been better to wait until she was more practiced, but there was no guarantee she'd have another chance. Varick had once – long before she'd ever touched the cursed stuff – described how magic had been used to improve crop yields in farming, in quite some detail.

A hundred or so paces from her was a tree, where blossom buds were beginning to peek through. Presumably, for the first time in almost a century. Drawing closer, she concentrated on a single bud and gently encouraged it to bloom.

It imploded. Broken petals fluttered to the ground; the stem wilted.

Focusing on another bud, this time Adria devoted more energy to shaping the magic before she released it, trying to follow the process the book had described. The effect was the same.

The more disheartened she became, the more eager the magic seemed to be. She couldn't stop. She tried again and again, with no success.

Lamenting the damage she was doing to the tree, she sought to think up another way to practice but drew a blank. Turning her attention away from the new buds, she tried to encourage the broken stems to once again grow hale.

With a full fifth of the foliage having been desecrated, she had no choice but to head back to the inn. Hopefully, before Varick returned and asked where she had been.

CHAPTER 36 – NOBILITY

The girl was up to something. He was sure of it.

Having intentionally left her alone for a few hours, he'd erroneously assumed the innkeeper would provide an update as to her activities on his return. Whether he was telling the truth when he claimed not to know, or was merely withholding the information, he could not have said. Either way, it was infuriating.

In the long run, her disobedience was of no consequence to him, but for now, he wished to know whether she was loyal – if she could be relied upon. There was more than one way to stab somebody in the back.

Varick showed no interest in how she'd spent her day and merely rambled on about how much he'd impressed everyone. Evidently, the events of Southfern had been all but forgotten.

Adria was daydreaming rather than listening, but her thoughts were still on Varick. How was it possible he could simply cast the responsibility for five deaths out of his mind? Did the ability come from having lived a long time?

She couldn't help but think life would have *more* meaning rather than less, if she had been in his place. If she were to be privileged enough to have a life the length of four or more normal lives, she would surely do her best to lift others up and treat their shorter lives as being more precious.

But then this was Varick she was talking about, and since when had he ever thought the same way as she did... about *anything*.

"We're still staying the night, then?"

Varick stared at her instead of responding.

"What's the matter?"

"You just interrupted me mid-sentence. As though you weren't even listening to me! I feel as though I should start over. Care to explain yourself?"

"Oh, I think I got distracted. I got the general gist of what you were saying. Congratulations on how well you did today; it sounds like it was worth the stopover."

Varick frowned, but let it go. "Yes, we're staying here tonight. Make sure you're ready to go early tomorrow. And whatever the matter is, make sure you've snapped out of it by then."

"Oh. I was hoping we might stick around in the tavern for dinner."

"Fine." He nodded to the server and asked for a couple of bowls of stew. They waited in awkward silence, so it was a relief when they arrived quickly.

Adria, happily tucking in, thought it tasted pleasant enough, so it was something of a surprise when Varick stood up and yelled, "This is what you thought was fit to serve me? Where is the meat!"

She shrank into herself, wishing she wasn't sitting at the same table as him. Or that she'd eaten in her room after all. The food was no different to what she was used to – carrots and parsnips made up the bulk of it. It would have been nice to have a bit of potato with it, and the beetroot had stained everything a pinkish-purple, but it wasn't anywhere near the worst fare they'd eaten; and it was pleasant to have been served something piping hot.

Each and every one of the other customers looked like they felt just about as awkward as she did. The waitperson had run off to fetch the owner; Varick was still standing. What he thought he was going to achieve, Adria had no idea.

"I'm sorry to have offended you, sir. Could you tell me what I can do to rectify this?"

Please… just say it's fine, Varick. You've had your apology.

"I want real food. Something you would actually consider fit for a king."

"I'm afraid this is all we have that's fresh. In time, we might be able to widen the variety of produce we can serve, but I fear that may take two to three years…"

"You have had all day; surely you could have procured some meat. Or fish, otherwise." Varick was not going to back down. Now he'd made a scene, he needed to prove his point.

Adria scrambled about, desperately trying to think of a way to let him walk away whilst keeping his pride – but she was drawing a complete blank.

"I regret we did not have the foresight, nor the knowledge of anywhere which would have had such ingredients available within a suitable distance. Is there anything I can do to make this up to you?"

"I will have a think."

Adria could have predicted it; Varick had no clue what he'd been trying to achieve with his supercilious stunt. If he'd been hoping to show everyone he was a man to be respected, as opposed to a petulant child, then he'd somewhat missed the mark.

Varick sat back down, still scowling. The innkeeper

lingered for a minute, shifting his weight from foot to foot, unsure whether it was safe to make a break for it. As he turned to go, Adria gave him a half smile, hoping he could see the contrition in her eyes.

Quickly finishing what was left on her plate, she bid Varick goodnight. It was early enough that she ought to be able to get a good amount of sleep before their early start.

Instead, she found herself lying in bed thinking.

Or more like, *trying* to think, because her brain was busy producing nothing of use.

She needed to find a way to incapacitate him for long enough to pull all of his magic away. But she'd been trying to think of a way to imprison him for weeks with no ideas – did the fact it would be only for a few minutes rather than a lifetime really change anything?

He needed to be held securely. If she left even a drop, not only would she fail in her attempt, but she'd have missed her chance for good; there was no way he'd let her get that close twice.

In fact, he would probably execute her without a second thought.

She shifted on the bed, and the shaft of a feather poked her in the back. Thinking of the proprietor's reaction if she went downstairs and complained the bed was uncomfortable almost made her laugh. Instead, she choked back a cry. This could be her last ever night in a bed.

No, she needed to focus on how she could fix things, not on her own fate. What if she tried to drain him now, while he slept? It seemed like too much of a risk. She'd have to go slowly so as not to disturb him, but the more time she took, the more it would increase the chance of him waking.

Adria kept coming back to it – mostly because she had yet to think of anything better – and dismissing the idea all over again.

If he woke up and they lost contact, it'd all be over.

There was also part of her which knew that if she attempted to make her move while he slept, then her best chance to end this for good would be right then and there. She couldn't spur herself into action; the thought this might be her end loomed too closely, and to be the instigator of her own demise… that was a tough choice to make.

She hoped a time would come when the decision was made for her, and she'd have no option but to act. When they reached Ember House would be her preference – as well as being familiar ground, it would give her more time to prepare.

Her eyes drooped; in that middle state between awake and asleep, a thought occurred to her. She hoped she'd remember it in the morning.

CHAPTER 37 – TEARDROPS

Adria was waiting patiently at the stables when Varick arrived. He gave her no thanks for making the effort to be up and ready, but it was better than earning his ire.

For a moment, she was reminded of a time not that long ago when she cared about what he thought and had done her best to please him. Her days were still easier when he was in a good mood, but the dynamic had changed entirely.

In a way, things had been simpler when she'd blindly followed him. Her curiosity would never have been entirely assuaged, and the peace would not have lasted, but the weight of responsibility sat heavily upon her now. It was a coward's thought; she might have been happy in her ignorance, but being selfish would have made her almost as immoral as him.

Directing Cotton to catch up, she dwelled on her remembered thought from the previous night as they rode.

If she used his magic to bind him, there was a chance he wouldn't be able to remove it. It was *his* magic, so it ought to respond to him... but while they were in contact, hadn't it denied him previously? Varick hadn't realised what had happened, surely that could only work to her benefit.

Although she hadn't been able to shape his magic into anything useful, she felt confident she could create a bind using the magic in its raw form. It was a bold assumption, given her previous day's attempts had all spectacularly failed. Perhaps the magic's influence on her mind also lent her some of Varick's supreme overconfidence.

Practice would be crucial, but how to do so... unless she used her own arm? The thought was horrifying after what she'd done to the buds and petals.

Adria stared at her hand on and off until she couldn't put it off any longer. It was necessary for Azeileah.

Closing one eye – as much as she'd have liked to, she couldn't afford to close both – Adria tried to let out the magic as gently as possible. Relief came immediately. From the moment it began to move, she could tell it was entirely under her control. Slithering across the surface of her skin, the serpent-like thread was translucent and imperceptible – but it didn't matter because she could feel where it was in order to direct it.

She was transfixed. It was like having a pet, except it was hers to command. She felt... *powerful*?

"What's happening?" Varick sounded agitated, and her focus broke. The magic dissipated, vanishing into the air. "What was that?"

"What do you mean? Like a sound?"

"No, it felt like... but it's gone now. Were you doing something?" He narrowed his eyes at her warily.

Adria almost gasped, as it dawned on her that he'd sensed her use of his magic. Recovering quickly, she did her best to keep her face impassive; the last thing she wanted was for him to realise what she'd been doing. "I don't think so, like what?"

"Stop a second." Frowning, he continued studying her. "Were you using magic?"

"Not that I'm aware of. Maybe it was leaking out from me because I'm not controlling it properly?" She'd said that too quickly… it would cast suspicion on her.

Varick looked at her oddly. "Hold my hand a second."

Feeling she had no choice but to comply, Adria let him touch her. Taking slow, deep breaths, she tried to remain level-headed as he looked around inside her. Her body trembled, and she felt sure he'd be able to tell how uneasy she was, if nothing else. Could he sense how fast her heart was racing?

"You're certainly holding a lower level of my magic now. Whether I believe you that it's been leaking out is another matter. I don't think you have enough in there to do any damage, at least."

Holding back a smile, Adria relaxed her tension. He hadn't found her hidden second container; she'd successfully managed to cloak it. Her control was better than she'd realised.

There was still more to do, though. Not until she managed to determine whether or not he'd be able to remove the binds would she consider herself truly ready. Or, at least, as ready as she could be.

And she'd just missed her chance to test it.

For the first hour or two of their journey, Adria remained hopeful Varick would make contact with her again, and she would have her chance. From thereon, her optimism began to waiver.

She could not quiet the constant worries which had taken hold in her mind. Had she made the wrong choice by deciding to wait until they reached Ember House to make her move? She'd convinced herself that would be her best place to make a stand, but what if her magic worked differently once she was inside the glamour? There would be no way to know.

Had it been foolish to rely on the hope that when Varick made his attempt on the Jhardis' lives, it would give her the cover of having killed him in self-defence? To think that perhaps, if she failed, there might be someone else to step in and make the final blow?

Part of her was confident she'd feel stronger making her move on familiar ground, even knowing it might give Varick a bigger advantage still.

Admitting as such was hard, but most of all, she wanted to see her home once more; or, at least, the closest thing she'd ever had to a home.

The countless uncertainties mixed together until doubt consumed her, overpowering her sense of revenge and need for justice. She tried to quash all her thoughts, wanting her mind to go blank. It needed a rest. Hopefully, it would be possible to find inspiration once she felt fresh again.

Overnight, she took no magic from Varick while he slept, staking everything on the hope he would begin to overflow and seek her assistance.

They had reached the final stretch, and she couldn't shake the feeling she was walking to her grave. Although she'd made peace with this – her greatest hope being that she wouldn't be going alone – her nerves were still uneasy.

Varick, consumed by his own thoughts and plans, muttered to himself but made little conversation. Her eyes kept flicking towards him, hoping he might show signs of wanting relief. He usually did, but today he seemed distracted by their approaching destination. Adria knew she couldn't ask him. Whilst enquiring whether she should take some magic might seem simple enough, he could always tell when she had an ulterior motive. He was annoyingly perceptive.

Tenebrae loomed overhead even now, and she had already accepted that she'd simply have to pray the binds worked, when Varick unexpectedly dismounted.

"Take a little of my magic, and then let's finish the last of our food. I want to be at my full strength and *sanity* before I face the next stage of my journey." Adria's heart perked up in response, her concentration wobbling along with her hand. Instead of allowing him to send his magic through her, she was readying her own to go in the opposite direction.

The magic already inside her responded gleefully. Almost as though it were as much *hers* as it was his own. Adria fought with it, doing her best to hold it back and only release a little. Once she had tamed it, she directed it.

Where they made contact, her snakes crawled over his hand, unseen.

She couldn't siphon any magic while she was creating the binding around his hand – it was the same restriction that prevented Varick from using magic while *she* was siphoning – so she worked as quickly as possible. The second they were in place, she sipped from his well. Her stomach flipped with relief when she confirmed she could still do so.

While she drew some of his magic away, Adria investigated Varick's power source. She wanted to understand what was preventing him from using the magic himself. While they were connected, and it flowed away from him, he wasn't able to redirect it. She had thought it was because the magic responded to her own will in preference to Varick's, but now she realised that wasn't necessarily the case. The magic wanted out, and its easiest channel was the one already open to it. For all his endless well of power, he wasn't able to overpower its desire to escape.

Even if he had intended to expel it himself – to release it through one of his quick, lethal blasts – the magic would have had to be redirected from its current course, which was too much of a struggle.

Adria paused to reinforce the walls of the stream flowing towards her. There were no signs he was beginning to break through them – she could feel him straining – but when she attempted to drain him fully, she'd be holding him for several minutes at least. Having determined it was possible, she knew she'd be able to do it again when needed.

Now, she just needed him to try and break contact with her. Knowing Varick, this attempt would come at any second…

"What… what is this?" As soon as she felt his slight tug, she called off the magical restraints; they disintegrated immediately. Although he had been unable to use magic while touching her, this hadn't been sufficient to confirm he wouldn't be able to break them himself. His inability to remove his hand was what she had sought to prove. She had learnt what she needed to.

She frowned at him. "What's the matter?"

"I couldn't move my hand for a second."

Adria rejoiced. Finding it difficult not to smile, she thought it best to respond mockingly, in the hope her words would better match her facial expression than a denial would have done, "That's ridiculous. Do you mean you got a cramp?"

"No, I…" He made a fist, then released it several times, testing the working of his hand. "It must have been, I suppose."

"It'll be from holding the reins too tightly. Is it okay now?" She made her way to Varick's satchel and began sharing out the food, hoping the distraction would take his mind off it.

"It aches a little. Wait, how much are you taking there?" He reached over and took one of her pieces of bread. "I'm the one who needs to prepare himself, and I'm hungry." She wanted to complain, but instead, she used her indignation as fuel. It was ironic he was complaining about her taking too much food when the bigger question was how much she'd taken of his magic.

She was readying herself too… anticipating their long-awaited confrontation would be just around the corner.

CHAPTER 38 – EXPECTATIONS

He should have felt something, but he didn't. There was no excitement – mild anticipation perhaps, at a push – and no uncertainty.

Sometimes, it seemed as though there was little left for him in this world.

Pride would not let him back down.

He hated these moments of clarity that compelled him to question the meaning of things. They always made the passage of time seem slow and laborious... made him forget why he wanted to take back his rule in the first place.

The scent of freshly cut grass brought with it an overwhelming sense of familiarity. It wasn't something she'd ever dwelled on or appreciated before, nor was it something she'd consciously missed. Yet here it was, and it made her eyes water. She wanted to lie down and enjoy it, along with the unobscured rays of sunlight.

They had approached from a completely different angle to the one they'd left by. Having not been required to climb Tenebrae to re-enter, they'd taken the trading route commonly used to reach Freeway for its weekly market. It had brought them around to the same gardens where Adria had lingered for much of her youth.

The rest of the Island may have been recovering, but on passing through the glamour, she knew the haze sitting over the sky hadn't yet cleared. Nowhere felt quite so alive as it did at Ember House.

Seeing the Adria flowers still in bloom across the mountainside, she felt a pang of sympathy for Varick. Then immediately hated herself for it. She may have once felt something for him, but even that had all been a deception.

Manipulation.

Don't think about Alis.

Hopefully, Varick had been wrong, and Alis's black arrow wasn't the only thing that could end his life.

It was a time for lingering, for enjoying being home – but based on the speed with which he marched across the lawn, Varick didn't seem to agree.

Adria wasn't sure what she'd expected, but the pair of them making their way towards Ember House went ignored by most of the occupants. It was a huge shift from having been stared at and disliked wherever they were. Although she knew that had not necessarily been *Varick's* experience of the populace, it had certainly been her own.

"Where are you going?" she asked him without thinking – too distracted by trying to absorb all the details in case it was her last time walking down this path she'd taken for granted a thousand times before…

"*I* am heading towards the Jhardis' quarters." He turned towards her and frowned as though the thought had only just occurred to him. "You should wait here."

"I will not." He continued walking, and she hurried after him, relieved the conversation hadn't gone any further. It was strange to be walking around the eastern side of the house, to an entrance she'd never used. Had never expected she *would* use.

Except. If she'd returned with Alis, perhaps…

Adria gulped, then took a couple of large strides to catch up again. Maybe soon, she'd be joining her.

Varick paused in front of the large, banded door, then knocked. Four loud thumps.

Her mind detached from her body; her surroundings became surreal. While she stood still, the world moved around her.

For now, likely no one would be able to tell there was anything wrong with her from the outside, but she needed to ground herself before her internal battle began to show.

A suited gentleman answered the door. Adria was unsure who he was but inferred from Varick's reaction that it wasn't the Sovereign himself. She wasn't sure how he knew – it must have been a judgement made based on his dress.

"Do you have an appointment?"

"We have news." Varick's smile was unsettling. Would others notice its *wrongness*, when they didn't know him as well as she did? "I believe the family would like to hear of Lady Jhardi's demise."

"Granted, they may." Did the man's lip tremble ever so slightly? "And who should I say is to be delivering such… *unfortunate* news?"

"A friend. The name's Varick." He held out his hand by way of greeting.

When the man did not shake it, Varick turned to Adria and shrugged – evidently amused by the slight – then moved his hand to his hip. The interaction made Adria overly aware of her own hands, and she found she suddenly had no idea where to put them. *What do I usually do with them?*

The housekeeper, or butler, walked away, and she wasn't sure if they were supposed to follow. When Varick strolled after him, the decision was made for her.

He'd obviously decided the pair of them posed no threat. It was an oversight, but perhaps it had saved his life, as surely Varick had intended to gain entrance Ember House, at *any* cost.

He stopped in a nicely apportioned drawing room, empty of any other people.

Based on the limited seating space – a two-seater chaise and a couple of armchairs – it appeared they did not often entertain guests. A rug and a display case were the only other furnishings. The trinkets on show might at one time have interested Adria, but there was too much currently on her mind for her to give them more than a passing glance. They were delicate… Adria wondered whether soon they might be broken, and she would have missed her only chance to look.

Out of the corner of her eye, she saw Varick making himself comfortable. Instead of joining him, she chose to assume a standing position by the bay window. She had heard about the family's private, walled garden. Who tended to it, she wondered, given the servants did not come here?

After a few minutes, with no one having arrived, she took a perch on the window seat, hoping it would enable her to observe any impending conversation without being fully part of it.

Eventually, the door opened, and Lord Dann walked into the room, his face solemn. He shook Varick's hand warmly and Adria admired his willpower. "Welcome, to our home. I hear you bring poor tidings?"

She let out a small sigh, relieved he hadn't attempted to strike down Lord Dann at first glance. Perhaps if he'd shown any signs of reaction on hearing Varick's name, things would have played out differently.

She would have been too slow to act if he had. Adria silently chastised herself – but was still none the wiser as to how this meeting would play out, and therefore felt no more prepared than she had moments earlier.

Alis had once said that Varick's first name hadn't been known to her, and Adria couldn't help but think it had been a calculated move, to not have provided his family name at the door.

The sigh must have caught Lord Dann's attention because he seemed to only then notice she was there. Had a flicker of recognition might have passed across his face?

Her dour expression certainly matched the occasion, however, her mind was less on Alis and more on fear; anticipating Varick might, at any second, attempt to strike down their host. Hopefully she would not fail this almost-stranger who looked nothing like his sister.

"I do. And I'm not sure where to begin." Varick's words unintentionally relieved the tension she had felt starting to build.

"I must beg you to wait for my parents. They are composing themselves as we speak."

A tear fell down her face. She hadn't known it was coming; only the trickling sensation on her cheek alerted her. Biting her lip, she turned towards the window – hating to look away in case something went afoul, but for the moment unable to look on.

Now wasn't the time for her emotions to get the better of her, but it was hard not to be human. At least Varick's magic hadn't *yet* taken that away.

"Is Stanmore fetching you a drink?" Lord Dann was pacing and seemed unsure what to do with himself. "No. Might I get you a drink then?"

Certain he was addressing Varick –assuming he thought she was his attendant – Adria didn't respond.

"I'd love a cup of something hot, thank you. I'm sure Adria would, too."

She frowned, wondering why Varick might be concerned for her comfort. *Why now?*

When they'd been outside, she had wanted time to pass slowly, but now it was the opposite. She wanted it to be *over*… and yet, she still wasn't ready.

Alone with Varick again, she couldn't help but wonder if she truly had it in her to do what was needed.

It might have been best to make her move now; perhaps her own reputation no longer mattered… but something, be it fear or self-preservation, was stopping her. It was just as well because the Sovereign and his wife chose to make their appearance. If they had intervened, and tried to pull her away from Varick during her attempt to deal with him, it would have been disastrous.

Thankfully, this time she was spared from introductions and able to maintain her spot on the edge of the cosy room. The mug of cocoa she was handed smelt delicious… *surely*, Varick wouldn't do anything until he'd finished his drink?

Not for the first time, she wished she knew more details as to what he had planned. It wasn't like she hadn't had ample time to ask him, but he'd been non-committal, and Adria hadn't wanted to seem like she cared.

She hadn't expected the suspense of this final bout of waiting to be quite so painful. *What was his intention in making them suffer before he struck?*

Never mind… she'd likely answered her own question. Hadn't he done the same with his own father?

Between sips from his mug, Varick began recounting his promised news of Alis – but the more she listened, the more he diverged from the truth. It was unlike him; she'd never heard him lie before.

Although technically, there was nothing within his words she could pinpoint as being inaccurate. It was more like he'd twisted his telling of the day's events, and omitted key details.

In his version, Lady Jhardi had died to save Adria. "I could only watch as she leapt in front of her, preventing the attack from piercing her heart, but sadly losing her own life in the process."

He mentioned almost nothing of himself.

This was not going to help them be sympathetic towards her... quite the opposite. *Why aren't they suspicious of him? Don't they wonder what happened to their fugitive?* As frustrating as it was, the answer, however, was clear. They were too devastated by the death of their daughter. That, and Varick's charming manner disguised his threatening nature far too well.

"What was it that killed her?" Lord Dann asked, and Adria felt a flutter of hope.

"That would bring me to my other news – or perhaps you have already heard? I know not whether this information will be equally grave or, on the contrary, if you might consider it a blessing. Magic has returned to Azeileah."

"It was magic, then? Her training attempted to prepare her for such an assault, but of course she'd no real experience of it. I wondered how a bandit could have prevailed. Why *her* though? Was it targeted?"

He was becoming suspicious of Varick, she was certain, but his parents – *Alis's* parents – were not sufficiently hale to process the duplicity.

"I believe they were after Adria, having seen her spending some of my coins. Your sister's actions were truly selfless."

The Sovereign's wife arose. Saying nothing, she nodded

as a means of excusing herself. Her husband made to follow after her but first paused and invited Varick to join them for dinner.

"Regretfully, I must decline."

The simple statement put Adria back on high alert. She barely registered his request for another audience tomorrow, once they'd had chance to digest the news.

Now she focused, she could sense Varick calling on his magic – despite never having noticed such a thing before. Either the practice she'd undertaken had improved her perception or, more likely, it was due to her circumstances, and the intense concentration she currently applied. She knew without a doubt that he was readying himself.

It was something of a relief to think that, very soon, this might finally be over.

CHAPTER 39 – SECOND THOUGHTS

Hand to his chin, Lord Dann was deep in thought. With his mother having left, there was space next to him on the chaise, and Adria made her way over.

He bristled in response. "Give me some time, please, then I would like to also hear your recounting of my sister's death."

She nodded, without taking her eyes off the perceived threat.

It was possible Varick would strike now but, ever one for dramatics, she suspected he would announce his intentions before he actually did anything.

She hoped.

He knew she was watching him… but he could not know what she intended to do to stop him.

"There is something else we must discuss."

Lord Dann did not look up.

"I *said* I have something to say!" Varick bellowed. Even Adria twitched at his frightening tone.

Lord Dann stiffened, his entire composure changing as he was put on his guard. She could, at last, see the nobility bred into him, instead of the affable bachelor. "If you mean to ask me for a reward for bringing such ill tidings, then I do not think *that* was the way to go about it."

"Do not dare to insult me like that. Did I not see you wondering why I hadn't given my full name? Were you afraid to ask? This is *my* property, and all I am doing is making sure you *understand* that I am reclaiming it, before I do so. I am Lord General Varick Azeileah. Before this evening is out, I will be *King* Varick Azeileah. As I was before the Jhardis were here and will be long after they are gone!"

Adria considered acting now, but if she waited a little longer it might be to her advantage. She needed to be sure Lord Dann fully perceived the threat to his person. She wanted to be his rescuer, not Varick's assassin.

Or, at the very least, both.

Lord Dann at last stood, so he could look Varick directly in the eyes. He was a hand's width taller, meaning he was the one looking downwards. "Say more if you must, sir, but I believe it is past time for you to depart."

"I will not be going anywhere. You, on the other hand…" He smirked, but Adria could see no madness in him. He knew what he said and did, and for the moment was thinking rationally. "I feel no regret for killing your sister, as I will not when you and your Sovereign also lie at my feet."

She lunged for him.

All that talk where he'd shifted the blame towards Adria for Alis's death… it was *her* he'd been trying to goad. Varick couldn't have cared less what the Sovereign family thought as he had always intended to kill them. It was obvious now.

Clasping her right hand around his left wrist, she turned her mind towards the pools of magic writhing inside her. She had moments before he used his free hand to throw her away from him – and if he did that, it would be over.

Adria had felt strong, but his wrist was thick, and more muscular than she had expected.

Bind. She called out in her mind. *Please, bind him.* The snakes came slowly and she worried it would not be enough to immobilise him. But Varick did not move. With this small measure of success, her confidence returned. When commanded, the snakes stopped slithering and remained in place.

The glamour hasn't hindered me; this is actually happening.

Having faith he was incapacitated, she tugged, stopping only to reinforce the walls of the channel through which the magic flowed, so that he could not fight her.

She didn't have time to stop and think, to process what she was doing, and it was just as well – her focus had to remain on Varick and him alone. The rest of the room – even Lord Dann – had blurred around her as she concentrated.

The level of exertion required to see it through came as a surprise.

A pained countenance began to creep onto Varick's usually expressionless face.

There was so much to take, far more than she'd ever held before, and she'd only just scratched the surface.

Her mind felt torn between several different places. She created new, larger receptacles to store the magic, kept Varick secured, and siphoned, all at once.

Adria had to be absolutely certain she had taken every drop.

It was unlikely, on account of his arrogance, but possible Varick also had vessels hidden throughout his body. He certainly had enough magic to fill them. Once she thought she had created enough containers, she turned her attention to checking the rest of him.

She felt sick as she explored his limbs, the sensation akin to crawling through his body. The feeling of familiarity, like she already knew every inch of him, was almost worse.

It was too much for her... She was only one person.

All the magic was running towards her now, as though it recognised Adria as its new home – or it mistakenly thought this was a way for it to be free. The sensation was nauseating. She felt like a host... or some vile container for *evil*. It didn't belong inside her, but it clung to her instead of resisting.

Why wasn't it resisting?

"I found a way to bring her back." Adria slowly became aware Varick was talking. She had been so focused on keeping the magic in check, she'd forgotten she was actually killing him. And now he was talking.

She was completely thrown.

"I was experimenting. After I threw out my magic and only had that tiny bit left... before I used the last drop to lock myself in that room... I wasn't sure whether my mother's body would remain in stasis anymore, so I found a way to revive her regardless. I wouldn't have risked locking myself away otherwise."

"No." She stopped, hesitating.

"Don't do this. Please. I can help you bring her back. It's only been a few weeks – it'll be easier with so little time having passed. Adria, stop." His whiny pleas were anathema; he sounded genuinely afraid.

"Shut up!"

"Alis."

She couldn't... it was too big a decision... she had to stop.

No, she couldn't stop. But... hearing Alis's name almost broke her. Adria was supposed to be strong... but she was failing her test.

She felt Varick tug slightly, as though gaining a little

traction against her. It was too late.

She released him.

Varick's body slumped to the floor, the last bit of magic taken away. Still conscious, but weak, he began to crawl towards the door. Only the man was left now. The man she'd first met under the mountain. Clever and mean-spirited but devoid of malice and hatred. *Mostly.*

How long would it take before his magic began to regenerate?

It was now or never.

It had to be a split-second decision. She either followed through or let go.

"Finish him!" Lord Dann shouted. But the choice had to be her own.

Adria let out a burst of uncontrolled magic.

There was no suspense – he could not have survived it.

Bile rose up in her throat, and she swallowed it down. She had expected to feel guilty, but Varick had weaselled his way into her mind and replaced her conscience with something else. *Regret.* He had dangled a carrot in front of her, and she had turned her head.

She'd had no choice. But…

"I need some fresh air." She ran out, leaving Lord Dann to deal with the body.

CHAPTER 40 – AFTERMATH

The world has healed, but who is there left to step forward now I am gone? What will you do, girl? Can you fill such large boots?

Adria gasped, certain she'd been talking to Varick. She couldn't possibly have been. "No, I was asleep." The sound of her own voice helped her distinguish between what was real, and what was only in her head.

She wished she'd been allowed to return to her old room, but the Jhardis had insisted she sleep in one of their guest rooms.

The place felt lifeless. The windows were obscured by heavy velvet drapes, and behind them, the glass – though clean – was held together by flaky, wooden frames in need of painting. It was spacious, but there was no furniture other than the four-poster bed, which matched the deep violet curtains and boasted gold tassels hanging from the upper frame.

There was nothing wrong with the room, and she couldn't see any traces of dust, but it didn't look used or *lived in.* She tried not to think about how long it must have been since anyone had actually lain in this bed.

Until now.

Being relegated to such a chamber confused her already

tortured mind.

She felt like a ghost.

Adria was yet to fully comprehend she'd survived. That her plight had ended.

The light creeping in through the gap in the curtains told her it was a reasonable time to go to the breakfast room, so she washed and pulled a tunic from the commode.

After eating, she'd travel outside of the area and release some of Varick's magic. Whilst she still felt in control, it wasn't worth the risk. She'd seen what it had done to him.

She would know if she wasn't okay, wouldn't she?

Releasing it all wasn't a consideration, but for now, she needed to ease the tension a little and expected even a small amount would make a sufficient difference.

Deciding the best course of action to take with regards to the rest of it would require careful consideration. Hopefully, Varick's journals would guide her towards a solution. Should the worst happen, and she let his magic free only to unintentionally bring the curse back upon the land, she needed to know how to remove it again.

Learning how to store the magic in the portholes *might* avoid the issue, but on balance, she felt it was equally probable as to whether doing so would or wouldn't bring about the curse. Yet, releasing it now, while it remained raw and formless, would not be an option unless she was desperate, of that Adria was certain.

Varick had cast it out in anger, which was as good an explanation as any for why it had done such widespread damage.

Even now, she could feel the magic's dark and aggressive nature as it clamoured inside her. Her own expulsion wouldn't be so hostile, and it might not have such devastating effects if she released it more mildly – but over time, there was a risk it would still result in the same, gradual rot... that the plants might once again wither and fail. Her gut told her they likely would.

In truth, she needed to learn how to shape it. Changing it from its base form of pure, raw chaos into something usable might temper its fury.

Before she could have the necessary space to fully process her change in circumstances and begin to plan for the next few days, she had to get through what had, unsurprisingly, turned into a rather uncomfortable breakfast. She even took a second piece of toast, then tried to draw out spreading her butter, just to avoid the conversation.

The family were clearly trying to be polite, however, Henrietta – that was how she had been asked to address Alis's mother – was still very upset.

All three of them were doing a very poor job of concealing their fear of her.

The conversation skirted around anything important, focusing instead on their daily activities and the weather. *I'm not going to declare myself the new Sovereign*, she wanted to yell; but she didn't. She sat there quietly and attempted to maintain as much dignity as she could.

Lord Dann had already seen her at her worst, and she cringed at the thought of what his opinion must be of her. Even if she knew she'd been incredibly lucky. In every scenario she had anticipated, surviving the fight had meant being accused of murder and immediately incarcerated.

Adria had no idea what she was going to do with herself now – but was certain ruling the Island was not it.

No... she did know. She had to find out whether it was true – if it really *was* possible to resurrect someone this long after their death.

Varick never lied.

Once she used the magic, it'd be gone. She had no way to regenerate it. She'd cling to it until she knew.

Perhaps she wouldn't release any of it today, after all.

"Would you mind if I paid a visit to Lucis Palace before lunch?" The faces before her looked shocked, so she quickly added. "I was hoping I might find some of Varick's journals. Honestly, I'm not intending to take over his crusade. You have my allegiance and I'm happy to assist you in any way I might. I'd like to know a little more about magic, that's all."

"But what might you do with that magic? You have to understand..."

"You're right." She wanted them to believe her, but the best way to ensure this would have meant revealing that her supply of magic was finite – and Adria really wasn't sure whether she ought to. Whilst she expected she held sufficient power to last the rest of her life, revealing any weakness was still a huge gamble. She didn't really know these people. "The magic is raw and untempered. I would like to ensure I do not become... like Varick."

After she'd said it, Adria realised there had been more truth in her statement than she'd first realised.

"And what do you plan to do after that? Don't you have a home to go to?" Lord Dann eyed her sheepishly from over his porridge. She had been mistaken when she thought he'd recognised her yesterday; he had obviously never noticed her while she'd lived at Ember House. Adria wasn't surprised.

"Didn't Alis explain before she... left?" She gulped at their responses to her name. "I'm from here. I was an orphan you took in. I was assigned to carry food up to Varick. He... He tricked me into releasing him." Yes, let her put it that way. It was sort of true, at least.

"My magic – before I knew I had any – began to pull

away the glamour and it woke him up. It shouldn't really have worked that way. I couldn't absorb any magic until we first made physical contact, but then I guess there's a lot about it I don't know yet. Maybe the glamour itself was enough exposure to his magic for my body to subconsciously begin fighting against it..." She let her words tail away. She had been rambling, mostly trying to make sense of it herself rather than addressing her words to her current company.

"Physical contact?" Dann's eyebrow raised. His parents also stared at her curiously.

"I just mean when he grabbed my hand and pulled me inside his prison." Adria folded her arms, uncomfortable with their insinuation and frankly a little angry, even though – had she thought about it – it was a predictable question for them to have asked.

"And my daughter?" Henrietta asked, her voice trembling a little, "How much of what he told us was true? Did she really die to protect you?"

Adria had been waiting for the question. That didn't make it any easier to answer. "In a way, she did, though I dare say that was not her intention. When he… when Varick grabbed me, she held her fire. He was trying to save himself; I think he knew she was too noble to strike me, and I regret that she did not have another opportunity to…" The toast turned to ash in her mouth.

"Where is she buried?" The Sovereign asked, giving her no chance of a reprieve.

"A graveyard in Cent." Adria sincerely hoped this was the truth. She was a little ashamed not to know definitively, but now was not the time to admit as such. Truly, she felt like an interloper, and wished only to excuse herself so the Jhardis could grieve in peace.

The silence dragged on, until it became uncomfortable.

"As I would like to stay for a while, I don't know whether you might be able to please find me some lodging? My old room would be fine, although maybe somewhere a little larger..."

Henrietta nodded.

"And I was hoping that, perhaps, you might employ me as an advisor in some capacity. I fear I could not go back to my old life after all I've experienced of late."

Adria knew she was pushing them. She was pleased that it had turned out she was not above asking for what she needed. Although she had not yet decided what she wanted her future to hold, having somewhere she could return to would be comforting.

They agreed to consider it, which was likely as much as she could have hoped for.

When, at last, the Sovereign excused himself, Adria promptly did the same.

CHAPTER 41 – FREEDOM

The walk towards the stables was strange – familiar but a little awkward. Recognising Arron, Adria enquired after Velvet. She could've taken Cotton, but Velvet knew the route, and, truth be told, she had long wished to see her again.

"We've been exercising her, though not as often as we might. It will do her some good to see you... Look, she's perked up something huge just at the sight of you." As if she'd understood their conversation, Velvet whinnied.

"Might I ride you?" Adria asked out of politeness, then climbed upon her old friend. It had always been the most pleasant part of the journey, and she tried to enjoy it without thinking about what lay ahead.

Once they reached the foot of the mountain, that was no longer an option.

Her body remembered the steps – which ones were a little narrow, and the many spots to avoid – but it was slow going. The wind whipped at her, and she couldn't think why the chill hadn't stuck in her mind; surely, if it had, she would have thought to bring a hair tie. With the strands blowing across her face, she felt a little wild and untamed.

Despite all the walking she'd done, the steep climb up Tenebrae was exhausting. She didn't reach the top until far later in the day than she'd hoped, and by then she was desperate for shelter from the sun's rays.

Standing in front of the main door, Adria remembered the seal. The small amount of magic she tested it with was insufficient to make it yield. She would have to use more.

Unless... she sought out the side entrance. With the barrier enclosing Varick's cell removed, she should be free to use it as both an entry and an exit.

It wasn't just conservation of magic which motivated her. Perhaps in time, she might break through the front door, but for now, Lucis Palace would remain closed. Anyone who knew about Varick's cell might find the side doorway, but there were very few who did; of those, Lord Dann might be curious perhaps, but she found it difficult to imagine the Steward making the climb.

Even if someone else found it, they might not figure out how to open it. Only the bottom third slid open, and it was heavy; you had to know exactly where to place your weight.

She made sure to close it behind her.

Climbing through the hatch was unpleasant, not only because it was dark and narrow, but also as a result of the memories it brought back. She shuffled along the floor with her eyes closed, thankful when the inner slot opened for her, to have this confirmation that she wasn't trapped.

As she climbed out into the small room, she felt sick at the thought of someone having been sequestered in there. Now was not the time to feel sympathy for the man she had just... *don't do this to yourself, Adria.*

Oh, but you deserve it.

Adria winced. For a second, she'd believed that thought had been Varick's.

Don't think about the affliction. It isn't you; it won't be you. It was him, not the magic. He allowed it to twist him.

She righted herself, then took several calming breaths. The short crawl had left her clothes filthy. It was a shame to finally be able to wear nice clothes and already have ruined them, but presumably they could be washed. They might not be as good as new afterwards, but salvageable, she hoped.

Less easy to recall than the climb, was the way to Varick's bedroom. She had only been there once and hadn't been fully paying attention at the time.

The first part was simple, she needed to follow the servants' corridor into the main house… but then, somehow, she did not come across the dining room like she had expected.

It didn't matter. If she explored the palace instead of seeking Varick's journals, there would always be tomorrow to make better progress – and whilst there was nothing productive about wandering aimlessly, it did satisfy her curiosity somewhat.

The place was so much larger, and more labyrinthine, than she had imagined, despite having seen part of the lower level previously. It was fascinating.

As she might have guessed, almost everything was gold and over-wrought. Bedroom after bedroom contained elaborately sculpted beds, with fancy headboards and intricate detail fashioned into the legs; to the extent she began to wonder if she'd even recognise Varick's bedroom when she did find it.

It seemed like such a long time ago that she'd been here. These had been the longest few months of her life.

Pulling an apple she'd taken from the breakfast table out of her pocket, Adria rested on one of the beds. She realised she had no idea what time it was.

☆ ☆ ☆

When she woke up, her first thought was that she'd left Velvet waiting outside for her. Light shone through the tiny window, and she had a feeling she'd slept all through the night. There was something about this place that resonated with her.

It's because I called it home. My magic recognises it.

Not I, he. *Him.* Varick. What was wrong with her? Adria tried to shake off her sleep. She had intended to revisit Lucis palace today anyway, so there was little point in her climbing back down just to return, even if she hadn't eaten anything.

Velvet would surely have made her way back to the stables by now, and her hunger wasn't bothering her anyway – perhaps it was a side effect of being sustained by the magic. Sometimes she was afraid of how little she truly knew about it. Those were the moments when she felt it roiling inside her; thinking it owned *her*, rather than vice versa.

She took a sip from her canister, pleased to have some water. Not to quench her thirst, but because she'd come over hot and flushed.

The unnatural, pristine state the palace had been kept in no longer unnerved her, but she wondered if it would begin to gain dust now Varick was gone. Presumably not, as it must have been the seal placed on the door which had caused such an effect, and the people who had created that were already long gone.

In that case… did that mean if Varick hadn't reclaimed his magic before he'd died, the curse would have endured for an eternity?

It was a frightening thought. She was glad it hadn't occurred to her earlier.

Her exploration took her up into the towers; to where she might have expected to find Varick's laboratory if she hadn't known it to be hidden under his room. Instead, she discovered sewing rooms – the only interesting thing about those being the panoramic view from the window – and an observatory.

It was with no small amount of disappointment that Adria determined she was unable to operate the telescope. There was nothing instinctive about it – or, at least, not to her. She still found herself drawn to it... towards this one room which wasn't brassy or ornate.

It was a large open space, which had been furnished with only the long, plain tube in front of the window and two narrow sofas. The floor was tiled in different shades of brown and mahogany, laid out in a pattern, and the cylindrical shape of the room should have made their placing awkward, but there was no evidence of a struggle. They blended seamlessly into the unusual walls.

These were inscribed with what looked like more carvings, but on closer inspection, Adria realised they were constellations. Maps of the stars. She trailed her fingers over the detail, wondering if this was an interest Varick had pursued but omitted to mention.

It was Dayne's.

Dayne? Who... oh, Varick's middle brother.

No, he was the eldest.

Adria shook her head. She remembered Varick's dream now – if that's what it had been. For a while she'd been wondering if it might have been his subconscious she'd unintentionally invaded.

She clung to the sides as she wound back down the spiral stairs. They seemed more precarious now than they had on the way up. Although she could have lingered, it was time she returned to the first floor; she was certain that when she'd been with Varick, they'd only ascended a single set of stairs.

There were dozens of rooms, but she spent little time

in each, only peering in to see whether any of them looked familiar.

When she found the one she sought, Adria knew instantly.

Unable to stop herself from examining this space he'd once called his own, she walked inside – then paused, wondering what exactly she was expecting to find. The vanity desk and the obscene mirror atop it drew her attention the most. The drawers held only a comb and a pen. There were no papers or books. It was too tidy – empty of any real possessions.

Hadn't his parents known him well enough to see he was hiding something? Or had they simply not cared?

Leafing through the clothes in his wardrobe revealed dozens of almost identical outfits.

His water closet held an enormous, gold-plated bath.

Or, more likely, it was solid gold.

She could be rich if she wanted. There was so few who knew how to enter Lucis Palace and it was very unlikely anyone would hold an inventory of the place after all this time. Even if they did, would they really go meticulously through room by room to check it?

Who would all this wealth belong to now, with Varick no longer around to inherit it?

Nonetheless, it still felt enough like stealing for her to hold back. Conversely, Adria had no qualms over taking Varick's books and journals – although she had at least apprised the Sovereign of her intentions in that regard.

It was a shame the dresser drawers did not contain any old correspondence, but having determined there was nothing of interest in his room, she was forced to turn to the trapdoor. Now Adria knew it was there, she could discern the outline that had remained hidden from her when Varick had originally surprised her with its presence.

Lying on the floor, supporting most of her weight with her right hand, Adria peered over the lock. Holding her breath, she pushed a tiny impression of Varick's magic into it, releasing it as soon as she heard the click. She almost slumped to the floor in relief.

The fear she might fail to open it had been playing in the back of her mind, such that she'd delayed finding out for as long as she could. After all, she had been unable to remove any magic from the portholes.

Varick had claimed his imprint was the key, rather than his magic, but as Adria had suspected, these were part and parcel of the same thing. His magic held sufficient memory that the lock had recognised his presence.

Varick must have begun to regain his magic from the second she'd released him from his cell. It wouldn't have surprised her. He'd never directly said he hadn't.

Her fingers teased the edges, prising it open.

His main workroom was directly below this. All she had to do was climb down, pick up some books – whatever she could carry – and return down the mountain. It would only be a few minutes of discomfort and she'd leave the trapdoor open; she wouldn't be confined.

Once she'd read her first selection, she could come back for more anytime she wanted. Even in the unlikely event someone made it into the palace, there was no risk at all of anyone else gaining entrance to this place. She truly had the knowledge all to herself.

CHAPTER 42 – STASIS

She wasn't quite so afraid this time, but it was still dark, dingy, and unpleasant. The shaft above her let some light through, though it wasn't enough to be of comfort, and Adria worked as quickly as she could.

She barely looked at what she was picking up – it was difficult to read the titles down there anyway.

Varick had left the lantern they'd used beside the exit door and likely there wasn't another, so she didn't bother to waste time searching for one. Ultimately, she intended to do her best to read everything she could find, so the only real danger was if she picked up works that would be too complicated without having read some of the more straightforward material first.

With her hands full, she attempted to climb back up the stairwell – but after almost falling, she was forced to abandon several books.

Only once she was no longer overloaded, was she able to keep her balance.

It was just as well she'd realised now, as she had still to climb the mountainside carrying everything – on her next visit, she'd remember to bring a basket.

By the time she reached the bottom, she was exhausted. Not tired mentally, but her body ached and screamed with lethargy.

Velvet wasn't waiting for her.

Adria was worried something might have happened to her, but then realised it was herself who'd been the flaky one. Velvet no longer trusted her to come back. Knowing she would have slept at the stables, after having been groomed and fed, she'd hoped the pony might return for her today, but it had been silly to think Harlan would have let her out alone.

She'd been looking forward to riding, but the walk wasn't strenuous in comparison to the descent, and despite her initial disappointment, she found she didn't mind it so much.

Having gone via the stables, to reassure herself Velvet had successfully made her way back, there were still a couple of hours of daylight, so Adria laid on the lawn. She'd been planning to read but instead found herself people-watching.

It was strange to observe everyone else milling about, ignoring her.

Although hadn't they *always* ignored her? Why had it been like that for her? Suddenly, she felt like she'd never fit anywhere. Never had… never would.

Never mind.

She quashed the voice; it was only scaremongering. It wasn't really her.

Adria thumbed the spines of the books she'd taken. She'd promised herself she'd wait until she reached the house to see what they were. It had kept her going; had prevented her from turning back and staying another night at Lucis.

She was already feeling addicted to the palace. It was strange to think she'd ever considered it a monstrosity. There was something there that called to her like nowhere had before.

It's home.

It was only as the sun began to set that Adria realised she didn't know where to go. Presumably, a room would have been set aside for her, but whether she should use the main entrance or the family entrance…

Unsure and hungry, she made her way to the dining room where she had previously spent so much of her time. If she found the Steward while she was there, then so much the better.

She piled her plate high, no longer caring for appearances. Besides, she fully intended to eat the whole lot. Choosing an empty bench against the back wall, she balanced the books in a pile on the floor by her feet.

When someone took a perch next to her, she didn't need to look up to know who it was. He was the closest thing she'd ever had to a father.

Had he acted in a fatherly way towards her? He hadn't protected her, but he'd had no choice. She wasn't sure she even cared; it wasn't like she had any other paternal figures to compare him to, and she'd managed fine without one.

"I hope you're well, Adria."

"I am, thank you. Somehow."

The Steward patted her back. "You haven't missed much here. I admit, I'm a little envious of your travels. Perhaps one day…"

Adria turned and smiled at him, newly feeling like she was the more mature one between them.

"I've had a room made up for you. I thought you might prefer to be on this side of the fence, so to speak. It isn't your old one, but I'm sure you'll find it quite comfortable."

"Thank you. I appreciate it. I intend to stay here for a time – I trust that is okay. I've helped myself to food this evening." She grinned. "I hope I'll be welcome on other days too."

"Of course. I'll see that the arrangements are made."

The new room was around three times the size of her old one, which was to say, it comfortably fit a bed and a wardrobe. A selection of clothes had also been relocated from the guest room she'd used a couple of nights earlier, which meant she didn't have to waste time looking for any. It was nice to have something different from the standard uniform too.

Seeing there was no desk, she sat on the bed, with her back against the wall.

One of the books she'd chosen was a journal of plants, and another was an introduction to the use of various farming tools. Adria had yet to determine a need for either of these, which left her with four others – three journals and a general notebook.

She opted to start with the notebook, expecting it would be the quickest read.

Varick had taken some of his favourite ideas for inventions and replicated them in their own separate book. She enjoyed looking through it to begin with, but his thoughts became increasing convoluted and twisted. She considered the possibility she might return to it later, but for now, Adria needed to put it to one side.

Each journal only covered several months, which suggested there were going to be an awful lot of these for her to go through. She might even find she needed to home in on a particular time period – but which? It had to be one of the later ones… hadn't he said he'd stepped up his research immediately before entering stasis?

So, then, it was just a matter of how to identify these.

For the moment, however, she was happy to have had some measure of success, and to spend a while leafing through those she had already retrieved.

Adria spent day after day reading, stopping only to return to Lucis Palace once a week.

Had she not needed to eat, she probably would have camped atop Tenebrae. Only her desire to remain visible around Ember House – she was certain the Jhardis would have someone keeping an eye on her – prevented her from packing several days' worth of supplies and hiding away up there.

While she had uncovered enough information on the shaping of magic that she finally felt she might have a chance of succeeding when she next took the time to practice, Adria had yet to find any of the experiments he'd been doing on resurrection. She'd begun to accept his notes were stored wherever in his catacombs he'd been conducting these.

He'd alluded to there being a number of side rooms only he could find, and the more she learnt about his methods, the more Adria began to despair of ever finding what she was searching for.

The idea of shutting herself under the mountains pretending – to herself – that she was searching for his secrets became increasingly appealing.

Her latest batch contained the most recently dated ones the room had held, but there was still nothing – and annoyingly, Adria wasn't sure of the exact year she was looking for. She was persisting in reading them, albeit half-heartedly, when there was a knock at the door.

"Come in." Adria was surprised to find it was Lord Dann paying her a visit.

"I came to see if you were okay," he admitted before she could ask him what he wanted.

"Oh."

"That says it all." He took a seat next to her and put his arm around her. She tried not to squirm – but he sensed her discomfort and immediately moved a pace away. "Care to talk about what it is you're looking for? This obsession has gone beyond anything I can understand, but maybe you could explain it."

"I knew you were spying on me."

"I wouldn't have called it spying, not exactly. I was worried about your wellbeing after your confrontation with… that *man*. What I've seen hasn't reassured me."

"You still came to check up on me, though." She dipped her head, brushing her eyebrow as an excuse to partially obscure her face.

"I thought you might want someone to talk to. I can see you have no one. I can go away if you like? I didn't come here to upset you."

Wasn't that just the truth of it? She had no one. Adria burst into tears.

Perhaps he *would* have been supportive of her endeavours, but more likely he'd want to see his sister laid to rest.

Selfish.

She was doing this only for herself.

And why shouldn't she? Who else was going to do anything for her?

Before she lost herself in the catacombs, she realised she ought to retrieve the body. At least then, should she not succeed, Alis could receive a proper burial. Now she thought about it, the townspeople of Cent were unlikely to have done anything other than pocket the coins she'd given them. Even if they *had* followed her request to treat her body with respect, Alis deserved to be back with her family.

"I guess you aren't going to tell me," Dan said, rising to leave. "But I can see something has occurred to you, so hopefully, this helped a little. If you need me, just come to the other side of the House, and I'll do my best."

Having excused himself, he didn't leave. Adria frowned at him.

"There was one other thing," he added. "I wondered if you might hold any interest in marriage. In marrying *me*."

She looked at his face discerningly. Surely... "I don't think that would suit either of us. Can you disagree?"

"Not at all, but my parents thought it would be beneficial, given how strong your magic is, and I promised them I'd ask. I can't pretend I'm not relieved you have turned me down." He smiled warmly. "Perhaps you might say I tried my best to persuade you, should anyone ask."

She laughed, nodding. Only once he'd left did she wonder if rejecting him outright might have been a mistake. Had she said yes, it would have given her a purpose and a way of influencing the world.

Adria ran after him. "Wait." He turned back, looking nervous. "Come back a second, please? Do you think you could instead consider me as an advisor? I mentioned it once before, and... when you asked after marriage, I acted on my gut to refuse, but I'd still like to do what I can to help Azeileah. Especially since I've learnt so much about magic and how it can be used for progress and welfare."

"I'd like that, Adria." He brushed his hair away from his eyes and let out a small sigh. His gestures were relaxed, natural – so unlike Varick's had been. "I get the sense you are talking about sometime in the future rather than right now – so come and find me when you're ready, and we'll sit down and work out what we can do together."

He made to give her a hug and pulled back at the last

second, remembering she didn't like to be touched. Adria was impressed. Hopefully, this was an alliance – a relationship – which could work to both their advantages.

"I believe I'm going to be taking a short trip, but I'll be returning soon."

CHAPTER 43 – NECESSITY

The trip to Cent was hard going – and lonely. Adria trudged along, alternating between walking and riding Cotton. She hoped Velvet would forgive her, but the sturdy pony would not have been cut out for the trip.

She hated it all. The hiking, the camping outdoors, the stopping at various villages for supplies… where they either ignored her or worse, asked after Varick. "He's fine," she would spit out. When they probed her further, she'd started pretending he was in a jail cell.

She wasn't sure why she'd been telling people that, but she'd yet to think of anything better. It was certainly easier than saying she'd murdered him.

Hopefully, these people, whose worship of Varick seemed to have only grown, didn't turn against the Jhardis as a result.

Adria was surprised they even remembered her when Varick was all they'd cared about. All she wanted to do was buy food and leave.

If the travelling hadn't already been unpleasant enough, her days were made worse by the lack of company. There was no one to distract her from her mission and no relief from the heavy weight on her mind. Revenge was no longer a welcome distraction.

She felt hollow.

At her lowest moments, the magic overpowered her, but its schemes were subtle now. It whispered malevolent thoughts. Adria needed to master it… and sometimes it felt like she was almost there… but when her spirits were the darkest and her motivation to keep going wavered, control began to slip away from her.

It's because you stop trying and let it in. Sometimes you're curious what it will say.

Confident she could use magic to defend herself, Adria didn't bother staying at any of the inns along the way. Ever since she'd seen Dayne's observatory, she'd found being outside in the fresh air reassuring; it had become worth the discomfort of sleeping on the hard, rocky ground.

It also meant she'd been saving the allowance Lord Dann had provided her with and would be able to use it for something else. Once she'd completed the task ahead of her, she'd promised to treat herself to a new cloak and boots.

☆ ☆ ☆

Arriving in Cent, Adria beelined for the inn where she and Alis had stayed.

She'd been happy there. So happy the memory of the rest of her life now seemed faded. Although, hadn't they argued? It all seemed like it had happened to a different person now.

"You're back!" The innkeeper greeted her more cheerily than anyone else she'd seen. "And where's your companion?"

"Oh, Varick is… he's indisposed."

"The tall, serious lady? You two were quite the contrast."

Of course he hadn't meant Varick, he hadn't even been her travelling companion while she'd stayed here – but it was the first time during her entire trip that someone had actually asked after Alis.

"Ohhh. She…" But if he didn't even know she was dead, he wasn't going to be able to direct her to where they'd buried her.

It had been a poor start, and it didn't improve much from there. She described Alis to the mayor and then the merchants, but nobody knew anything about where Adria might find her. If they were telling the truth, they weren't even aware a murder had graced their town.

She fretted that the bystander might have simply taken her coins. Presumably, they'd also dumped the body somewhere, or the townspeople would have heard about it. If she could track him down… but the whole aftermath was a blur. Adria could barely remember what he'd looked like.

Dejected, she went back to her room and pulled out one of Varick's journals. They'd languished, ignored, at the bottom of her bag for the rest of the journey – she'd managed to kick her obsession with them while travelling – but now she needed to find herself purpose.

Her guard down, she fell into a sort of trance. She heard Varick's voice reading the words to her… could picture him frantically scribbling away as his advisors called to him for assistance.

"He's ignoring us again."

She was back at Lucis Palace, sitting at a desk just inside the entrance to the catacombs – the voice had reached her through the trapdoor. Relaxing her hand, she set down the pen it had been tightly clutching. Ink stained most of her palm. She knew she'd fallen asleep, but the disorientation was confusing.

"Varick, they're going to leave if you don't come up now!"

Where was he? It was too dark down here… Adria

ascended the stairs and peered into his bedroom. Someone grabbed her arm and dragged her through.

"Hey! Get off me!" Her voice sounded deeper than usual. Pulling away, she touched the back of her head, where something felt too tight. Her hair had been plaited and tied off with a cord... and the texture was off. "Am I... *Varick*?"

She received a couple of odd looks in response. "What did you do to yourself now, your Highness?"

"How do you mean?" Was this a dream or another memory? Had she somehow been Varick when this had happened? Had she travelled in time?

Adria, suddenly fearful she might change the day's events and thereby cause unpredictable repercussions, didn't want to speak.

"Another time, Varick. For now, the Lian-Ren delegation is waiting."

"I can't, I'm not..." Wait – he said *Lian-Ren*. She recognised the names as being two nearby islands. She was being asked to meet people from outside Azeileah. Maybe she could learn something. At the very least, it would be fascinating. She changed tack.

"Not what?"

"I'm not *dressed*. Wait outside my door while I put on some more suitable attire, and I will be with you shortly."

☆ ☆ ☆

Adria's head ached. She must have been asleep, but it felt more like she'd been physically displaced. For a few minutes afterwards, her limbs hadn't even felt like her own.

Worse, she couldn't reach her magic. It was as though it had gone entirely – she'd lost it because, at the time where she'd been, it had been Varick's. Except she'd been Varick. Her head hurt some more, but she felt a reassuring rumble; whatever had been blocking her magic had receded.

She had no idea what to do with herself. She'd come all this way and wasn't going to give up, but it seemed hopeless all the same.

Pulling herself together, Adria meandered over to the street where everything had happened. She planned to knock on the nearby doors to see if anyone might recall anything, but before she started, she took a seat on the ground.

In this exact spot, she'd wept over Alis.

The idea of speaking to people no longer seemed quite so appealing. Now was a time for wallowing.

She ran her fingers across the stones as if the ground would remember having soaked up her blood. With nothing to see, she closed her eyes, and focused only on her fingertips and the pounding of her heart.

The sun was out, but there was a breeze, and Adria began to shiver. She'd been sitting there for hours, reliving what had happened that day – this time without the denial or disbelief.

The chill had seeped through her entire body, but she couldn't move.

A hand on her shoulder disturbed her contemplation. "You've been out here for a while, lass. I've been watching through my window while I potted about with my errands. I thought you could use some water."

Her mind was yet to catch up with the spoken words, but Adria found herself reaching out to take the offering and gulping it down. Gradually, her eyes focused on the lady in front of her. She was grinning, presumably feeling validated at having been correct in her assumption.

"Thank you. It was very kind to think of me." Adria

fumbled with the empty cup.

"Water can't have solved your troubles, though. Is there anything else I can do to help?"

"Actually, there might be. If you don't mind. My friend was killed a few months ago, just here. I've been hoping to find out where they might have taken her."

She frowned, clearly thinking the question over, which Adria took to be a positive sign. "You weren't with her for some reason?"

"I was dragged away," Adria sobbed with guilt, knowing she'd been persuaded to leave mentally rather than physically, and feeling cowardly as a result. "I was afraid he'd kill me too and… I was weak."

"No need to ask me for forgiveness. Your problems are your own. I might be able to help you, though. Not personally, mind, but I know who you can ask."

☆ ☆ ☆
 ☆ ☆

Adria had already checked each of the stones in the graveyard. Being on the outskirts, she'd searched the place thoroughly before even approaching the town, turning up nothing.

Now, she was returning to seek out the gravedigger.

With the evening only a couple of hours away, it wasn't ideal timing, but she couldn't leave the lead unexplored.

By the time she reached her destination, it would be dusk.

At first, she thought the place was deserted like it had been earlier, but as she approached, she heard a sifting. Following the direction of the sound, she drew close enough to see movement.

"Hello?" A deep, hoarse voice called out.

Adria started, afraid for a moment, forgetting the magic made her a worthy match for almost any potential assailant. "Hi there! I was looking for some help. I was told you might know the answer to my question. If you were able to please spare me a few minutes…"

"Let me just finish up here." Up close, Adria could see he was watering some flowers at a plot which had been attended to far more lovingly than any of the others. She wondered if it might have some personal significance to him.

"Of course. You're Bernard, who works here, aren't you?"

He grunted, which she took to mean yes. "And you are?"

"My name is Adria. I'm hoping to find where my friend was laid to rest. She didn't know anyone here, but this is where she died. In the town, I mean." He didn't answer, so she added, "It was a few months ago now."

"Rings a bell. What is it you're wanting?"

"I wanted to know what has become of her." She rubbed her arms – still goose-pimply, despite having warmed up during her walk over. "Have you buried any unknowns recently?"

"Yeah, there was someone; she'd be at the other site. This section is the older burials. New ones are in the woods over there. Best wait until it's light to go visit. I can show you where it is. You won't find it otherwise, as it's unmarked."

"I guess that would be best. If you're sure we can't go now, that is?"

"You see any light over there? Want to go wandering about in those trees right now?" She was desperate and would have said yes, but his tone left no room for objection. "I'll see you at midday tomorrow."

Adria felt relief of a sort, but her anxiety had prickled

too. She wanted it to be over with – to see the grave and know she'd found *her*.

She'd wanted to have some time to grieve by her side.

With Bernard not being around until lunchtime, the only practical thing to do was make advance arrangements for the trip home. She wasn't sure what a fair price was for a cart, but she had a horse already and felt sure the latter had to be the more expensive of the two.

Being an outsider, Adria knew they would inflate the price she was quoted somewhat, but hoped they would still treat her reasonably. In this one sense, it would work in her favour that they didn't know *whose* body she was enquiring after.

By lunchtime, she had transport agreed and provisions for the return journey packed. There was only one thing she was missing.

Although she'd worried he might be late, or not show up, Bernard was waiting as promised. She followed as he led her through the trees, while trying to memorise the way – even though she didn't truly believe he'd abandon her in the middle of nowhere. He seemed like a reasonable person.

There were a couple of dozen graves in the area, but Bernard walked past these to another. There was nothing to demarcate this plot, but the ground was a slightly different consistency and colour to the nearby soil.

"This is the overflow. Other site got full. We've put her out here, but couldn't see any point in paying for a headstone given it'd just say 'unknown'."

Except she *had* given them money for one. Adria gritted her teeth.

"Thank you. I have a cart ready, but unfortunately, I won't be able to bring it close enough. Do you think we'll be able to carry the coffin between the two of us?"

"Hold on there. You've jumped around a bit now. What's this talk about moving her? Why would you want to do that?"

"She needs to be returned to her family."

"That's simply not practical, lass. First off, there was no one to pay for a box. Second, I don't think she'd be fit for travel."

"Right. I'll buy her one, return here with a shovel, and *then* we'll move her." He remained unpersuaded. She stared at him until he shook his head. "In this hole, you've buried Lady Jhardi, the Sovereign's daughter. I am sure they would not be happy to hear I have been unable to bring her home."

He looked like he would object, or at the very least contradict her, but thought better of it.

"You won't be digging with a shovel."

Adria frowned.

"Like I said, there's no box. If you start throwing a shovel around, it won't be pretty. It likely won't be, anyway, mind. She's been down there a while now."

She took a deep breath and wiped the sweat from her forehead. "Do you think you might be able to procure me a coffin while I begin work? Here, just take my purse; I'll trust you to be honest." Adria knew it wasn't the wisest of decisions, but she needed this over with – and a part of her wanted to be alone for the worst of it.

Down on her hands and knees, she began to rake at the mud.

CHAPTER 44 – SWIMMING

With Alis newly placed in stasis – one thing Adria *had* been able to determine how to do from the journals – she now rode next to her on the cart. It was an awkward position from which to hold the reins, and the constant reminder of her friend weighed heavily on her.

Alis's oval stone had been clenched in her fist, and Adria now turned it over in her palm as her friend once had. She'd often wondered what the significance of it was, and now she knew it was a stone and nothing more – yet the feel of its smooth surface was comforting.

Between the cost of the coffin and having needed to buy a second horse, she had nothing left. Her provisions would have to last her the entire way.

And it was slow going.

You're not alone.

"Alis, was that you?" Adria could have sworn she'd heard something. "Alis?" She rested her hand against the side of the wooden box as though she might feel movement within.

It's the magic.

The magic? The magic was making her hear things? That didn't make sense. Unless this was what had happened to Varick. "I'm not like Varick. I'm not."

She needed to release some of it. "No, I can't, I need it. Or this would all be for nothing."

Adria did her best to shut her mind down, focusing on nothing but the horses, cart, and road. All she had to do was get home. She was used to pushing herself up the mountain with only the goal of bringing Varick food in mind. She could push herself for this now, too.

The modest rations of food she allowed herself did not seem to hinder her persistence, and, if anything, she had adjusted to the meagre portions. Throughout the night, she had minimal rest and continued travelling as much as she could.

Only when Adria passed Kings'land did she almost waiver. There were a lot of people there, likely still in need of her help. With Alis in stasis, she could afford the delay.

Yet, with no money and limited magical prowess, she realised there was little she could actually do. It would be better to return and help them as Lord Dann's advisor when she would have the means to effect real change.

Her mind was made up. It wasn't a matter of prioritising Alis over them. Postponing her visit now would mean she was certain to return able to offer them a better prospect later.

She wanted – needed – to persuade herself she still had a conscience.

That the person she was most afraid of wasn't herself.

Adria made a vow; if she was doing this one incredibly selfish thing, she'd do her best to help others after. She wouldn't give up on Alis, but she would do everything she could to help Azeileah thrive – as it had under Varick's reign.

Everyone else was gone now... Alis, Varick. She had survived the two smartest people she knew, and it wasn't clear to her why or how.

Tricks and manipulation.

The unpleasant voice was gaining a foothold.

☆ ☆ ☆

Lord Dann wasted no time arranging a funeral, and Adria was left to watch him coordinate the event, make all the decisions, and pay the expenses. She felt lost, and worse, mindless. Her thoughts were becoming less and less her own.

She assumed it was grief causing her lapse, but there was always a worry in the back of her mind that the magic would overpower her, and she'd lose control over her mind or body. There wasn't even anyone for her to discuss her concerns with; perhaps Lord Dann, in time, but not while his mind was so focused on his sister.

Alis would be buried away from the main thoroughfare, and Adria was reassured that she'd be able to maintain her privacy whenever she visited.

Wanting to find a means of occupying her time, the Steward found someone who could teach her to swim. She was thankful to him for the idea, and once she mastered the strokes, Adria discovered it did not tire her out as much as it should have. After a few weeks, she could swim length after length of the lake without stopping for a break at either end.

She couldn't wait for the funeral to be over. She wanted to stop feeling like a loose end and was desperate to get back to her research.

The ceremony didn't matter anyway; the important thing was bringing her back.

When the day finally came around, the emotions she'd been trying to suppress came flooding back. Arriving an hour early, she chose a spot near the front but against a wall. There was no one coming with whom she wished to share this moment.

It was okay; this wasn't the end.

The second it was over, she climbed Tenebrae – asking Velvet to go back at the point she reached the stairs, hoping the pony understood she wouldn't be returning. Adria knew she could survive on very little and expected her supplies to last her the week.

Adria was in exactly the right state of mind to enter the catacombs. Desiring somewhere alone and dark, where she could mope and feel sorry for herself, Varick's hiding hole was perfect.

It was difficult to believe she'd ever hated it so much down here.

With her three colours of wool, she'd be able to map out a few different directions whilst still being able to find her way back.

The room immediately below the trapdoor held nothing more of interest; she'd already taken from it anything which might have helped her. She needed to find the side rooms – places where he might have stored his more controversial work, or books left in the rooms where he'd performed his experiments.

There were more routes than she'd anticipated – and going deeper into the mountain risked disturbing other things. Adria didn't want to have to waste any of Varick's magic protecting herself from hordes of Djharlings – or whatever else might be lurking in wait – but she'd resigned herself to the fact she might have to.

At least I'm not defenceless against them this time.

On her seventh day of searching, she found an enclave that looked like it had once been occupied. Although low on food, a quick check of her basket revealed she had more left than anticipated.

Now she had discovered what she sought, Adria couldn't leave.

Unlike the other nights, she didn't return to the surface. With the hundreds of unused candles stored in one of the cupboards, she didn't need to.

They were further proof Varick had fixated on this room.

The scribblings within the books she found were erratic and hurried. They were more difficult to decipher, but by now she was familiar with his handwriting, and they were finally addressing the very thing she'd been looking for.

Only the melting wax marked the passing of time.

Adria had been awake for over two days, but she wasn't tired.

Varick had managed to raise Djharlings from the dead and had done so effectively several times before moving on to frogs and mice. The former he had managed only to bring into comas, and with the mice, he'd been entirely unsuccessful.

Yet Adria knew it *had* to be possible. If the Djharlings could be brought back, then she was convinced there was a way. Just like Varick had been.

At some point, she fell asleep.

Feeling a little weak on waking, Adria searched for some food, only to discover her pack still held several days' worth. Had she not been eating?

You're becoming like me.

That time, she was certain it was *him*. "Varick? How is this possible?"

You're weak. You've let me in.

"B… but you're dead! Did you come back? So then, it can be done?"

I'm inside you.

Adria wanted to vomit up the magic solely at the thought – but she couldn't. It had attached itself to her. So instead, she ate some mouldy bread and hoped she could fight him off.

You don't need food anymore; or sleep, not really. Maybe to rest your mind, but not your body.

"I don't understand."

You never were the brightest.

Adria sighed. "I get it. You didn't age. Is that what's going to happen to me? I always assumed you'd done that by choice."

She was met only by laughter.

He didn't go away. As she continued to read the books, every now and then she'd hear him in her mind. No matter what she did to shut him out, he mocked and jeered at her.

She wondered, of course, if she was imagining it – but if she were, it was far beyond her control. And he knew details she didn't.

Within one journal, he had consistently encouraged her to turn to page thirty-seven. She'd refused to skip ahead but her anticipation had slowly built. On reaching it, she'd found a blank page – much to the voice in her head's amusement.

Adria had no idea how long she'd been down there when she finished the final chapter in the final book.

There were ideas, but nothing that would lead to a concrete success. Unless… should she explore alternative passages?

When the voice told her she'd found all there was to find, she believed it.

If he'd known what to do – as he'd implied at his death – the secret had been lost with him.

You'll never know.

She began to suspect she could have brought this incursion upon herself. Had it been the way she killed him… having drained his very essence, she'd taken it inside herself?

Face in hands, she sobbed, mentally drained from her fruitless efforts.

☆ ☆ ☆
 ☆   ☆

The Steward led her away the moment she arrived back at Ember House. Adria had intended to take a bath and follow it with a meal in the dining room, but he insisted she go straight to her room. Only when she was inside, did he speak.

"Adria, you look like you've wasted away. It's been two months… Lord Dann even sent people to find you, but there was no trace of where you'd gone. I'm not going to ask what the truth of it is, but you can't walk around looking like you do right now." Seeing she was still processing his words, he continued, "I'll send you up a bucket with some water and a tray of food. Get some rest, and I'll come back in the morning."

She'd been okay until he left. Alone in the small room, she felt displaced. Sliding open the left-hand dresser drawer, she pulled out the wooden hand mirror and winced at what she saw. Her face was almost skeletal.

I said you didn't have to eat to live, not that you should stop entirely.

"Shut up!"

"Oh. I'll just leave it outside your door. Are you sure? It's quite heavy?"

"No, I'm sorry – is that the water. Please bring it in."

Adria stood facing the wall, too ashamed to be seen, muttering only a thank you to the ladies who'd carried in the small, portable bath.

The Steward had been right; she couldn't see anyone, especially not Lord Dann – whom she needed to respect her – until she recovered.

CHAPTER 45 – SEARCH

When Adria finally took a seat at the table with Lord Dann and his advisors, she had to quickly adjust her expectations. Everything she'd hoped they could begin work on immediately would need time to set up.

There was no 'quick fix' to the situation in Kings'land, for example. She could offer to transport food to them, but that would only improve their situation for a week or two; building them new homes would take time.

"Let's build them, then," she'd said – but the others had looked at her like she was a child.

"We need to hire builders. That doesn't happen overnight – we need to get references from their previous jobs, and we need a selection to choose from to make sure we receive a fair price. They won't be able to tender until they know the material costs."

"Okay, I get it; I'll stick to my own areas of expertise." It had been a poor start; she had lost a lot of respect before she'd really even begun.

"The other issue will be how the rest of the population react to this many people receiving handouts when they've had no support over the years." Before Adria could put her foot in it again, he added, "I think that is a matter for me to handle personally."

She would have walked away feeling depleted, but at the very end of their day-long session, Lord Dann ran through their individual responsibilities. Adria's role was clearly something he'd thought about in advance.

"Whilst Adria has not had the benefit of the political, social, and economic learning we have all been privy to, she instead has something none of the rest of us do, and that is a vast wealth of knowledge on the subject of magic."

She thought he was slightly overplaying that.

"All over the country, we are anticipating individuals may be newly discovering either they have magic or their children do. Adria, would you be willing to visit them and offer support?"

She thought on it for a few moments. Was there really any reason she needed to be near Ember House in order to experiment with her magic? She would have plenty of time spare while she was travelling, and could use this to practice. Maybe she'd even find someone who could help her find a solution.

Out in the fresh air, she wouldn't have to chase after Dharjigs. There would likely be plenty of recently deceased earthworms and insects ready and waiting for her to experiment on.

You can use your magic to seek dead things, too. Varick's voice was followed by a chuckle, and Adria shivered.

"I'd love to be of assistance."

"Great! We get together for a full day every two to three months, so just try and make sure you're around to give us all an update – and I'm sure you'll want to hear about everyone else's progress, too." He was making it clear Adria was part of the team.

It helped her feel at ease and reminded her of his good nature.

Adria's initial trips revealed that the only magic to have developed in individuals was very weak; too little to do anything and too little to be of danger.

She spent a year touring Azeileah to be certain, but it seemed likely it would be another ten years before those now being born came into their magic – and she suspected the new generation would be stronger.

There was therefore nothing for *her* to learn either.

Having left it until last, she finally visited North-Harbour, and could immediately see why Alis had loved it there. She lingered until she had no choice but to return to Ember House for their quarterly meeting.

Not wanting to report she'd given up, Adria went to meet Lord Dann and his advisors with a different type of proposal.

It was driven by self-interest. She wanted to keep herself busy and make sure they continued to include her as one of the team. Above all else, having exhausted her research in Azeileah, she hoped to broaden her horizons.

You really aren't much use to them. Murderer.

Adria almost fell off her chair.

"I think we should re-open our borders. We could either send an envoy – myself – over the ocean, or we could invite them here. It's time we re-established relations with our neighbours. We used to… there used to be regular communication, but I think when Varick sent out that blight everything must have come to a halt."

Lord Dann sat up in his seat, and Adria knew she'd piqued his interest. "An intriguing idea. It seems like a long time ago in our history, and we still have so much to do to enable Azeileah to finally recover, but perhaps I would like to be the leader to take that leap all the same. Adria, can you truly say you'd be happy to spearhead this?"

"I'm hoping they may know more about magic, so there's an incentive for me too." A little honesty wasn't going to hurt her case. "I thought perhaps we might start with the islands of Lian-Ren. The journey would only take a few weeks, and I already know a little about their people. From Varick."

"Let me think on this properly, Adria – and I'll have to consult my father – but I like your proposal. My feeling is we should follow this one through."

☆ ☆ ☆
 ☆ ☆

He'd yet to come back to her with a 'yes', but Adria had still gone looking for the team of tailors, hoping to have something suitable made. She needed rich-looking clothes, but she also hoped to impress them by imitating their style – even if her knowledge turned out to be a couple of centuries out of date.

Having interacted with their emissaries in her dreams was a far bigger advantage than Varick having simply told her about the islands. She wasn't sure exactly why she'd lied to Lord Dann by saying it had been the latter. For simplicity, she supposed, as there was no reason to keep it a secret.

Maybe to prove she wasn't Varick.

She'd told a few untruths recently.

She hoped they'd continued to learn the Azeilean language, despite the lack of contact between the nations.

It was strange to feel excited about something, after she hadn't looked forward to anything for such a long time. Perhaps she was simply optimistic that she might find someone there who knew how to revive Alis… but the idea of going over the seas filled her with anticipation.

When Lord Dann finally came to her, a full two weeks later, it was with better news than she'd expected. He had found her a ship and a crew. It was only a small vessel, and one in need of repairs, but he hoped they'd be complete before the month was out.

"It'd be nice to have more ships, but we've lost the knowledge. This one has been stored in a cove for the last hundred years. We'll need to ensure it's fully seaworthy before we go, but we have books, and we're learning."

Adria found herself returning to the library, desiring to learn about boats for her own sake. If an accident happened at sea, she'd be the only one with magic at their disposal; perhaps she could learn something about fixing holes. She poured over book after book – and, as it transpired, spent an equal amount of time reading what she could about Lian and Ren.

She waited all through winter, taking on board the advice of the crew leader and lady in charge of the ship's maintenance that delaying the trip would be safer. They lacked the experience to know about the currents further away from the shore, but the sea was always calmer around their own cliffs in spring, and travelling would be more pleasant in the warmer air.

They had no way to let their neighbours know they were coming, so a small rowboat had been built to enable someone to go ashore and treat with them before the rest of their party docked. Hopefully, they would agree to let their representative land, and the adventure wouldn't be for nothing.

Faced with time on her hands, Adria had been learning their language. She was already the most likely candidate to be their first contact and ambassador and had resolved not to leave any room for argument.

☆ ☆ ☆

From the moment she rowed up to the shore, when she was greeted by a hand reaching out to assist her, Adria stared on in amazement.

She had always felt plain and straightforward. Even through her supposed adventure across Azeileah, she'd followed the lead of others the majority of the time.

This was different. It was something – a *choice* – of her own.

She finally felt independent.

The flat, sandy coastline was a far cry from the rocky cliffs of her home, and she wondered whether the ground would feel soft and smooth beneath her toes.

There were no buildings or other developments in sight; beyond the beach, she could see only grassy fields.

With the vista giving away nothing of Lian – this being the larger of the two islands – the mystery of what new experiences this neighbouring island would hold continued to intrigue her.

"Hello. I'm Adria," she said simply, hoping her pronunciation was sufficient for her to be understood. Their languages had some similarities, and having heard them speaking in her dream, she'd been attempting to practice their accent.

She received a wide smile in response. "We heard a boat was approaching from the south-east and sent a welcome party."

"That's very kind of you. Yes, we have come from Azeileah in the hope we can establish a friendship. Might I bring ashore the rest of my company?"

She returned to inform those remaining on board that things were going well and invite them to dock.

They took a path through the meadow, until they reached a well-maintained, grit-paved road. Although at this stage the conversation was limited to introductions and questions about their journey, there was much to talk about, and the short walk passed quickly.

Her first glimpse of the nearest town did not disappoint. The stone buildings rose into the air, making full use of the space, and the streets were wide and straight. Each house had its own allotment, and their guide explained that local requirements decreed at least half of every plot should be used to grow vegetables, herbs, or medicinal plants.

Almost every intersection boasted a working well.

Adria imagined this was much as Azeileah had been, prior to its destruction, and couldn't help but feel a pang of regret. When Varick had described the world as he'd known it, she'd formed an image to go with his words, but of course the reality was far more enlightening.

Their hosts were gracious, finding them private accommodation and entertaining them daily with meals and music.

There was a level of guilt over their hundred years of silence. Lian had thought Azeileah destroyed by the curse. When they'd ventured over there to offer aid, they had seen nothing but levelled buildings and had not continued onwards to shore.

Adria could not believe it. She'd assumed there had been an argument with Varick and relations had faltered, but there was no bad blood and never had been.

They had magic, having never lost it, and were able to teach her how to manipulate it into something usable – to do something *other* than cause violent explosions – but they looked down on her questions about raising the dead, and she did her utmost not to persist in case it offended them.

She was invited to return, being told she was welcome at any time – and Adria thought they genuinely meant as much. Had she not needed to report back to Lord Dann, she thought she might have stayed there for an unspecified duration.

Instead, after six very pleasant weeks, she found herself bidding them goodbye, with the promise to return as soon as she was able.

CHAPTER 46 – SUNRISE

Fifty Years Later

"Adria, Lord Dann is calling for you. It's time."

She rose from her reading and ran towards the room of her Sovereign and best friend, knocking gently on his door.

"Adria, come in. Simone, Ollie, could you leave us for a little? I promise not to die while you're outside." Adria smiled at his two children as they left. Simone was already acting ruler, and Ollie had learnt diplomacy under her wing. They were grown up now, with families and children of their own.

Yet I still look as though I'm in my early twenties.

Taking a seat on the divan, she leaned towards the bed. "I thought I'd never again feel a loss as keenly as Alis's, but I do believe I'll miss you greatly."

"Adria." He looked at her sympathetically. It was the wrong way round – that was how *she* should have been looking at *him*. "That's what I wanted to speak to you about. I hope you won't get angry with me. We've been through enough together... I think I can speak my mind?"

"I won't, Dann. Tell me what you need to."

"For fifty years, you've been focused on Alis. You've travelled far further than anyone else from Azeileah – to places I have never had the opportunity to see for myself – and been a wonderful delegation leader... but all this time, I know you've still been thinking about her and... and it's time to let her go

Adria."

"I never told you, but Varick thought there was a way to bring her back. I've been searching for it."

"I know, Adria. I was there when you… when Varick *died*. It's time to put the past behind you now. Doing this… you think you've been doing it for yourself when really it's yourself you've been hurting. I'm sorry I didn't say anything sooner. I hoped you'd come to the conclusion on your own, but you were so determined."

Adria took his hand and nodded. A tear fell down her face, and she let him see her vulnerability. He was the one person who'd been a steadfast presence in her life, but it was true she had put her own existence on hold. It was almost poetic that she hadn't grown older while she'd done so.

Adria hoped he knew her lack of words meant she was reflecting on his suggestion. She was sad to think of his imminent passing, too, even though he'd lived a full, contented life. All she could manage was, "I'll try."

She stayed by his bedside for a little while, sitting silently beside Simone and Ollie, but when the time came, she left them to say their goodbyes.

Adria felt different, but not in the way she'd expected. Dann's words had made her reflect internally. A final gift to her.

She'd never quite been able to give up her search; she'd been hoarding Varick's magic, saving it up for when she would need it. Dann's permission to stop looking was different. It held more weight because she wasn't simply giving up; someone else, someone she trusted, had told her it was okay to move on.

Adria had loved travelling. She'd been lucky to experience more than she could ever have dreamt of, but he was right about her reasons needing to change.

She'd take baby steps; let a little magic out, to begin with, then she'd still have plenty left… just in case. Did she even want it anymore?

Magic is power.

"I don't want power, Varick. I never have."

It was going to mean letting part of herself go.

☆ ☆ ☆

Azeileah had flourished under Dann's rule.

Adria possessed a wealth of knowledge, and more magic stored up than the rest of the Island put together. As well as helping those with magic understand what to do with it, she'd known her own stores held great potential.

Once she put her mind to it, the ideas had begun to come to her. She'd poured over Varick's old journals once more and taken most of her inspiration from there – there was no denying he had obsessed over innovation and progress.

Now able to shape her magic, she built aqueducts single-handedly. She flattened roads, improving travel routes. The island was transformed in the space of a dozen years.

Only through this did she appreciate it wasn't holding the magic which had led to Varick being unable to cope; rather, it was the *use* of it that had addled his mind. Luckily, her own store did not regenerate, and although it taxed her mentally as well as physically, as long as she took time off – even when she felt as though she didn't need it – it allowed her to regain her senses.

Adria didn't notice it at first, but one day, she looked in the mirror and saw she had begun to age. Smiling back at her slightly older self, she traced the outline of her cheeks in the mirror. Instead of feeling old and weary, she felt refreshed.

The magic was almost depleted, and it no longer

weighed so heavily on her. Her body moved more easily. The aches she hadn't even known she'd suffered had gone.

"I haven't heard his voice, either. Not since…" but she couldn't remember when. "Varick, are you there?"

There was no response.

Adria returned to Alis's grave and released her body from stasis, letting her return to the earth; leaving herself with one single, remaining drop of power – only detectable because she was so accustomed to its feel inside her.

Once it was gone, Varick's catacombs would be sealed forever. Any secrets they might still hold would never be discovered.

Adria no longer minded.

When the day came to release her last ounce of magic, she imagined it a celebration. She would still be able to use magic while in contact with another who had their own supply, but she'd never again contain it within herself. Sitting on the mountainside, amidst the Adria flowers, she released it frivolously, in the shape of a balloon.

"Farewell, Dann. Farewell, Alis. Farewell, Varick. I think I might go back to one of those Islands now and enjoy a long, relaxing retirement." There were several she was particularly fond of; it would be a hard decision to choose. "Perhaps I'll even change my name and begin anew."